WAGON TRAIN REUNION

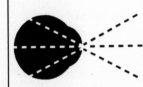

This Large Print Book carries the
Seal of Approval of N.A.V.H.

WAGON TRAIN REUNION

LINDA FORD

THORNDIKE PRESS
A part of Gale, Cengage Learning

GALE
CENGAGE Learning·

Farmington Hills, Mich • San Francisco • New York • Waterville, Maine
Meriden, Conn • Mason, Ohio • Chicago

GALE
CENGAGE Learning®

Copyright © 2015 by Harlequin Books S.A.
Journey West.
Thorndike Press, a part of Gale, Cengage Learning.

Thorndike Press® Large Print Gentle Romance.
The text of this Large Print edition is unabridged.
Other aspects of the book may vary from the original edition.
Set in 16 pt. Plantin.

LIBRARY OF CONGRESS CATALOGING-IN-PUBLICATION DATA

Ford, Linda (Linda Carol)
  Wagon train reunion / Linda Ford.
    pages cm. — (Journey west) (Thorndike Press large print gentle romance)
    ISBN 978-1-4104-7907-5 (hardback) — ISBN 1-4104-7907-2 (hardcover)
    1. Large type books. I. Title.
PS3606.O7395W34 2015
813'.6—dc23   2015005121

Published in 2015 by arrangement with Harlequin Books S.A.

Printed in Mexico
1 2 3 4 5 6 7 19 18 17 16 15

When thou passest through the waters, I will be with thee; and through the rivers, they shall not overflow thee: when thou walkest through the fire, thou shalt not be burned; neither shall the flame kindle upon thee.

— *Isaiah* 43:2

I personally know many who have suffered losses and events that have left them hurting, broken and filled with doubt and guilt. You know who you are. Through the love of God may you find healing and wholeness. This story is dedicated to you.

CHAPTER ONE

Independence, Missouri
May 1843

Benjamin Hewitt stared. It wasn't possible.

He blinked to clear his vision. If the man struggling with his oxen didn't look like Abigail's father, he didn't know a cow from a chicken. But it couldn't be Mr. Bingham. He would never subject himself and his wife to the trials of this journey. Why Mrs. Bingham would look mighty strange fluttering a lace hankie and expecting someone to serve her tea in a covered wagon.

The man must have given the wrong command because the oxen jerked hard to the right, yanking the wagon after them. The rear wheel broke free and wobbled across the ground, coming to rest against another wagon. The first wagon leaned drunkenly on one corner. A chest toppled out the back, followed by a wooden table. When it hit the ground the legs snapped and flew in four different directions. A woman followed amid a cascade of smaller items, shrieking, her arms flailing. Ben chuckled. She looked like a chicken trying to fly and she landed with a startled squawk on pillows and bedding.

Ben's amusement ended abruptly. He liked the idea of moving West but there had been times he felt as out of control as that woman.

"Mother, are you injured?" A young woman ran toward her mother. Making the comparison sparked by the wagon driver worse, she even sounded just like Abigail. At least as near as he could recall. He'd succeeded in putting that young woman from his mind many years ago.

She glanced about. "Father, are you safe?"

The sun glowed in her blond hair and he knew, though he couldn't see her face, that it was Abigail. What was she doing here? She'd not find a fine, big house nor fancy dishes and certainly no servants on this trip.

The bitterness he'd once felt at being rejected because he couldn't provide those things had dissipated, leaving only regret and caution.

She helped her mother to her feet and dusted her skirts off. All the while, the woman — Mrs. Bingham, to be sure — complained, her voice grating with displeasure that made Ben's nerves twitch. He knew that sound all too well. Could recall in sharp detail when the woman had told him he was not a suitable suitor for her daughter. Abigail had told him, with the same harsh dismissive tone, she would no longer see him, after a year and eight months of seeing each other regularly and talking of a shared future.

It all seemed so long ago. He'd been a different person six years back. Only twenty years old, he'd considered himself mature and ready to start life with a wife and home of his own. He had been full of trust and optimism.

Thanks to Abigail, he'd learned not to trust everything a woman said. Nor believe how they acted. Maybe he should thank her for that. Except he no longer cared enough to want to engage her in conversation.

Binghams or not, a wheel needed to be put on. Ben joined the men hurrying to assist the unfortunate fellow.

"Hello." He greeted Mr. Bingham and the man shook his hand. "Ladies." He tipped his hat to them.

"Hello, Ben." Abigail Bingham stood at her mother's side. No, not Bingham. She was Abigail Black now.

Ben darted a glance around. Where was

Frank Black? No doubt off spouting his opinions to one and all about everything and nothing. Ben never could see why Abigail would marry the man, though he knew well the reasons. Ben's family had lost their money in the Panic of 1837. Frank Black had not.

He turned his attention to getting the wheel in place. Several men groaned as they tried to lift the heavily-laden wagon.

"Over here." Ben waved to get the attention of half a dozen more and they lifted the wagon enough for the wheel to be put on again.

"The bolts need to be good and tight." He'd been elected as one of the nine committeemen and his task was to inspect every wagon in this section of the assembled group to make sure it was ready for the journey.

Mr. Bingham applied a wrench to the bolts. "I thought they were tight."

"Let me." Ben held out his hand and Mr. Bingham gave him the wrench. Ben turned each bolt a half turn. "Surprised to see you headed for Oregon."

"The economy here isn't what it used to be. I hear it's booming in Oregon. The land of opportunity, I'm told."

"Uh-huh." He checked the other wheels.

To his right, Abigail and her mother gathered together their scattered belongings.

"Mother, the table is ruined. Leave it behind."

"My own mother gave me that table. What would she think of this?" Mrs. Bingham clutched a splintered leg. "I'm grateful she hasn't lived to see this day." She tossed aside the leg and stared at the wagon. "How can your father expect us to live in this cramped space? This trip will be the death of me."

"Mother, don't say that. Besides, think of the opportunities in Oregon. A new society will need women with high standards to guide it."

Mrs. Bingham sniffed. "That's so I suppose." Her voice rose a degree. "But why must we crowd into one wagon?"

Mrs. Bingham and her daughter had not changed. They still measured every situation as a means to further their place in society.

He thought a person should be measured by their worth. This trip from Independence, Missouri to Oregon would be four to six months long over mostly unmapped territory. It would test all of them. Reveal their worth. Perhaps change many. Or it might destroy people unprepared for the challenges of the trail. People like the Binghams. Checking the wagons was one way Ben could ensure everyone made the trip safely.

He turned to Abigail. "Why don't I look at your wagon next?"

Her mouth dropped open.

Mrs. Bingham's lips pursed tight.

"She's traveling with us." Mr. Bingham spoke softly at Ben's side. "I guess you didn't hear that Frank died six months ago."

Frank dead? She was a widow? The words blared through Ben's head but he couldn't take them in.

"I'm sorry." He managed to get the words out, then hurried to the next wagon. His heart went out to her. He knew what it was like to lose people you were close to. But apart from that, her situation didn't mean a thing to him.

The noise of the gathered crowd assaulted his eardrums. Tin plates rattled as the women washed dishes. Babies wailed. How were the little ones going to endure the trip? Hopefully the moving wagons would lull them to sleep.

Five excited young fellas were shooting their pistols into the air and shouting — young men, thirteen to fifteen likely, on the cusp of adulthood.

"Oregon here we come."

"I'm gonna get me a buffalo."

"I'm gonna fight a bear."

Someone should warn them they should save their bullets for bears and buffalos. But he understood the excitement that almost crazed them.

A child screamed.

"You shot my baby," a woman screeched.

Ben straightened to see a little one in his mother's arms, a dark-haired little boy of about a year, if he didn't miss his guess. Blood stained both their clothes.

Women picked up their skirts and ran toward the pair. Abigail was among the first to reach them and knelt at the woman's side. "Let me see him."

She eased the woman's fingers from her son's side and lifted the little shirt. She glanced toward Ben.

Across the space her gaze found his. "It's just a graze but he needs it tended to." She obviously meant for him to take care of the problem. Did she see him as a man she could order around? He should inform her that he was one of the committeemen and as such, had some authority. He didn't intend to jump at her command.

But her opinion didn't matter because a child was injured and he knew who could help.

15

Ben grabbed the nearest man. "Go back to the wagon at the corner. Ask for Emma Hewitt. Tell her to bring her medical supplies."

The man took off like a shot.

Ben pushed through the crowd of women to Abigail's side. He spied a clean diaper and grabbed it. "Press this to the wound until my sister arrives."

He looked around for the youths who were responsible.

They saw him and began to slink away.

"Hold up there." He strode toward them.

Forced to face him, all but one of them put on defiant faces. "We ain't done nothin' wrong," one said.

"You could have killed a child and you don't think there's any reason to be apologizing?"

"I'm sorry, mister," said the only repentant one.

"Glad to hear it, though it's not me you should be apologizing to."

The boy took a step toward the bleeding child.

Ben caught his shoulder. "Hold on a minute. What's your name?"

"Jed. Jed Henshaw."

Ben would be remembering Jed. A lad willing to admit his wrongs could prove to be an asset in the months ahead. He held out his hand. "I'll take those firearms before someone else is hurt."

Jed immediately dropped his gun into Ben's hand.

"My pa ain't gonna be very happy with me." He hung his head.

The four others grunted and shuffled their feet but did not offer up their guns. The biggest, loudest, most belligerent of them spoke. "You ain't gonna take my gun."

For answer, Ben reached out and wrenched it from his hand. He reached for the others and they were released grudgingly.

"Here now, what do you think you're doing?" A big man edged between Ben and the boys. "You ain't gonna take my son's gun."

A crowd of men pressed close arguing about whether or not the boys should be allowed to retain their firearms.

"A baby was shot," Ben pointed out, but others said each male old enough to carry a gun should do so in case of some kind of attack. Ben pushed aside the big man crowding him and realized he was every bit as big. The man moved despite his attempt to stay planted. He addressed the boys. "I'd like your names." Only Jed had told Ben his name.

Three gave theirs, but the fourth only scowled.

"You don't need to tell him," the man at Ben's side shouted.

Ben cringed as the noise swelled. "There'll be a meeting of the committeemen at noon. Attend it and make your case. We'll all abide by the ruling as to whether or not you get your guns back."

Jed left the raucous crowd and broke through the cluster of women around the injured baby.

"Ma'am." He addressed the woman holding her baby. "I am truly sorry for behaving so foolishly. I hope your little boy will be okay."

Half the murmurs were accepting, half condemning.

At that moment, Emma rushed up with Rachel at her side. They made their way through the ladies and Emma dropped her bag and knelt to examine the injured child.

"It's only a flesh wound. It needs to be kept clean and covered." She sat back and glanced around. She saw Abigail at her side and gaped.

"Hello, Emma, Rachel." Abigail nodded toward the sisters.

"You're traveling with us?" Rachel asked. She stared at Abby. "Why on earth are you on this wagon train? Doesn't your husband's business keep you in the manner you prefer?"

"My husband is dead." Abigail kept her voice low but even so the women watched and listened curiously. "I am traveling with my parents." She nodded toward them. Her mother sat in a high-backed chair perched on the ground beside their wagon, her back rigid, disapproval written in every line of her face. Mr. Bingham stood at his oxen, looking like he was having second thoughts about this journey.

Emma hid her surprise better, focusing on the injured baby. She leaned back on her heels as if thinking what to do. If it had been a man injured, she might have cleansed the wound with alcohol, but knowing how much it hurt, he understood she was considering other possibilities.

Finally she turned to Rachel. "Would you bring me some warm water and a clean cloth?"

Rachel hurried to the nearest fire where a kettle of water stood and poured a little into a bowl. She glanced about for a cloth.

One of the women reached into her wagon and pulled out a square of pure white. "For the little one yet to come." She patted her stomach.

Rachel hustled the items over to Emma who carefully sponged the area then wrapped a dressing over the wound. "Keep it clean." She would be worried about infection. Emma grasped the mother's hands. "I'd like to pray for the baby. What's his name?"

The baby stuck his thumb in his mouth and clung to his mother.

"His name is Johnny. I'm Sally Littleton. And I thank you." She squeezed Emma's hands. Then they bowed their heads.

The women circling them also bowed their heads and Ben and the men removed their hats.

"Our Father in heaven, thank you for sparing Johnny's life. And grant our deepest desire that he recover from this wound with no ill effects. Amen." Emma opened her eyes and patted little Johnny's back. She straightened.

All this time, Abby sat beside Mrs. Littleton, one arm wrapped about the woman's shoulders, comforting her.

A man rushed up. "I heard my son was shot." He threw his hat on the ground and knelt before his wife. He ran his hands over the baby. "Is he . . . is he?"

Mrs. Littleton pressed her palms to her husband's cheeks. "It was only a flesh wound. Miss Hewitt tended it."

"Thank you. Thank you." He shook hands with everyone around him and introductions were made. "Thank God. Johnny is all we have left. Our other three died of swamp fever last year."

Ben's throat tightened. So many bore the pain of loss yet faced the great adventure full of hopes and dreams. Ben and his sisters, Emma and Rachel, shared the excitement. They'd eagerly sold the ranch and most of their possessions, bought three teams of oxen, outfitted their wagon with enough supplies to carry them across the continent to Oregon where they'd join their brother, Grayson. Grayson had gone out two years ago to escape the memory of his young wife's death in childbirth. He wrote often, urging his siblings to join him and for Ben to consider working at his store. After the death of their father late last year, they made plans to do so. Ben would do his best to see that everyone else on the train made the trip safely, as well.

As he continued inspecting the wagons in the section he'd been assigned, he overheard bits and pieces of conversation.

New beginning. Fresh start. Opportunity.

The final word rang throughout most of the conversations. It was the promise that filled them all with hope and determination. For a new beginning almost a thousand people were prepared to face the dangers this journey held.

Soon he was again engulfed by the noise of the camp as he went from wagon to wagon. Men yelled at oxen. Women shouted at children who raced about excitedly. Metal rang on metal as wagon wheels were prepared for the journey. Over it all hung the smell of hundreds of animals.

The poor oxen had to endure inexperienced men ordering them every which way without any real idea of how to direct the animals. Ben had taken the time to instruct both his sisters on how to drive their oxen. He planned to drive most of the time, though being one of the committeemen might necessitate he ride his horse along the wagon train to help convey instructions down the line.

He assessed those he was destined to travel with. An assorted lot to be sure. Many wore the clothes and had the markings of farmers. Others, like Mr. Bingham, appeared to be businessmen hoping for better times. There were small groups traveling together but most of the emigrants were meeting each other for the first time. There'd be plenty of friction as strangers were forced to learn to work together.

It was almost noon before he finished and returned to the wagon where his sisters waited with the meal ready.

Rachel looked ready to burst as he washed his hands and filled his plate. "I'll ask the blessing," he said, ignoring her impatience, and bowed his head. His amen was barely out before she spoke.

"I can't believe the Binghams are on this wagon train. How are you going to avoid running into her?"

He pretended not to understand what she meant even though he knew she referred to the relationship he and Abby had enjoyed back then. "There's a lot of people traveling together. We don't have to keep company with any we don't choose to." He said it as if that solved the entire problem of encountering Abby and he intended it should.

Rachel sighed. "I just don't want to see your heart broken again."

"It's not going to happen." Never again would he give Abigail the right to hurt him. He would do his best to keep a wide distance between himself and Abigail. Two thousand miles over several months lay ahead of them. But all he had to do was avoid her one day at a time.

Surely that wasn't impossible.

"Please stay with me," Mrs. Littleton said to Abby as her husband left to attend to other business. "I'm afraid to be alone at the moment."

"Of course." Abby sat beside her on a quilt. The blond-haired woman's blue eyes were friendly and welcoming. Her dress was well-worn but clean.

"You have a sweet baby. How old is he?"

"He's just a year old."

"I'm sorry to hear about your other children."

Mrs. Littleton bent over her son, caressing his brown hair. His brown eyes closed slowly and he slept. "Life can be hard at times." She looked into the distance. "I hope we can start over in Oregon without so many painful memories."

"That is my hope, as well, Mrs. Littleton." Losing her husband had necessitated her move back to her parents' home. But it didn't pain her the way losing her twin brother Andy had. That pain never went away but she had learned to let it sweep through her. It would then settle back into a steady ache. Perhaps in Oregon she could think of Andy without the pulsing pain and regret.

She hoped for more than freedom from her past with this trip. It was her chance for a new beginning. She had her private plans. When they reached Oregon, she meant to go her own way. She'd work until she saved enough money to set herself up in business. Perhaps she'd run a boardinghouse. All that mattered was she'd never again depend on someone else. But Mother had other plans . . . plans that involved marrying in such a way as to improve the social and financial status of the Binghams. Abby hadn't informed her mother yet, but she would not marry again. To her sorrow and regret she had learned a lesson about marriage that she didn't care to repeat.

Strange to see Ben on the wagon train. She hadn't seen him since she ended their relationship six years before. His light brown hair had been tamed some. Only one wave dipped over his forehead. He'd filled out, too, so his six-foot frame seemed all muscle and power. Even his blue-gray eyes had grown serious.

His expression when he looked her way contained only the cool disinterest of a stranger.

Not that she could blame him. Six years

ago, she'd dismissed him harshly because she knew no other way to end a relationship that held so much promise. She'd balked at the idea of marrying Frank. Begged her mother to allow her to marry Ben, the man she loved. But Mother had reminded her of her promise to take care of her parents and pointed out that Ben couldn't possibly provide for her and them. Nor could he offer a way of advancing them socially. His father's mercantile business had floundered in the depressed economy.

Mrs. Littleton turned to look into Abby's face. "You've had your losses, too, I can tell."

Abby's mind flooded with sorrow as she recalled kneeling beside Andy's lifeless body. He was but fourteen years old. If only she had spoken up and asked Andy not to ride that high-spirited horse. Instead, she had bragged to the snobby Isabelle that her brother could ride any horse they found. She had been wrong. She'd never told Mother or Father of her responsibility in Andy's death. Her sorrow and guilt had led her to promise Mother to take care of them. In her mind, she hoped she could replace Andy, become the one Mother counted on.

"My condolences over your husband's death."

Of course Mrs. Littleton meant Frank, but Abby could not find it in her heart to feel sorrow at his passing. Yes, it left her penniless and back home under her mother's rule, but it freed her from Frank's cruelty. She shuddered. She'd never told her parents what marriage to Frank had been like.

Mother had seen him as the key to a promising future for the Binghams and when Abby protested over his offer of marriage, Mother had reminded her of her promise.

"Marrying well is the best way you can help us," Mother had insisted as they discussed Frank.

"But I don't love him." Her throat still tightened as she thought of that day. If only her promise didn't bind her to do her mother's bidding.

"Love is a luxury few of us can afford."

"But you love Father, don't you?"

"I'm happy with our arrangement."

Abby realized later that love was nothing but a flight of fancy. But at the time she still believed in it.

Out of guilt and duty, and a desire to please her parents, she'd obeyed her mother and married Frank. To be fair, he'd been attentive and gentle when courting her.

That had ended the day of their wedding.

Mrs. Littleton patted her arm. "A new beginning will be good for all of us. And please call me Sally."

"I'm Abigail or Abby to my friends."

Sally chuckled. "Then I'll call you Abby."

Abby glanced at her mother still sitting nearby on her wooden chair. No mistaking the disapproving scowl. She sighed. She tried, oh, how she tried, to please Mother, but nothing ever seemed enough. Why, mother had even hinted that it was Abby's fault that Frank had died penniless. His grave had barely been covered over when agents from the bank had come and carried away everything but her personal belongings and had given her three days to leave the house. The harsh truth about her husband had been reinforced yet again. Not only was he cruel behind the closed doors of their home, he was foolish in business. She'd gone back to her parents' home. Where else could she go? Though it had reduced her to striving for her mother's approval and always falling short.

Mother would never let her forget her promise.

She remained convinced that Andy would have fulfilled all her dreams of advancement. And now she expected Abby to be the means.

"You'll need to find a suitable suitor soon," she'd been saying since they made plans to head West. "In Oregon, there are far more men than women. That means you can have your pick of the best."

Abby hated the reminder of her duty. Surely she'd paid for it with her marriage to Frank. However, one thing no bank, no demanding mother or cruel husband could take from her was her faith. God would provide the strength she needed for every test and trial. *And please, God, a chance to start over.*

Sally shifted and glanced at the sun overhead. "It's noon. I need to start dinner but I hate to put Johnny down."

"Let me hold him while you cook." Abby held out her arms. By rights she should offer to make the meal, but she doubted Sally and her husband would appreciate her efforts.

Sally shifted the sleeping Johnny to Abby's lap. "You never had any little ones of your own or did they — ?" She clapped her hands to her mouth to stop the words.

Abby understood Sally feared she might have brought up a painful subject — like she'd had babies and they died. "No, we never had children."

"I'm sorry."

Abby brushed Johnny's hair off his forehead. Oh, to have a child of her own to love and cherish, though she couldn't be sorry Frank had not given her one. It would have been a thousand times worse to endure Frank mistreating a child and she knew he would have if only to get at Abby.

She shifted the baby so she would look westward. In Oregon she hoped and planned and prayed she would find the freedom she longed for which, to date, had always seemed far out of reach.

Little Johnny fussed and Abby sang softly until he relaxed again. All the while, she watched Sally stir a pot of stew that had been simmering over the coals then slice a loaf of batter bread she'd baked in the tin oven. If Mother wasn't watching like a hawk, Abby would have asked Sally to explain how she did all that. Mother had forbidden her to ask for help from the women around them.

We're Binghams. We don't need help.

Abigail knew otherwise. If they were to make it across the great plains and over the mountains, Bingham or not, they'd need help because Abby had no idea how to manage under these circumstances. She'd have to learn by observation. They had a tin oven, as well. She'd try baking biscuits in it.

Mr. Littleton returned. "How's Johnny?"

Sally answered. "He's sleeping." But at the sound of his father's voice, Johnny stirred and held out his arms. Mr. Littleton took him gently, careful of the bandaging around the baby's middle.

Abby pushed to her feet. Her fingers trailed down Johnny's back then she stepped away. "I best go prepare dinner for my folks." She returned to their wagon.

Mother huffed as Abby set to work. "I hope you don't plan to spend a lot of time with the likes of those people."

Abby pushed aside annoyance. "Mother, it's a long trip. Those kinds of people will be our constant companions."

Mother pulled herself into her self-righteous posture. "You don't need to associate with them. Keep yourself apart until we reach Oregon and then we'll find you a proper suitor."

Ben's image as he faced those rowdy boys and then the questioning men filled Abby's thoughts. He was a noble and kind man. At least he had been at the time they courted. But that didn't alter the fact that marriage changed a man. Gave him rights to his wife that no law, no friend, nor even family could defy. She would never again subject herself to such ownership of her body and her rights.

She fried bacon and boiled potatoes. Even potatoes were difficult to cook over a fire. They burned on the bottom and were hard as rocks inside. Father ate them without a word. Mother nibbled at the food. Plain fare had never been her first choice. They both accepted a cup of tea. Abby sighed and turned her attention to washing up the few dishes, but her thoughts went round and round. She must become adept at all sorts of things if they were to survive this trip.

At Mother's request, Father took her wooden chair into the back of the wagon and parked it atop two chests. Mother followed and perched on the chair. She barely fit beneath the white canvas. Mother had brought as much as she could pack into the wagon which was far less than she insisted she needed.

Abigail had brought a minimum of belongings. A few changes of clothing, a warm coat, a waterproof duster, her Bible, a few of her favorite books and her mandolin. After Frank's death she'd learned how little material things mattered.

Abigail opened her mouth to warn Mother she wouldn't be able to ride all the way in that precarious position then she closed it without saying a word. Mother would soon learn or she'd find a way to remain there just to prove to one and all that she was a proper lady who shouldn't be expected to endure the heat and dust.

Not for the first time, Abigail wondered if this trip would destroy them. She shivered as she recalled Mother's words. *The death of them all.* Then she prayed, *Father God in heaven, guard and keep us.*

How many times had she prayed that on her own behalf when Frank scared her with his behavior? She wrapped her arms about herself and let the tears flow through her heart. Her eyes stayed dry. She wasn't about to bemoan the consequences of a choice she'd made. Though she had no idea that a man could pretend such sweetness before marriage and reveal such cruelty afterwards.

A walk would calm her. She hurried through the maze of wagons and tents and people to a place where no one was parked. Perhaps she could find a minute of peace.

A glance about revealed there was no one who would recognize her and she stood with her hands clasped in front of her. Anyone watching would assume she was peacefully enjoying the scenery.

They would have been wrong.

Slowly her emotions subsided. She rubbed

at her breastbone, knowing the ache would ease but not disappear entirely.

Oh, God, be Thou my strength. To Thee I flee for help.

CHAPTER TWO

The committeemen assembled to discuss the issue of the youths randomly firing their guns. Sam Weston the trail guide stood to one side. The tall, lean man stroked his bushy brown mustache as he observed the crowd with a steady gaze. He'd give his opinion if called for, but other than that he made it clear the emigrants would have to solve their own problems.

Ben wondered what he saw. An unruly bunch without any sense of working together? An eager assortment of men and women and children willing to do anything to get to Oregon? Likely there was a little of both in each of them.

Jed stood beside a gentle-looking man who seemed more fitted to tailoring suits than driving oxen across the country. No mistaking the father–son likeness.

The other youths also stood by men Ben assumed were their fathers or guardians.

Most family groups consisted of an assortment of people. Besides the teams of oxen, most wagons had a milk cow, a horse or two and various other animals in tow. Many families had offered to allow a single young man to accompany them, providing meals in exchange for help with the animals. Like the Morrisons who had young Clarence Pressman traveling with them. Few traveled alone. Miles Cavanaugh, one of the committeemen, was an exception. The journey would be more difficult for him with no one to help with the animals or spell the driver off or even cook meals while the other camp chores were taken care of.

The Hewitt wagon consisted of himself and his two sisters.

Mr. Cavanaugh chaired the meeting. "We are here to deal with the disagreement between Ben Hewitt and these young men. He says they were using their firearms carelessly which resulted in the injury of a child and he therefore confiscated their guns. Is that correct, Ben?"

"Yes, sir."

The father of the rowdiest boy stepped forward. "He ain't got no right. Why, he can't even say for sure it was these boys was responsible."

"Did you see one of these boys actually

shoot the child?" the chairman asked.

"I didn't but they'd been shooting and yelling wildly and there wasn't anyone else nearby shooting off guns." Let the truth speak for itself.

"See," shouted the belligerent man. "He's just guessing it were my boy."

"I didn't accuse your son," Ben argued. "Only said the boys were being careless and the baby had been shot. I suggest the boys get their guns back when we are on the trail." After a day or two, their high spirits would have subsided and they'd be less likely to shoot so carelessly.

"No," the angry youth yelled. "Ain't no one taking my gun from me."

Ben tilted his head toward the firearms stacked on the table in front of Mr. Cavanaugh. Obviously someone had taken his from him.

The boy tried to grab his gun. Someone pushed him aside and an uproar ensued.

Mr. Cavanaugh pounded his fist on the table. "Seems to me you're inclined to be a little hotheaded."

Ben would sure like to know that boy's name for future reference.

Apparently Mr. Cavanaugh did, too. "Son, what's your name?"

The boy hesitated. His father stepped

forward. "This here is Arty Jones, my son. I'm his father, Ernie. I say without a reliable witness, it's jest my word 'gainst his." He jerked his thumb toward Ben.

"I consider myself a reliable witness."

Ben jerked about to see who spoke. Mr. Bingham and beside him, Abigail.

"Step forward." Mr. Cavanaugh signaled them. "What did you see?"

Mr. Bingham kept Abby at his side as he pushed through the crowd. "I saw these young youths shooting wildly, as did my daughter. A couple of times I noted how they didn't always make sure the barrel pointed skyward before they fired. I was about to say something when the baby screamed. I saw him shot. As did my daughter."

Abigail nodded.

Ben stared. In his wildest dreams he'd never expected a Bingham to stand up for him. Yes, this was for the safety of all concerned, but still.

Mr. Cavanaugh turned to consult the other members of the committee, then nodded. "It is our decision that for the safety and peace of mind of all of us these pistols will be held in safekeeping until we are on the trail." He gathered the guns, pushed to his feet and headed toward his wagon.

"Thank you for speaking up." Ben spoke to Mr. Bingham, but his gaze darted to Abigail. Had she meant to defend him or was she only doing her duty? As if he needed to ask.

"It was clearly my duty," Mr. Bingham said, and Abigail nodded answering his question.

They left to return to their wagon and he did the same.

Rachel and Emma jumped to their feet at his approach.

"What did they decide?" Rachel asked.

"There was some concern that I hadn't actually seen the young fellas shoot the baby."

"They called you a liar?" Rachel rolled up her fists and looked ready to defend her brother's honor.

As usual, Ben found her attitude amusing and a little worrisome. He'd told her over and over that she must let him deal with his own problems. And warned her she shouldn't be so ready to interfere in a situation.

"Mr. Bingham stepped forward and said he'd seen the whole thing. They accepted his word."

Rachel's mouth fell open. Emma stared. She was the first to recover her voice. "Mr.

Bingham spoke up in your defense? What a surprise."

Ben shrugged. "He was only doing his duty out of concern for safety in the camp."

Emma nodded, her expression smoothed.

Rachel studied him for a long, silent moment. "Then why do you look so flummoxed?"

"I don't." Except he still couldn't believe Mr. Bingham had spoken up on his behalf. With Abigail at his side.

But Rachel had her mind stuck on the topic and wouldn't let it go unless he could divert her.

"The committee decided we will pull out first thing tomorrow. Those with cattle will go in one party. The rest of us will travel in another."

"We'll be ready," Emma assured him, and immediately started to gather up odds and ends of kitchenware.

Rachel did not back down. "I wish the Binghams weren't traveling with us."

Ben lifted a hand in a dismissive gesture hoping Rachel would see how little it mattered. "I don't see what difference it makes."

"I remember when she dropped you," Rachel said. "I saw how upset you were. I wanted to help."

"I survived and am stronger for it. Besides,

you were only thirteen."

"And now I'm nineteen and I'm still not old enough to watch my brother get hurt."

He shrugged. "Your big brother is quite capable of taking care of himself." If Rachel took it in her head to fuss about this on a regular basis she would make it impossible for him to pretend the Binghams weren't traveling with them. His stomach ached at the possibility.

"I hope so."

"You don't have to worry about me. I got over Abby years ago. I won't give her the chance to hurt me again." She was merely one of almost a thousand travelers, not anyone who would earn special attention from him. "All I care about is getting us safely to Oregon." He jammed his fingers into his trousers pockets. He would not fail. Not in any of his responsibilities.

The next morning, he discovered how challenging his responsibilities could be. Trying to get these emigrants organized and on their way was like trying to hold water in a sieve.

A man couldn't find one of his oxen and accused his neighbor of stealing it. Ben directed the angry man to search among the many loose cattle until he found his own.

A woman wrung her hands because her five-year-old son had disappeared. "I'll never find him in this bedlam," she wailed.

They were near the Bingham wagon and Abigail hurried over to see if she could help.

"What's his name and what does he look like?" she asked.

The woman stammered out a reply.

"I'll find him," Abby said to Ben. "You get on with your work." Without giving him a chance to say yay or nay, she started down the line of wagons, calling the child's name and asking if anyone had seen him.

He couldn't think if he appreciated her help or resented being ordered about by her. But he didn't have time to decide.

Mr. Bingham struggled with his oxen and Ben assisted him and gave him a few instructions on handling the animals. Mrs. Bingham sat on an upright chair inside the wagon. She wouldn't last long on that perch, but she would not look kindly at advice from him. He decided against suggesting she find a different place to sit.

He checked on the Littletons. "How is Johnny?"

Mrs. Littleton washed dishes with the baby on her hip. "He's fussy. Won't let me put him down."

"I expect he's frightened."

"My poor baby."

Ben was about to move on when Abby returned leading the missing child and turned him over to his mother who smothered him in kisses, then scolded him for running off.

Abby chuckled. Her gaze lifted to Ben's, her hazel eyes piercing right through his defenses.

How often in the past had her gaze done this to him? There was a time he welcomed it. No more. He wasn't good enough for her six years ago and nothing about his station in life had changed for the better.

He turned his attention back to his duties.

"The bank's been robbed!" A young man rode through the crowd shouting, "Fifteen thousand dollars missing from the new safe."

Men crowded around the rider. "Anyone hurt?"

"Did they find the thief?"

"Did he come this direction?" When the answers were no, the people were relieved to know the robbery would not involve them and returned to preparing for the journey.

The noise swelled with laughter, cries and shouts. Dust rose from the trampled ground. The smell of animals and woodsmoke tinged the air.

Mrs. Bingham had been riffling through a box of things at the back of the wagon. She straightened and signaled Ben, who rode over, his heart heavy. Whatever the woman wanted, he suspected it would be less than pleasant.

"My gilded mirror is missing."

Ben nodded. "You've misplaced it?"

"I have not. It's been stolen."

Ben sighed heavily. Such accusations without evidence served only to instill anxiety and mistrust among the travelers.

Mrs. Bingham drew herself up and gave him a demanding look. "Aren't you in charge of this group?"

"I am."

"First the bank and now a bunch of innocent, defenseless travelers. I suggest you do your job and find the thief or thieves."

"Yes, ma'am." Though he wondered if any of their group were defenseless. Everyone had a pistol or a rifle or both. All had axes and shovels. And he wasn't about to ride around demanding to know if someone stole a mirror. Likely the woman had misplaced it.

But he would do his job and keep a close eye on the Bingham wagon lest someone had targeted them as having valuable contents among their belongings.

Abigail returned to the wagon at that point. "Mother, what's wrong?"

Mrs. Bingham grabbed Abby's arm. "I've been robbed and this man is doing nothing about it. It appears to me he'll help only those he chooses to."

"Mother, we simply don't have time to worry about it right now. Everyone is ready to leave."

Ben rode away and didn't look back. Abigail was every bit as much under her mother's thumb as she'd ever been. Ben would not likely forget Mrs. Bingham did not approve of him. Therefore, Abigail didn't, either.

Abigail didn't have time to deal with her mother's fussing. Their journey was about to begin and she couldn't wait to get started. The future beckoned.

She joined her father beside the oxen.

"Well, daughter, we are about to see if your banker father can manage these huge beasts."

"You sound excited." Her own heart beat a rapid tattoo as she waited for their wagon to join the procession.

Ben sat on his horse, supervising the departure. He looked calm and in control.

She shifted her gaze away from him to the

wagons rolling out ahead of them. He traveled with his sisters. They must be so proud of him. And to think she might have been the one whose heart swelled with pride —

No. A life shared with him might have been filled with unexpected sorrow. She'd learned her lesson well enough not to care to repeat it.

"Come, boys," Father said, and the oxen moved out, following the others.

Abby laughed from sheer excitement.

Inside the wagon, Mother clung to her chair.

"Mother isn't happy about this adventure," Abigail commented.

"She's afraid of change, but we need it. We need to get over Andrew's death."

Abby's heart dipped. As always, guilt stung her at the mention of his name.

Father continued. "It's time to put his death behind us and look to the future."

"Is that possible?" If it still controlled them after ten years how was a trip going to change anything?

"I hope it is," her father said. "I believe this trip will change us all."

Abby hoped for the same, but change often came on the heels of adversity. She didn't have to think very hard to find it so in her life. Her future had changed when

46

Andy died. Again when the Panic struck and yet again when Frank died. And who could foretell which events would result in good and which ones in sorrow? *Father God, let this trip result in good for all involved.*

Sam Weston rode by. "Everyone ready?"

A roar of agreement answered him.

He rode on. "Wagons, ho."

Slowly the long line of wagons began to move.

Hundreds of people lined the route, waving flags and cheering them on. One lady ran forward and pressed a package into Abigail's hands.

"Some baking for the trip. God speed and safe travels."

Abby held the woman's hands for a heartbeat, and as the wagon lumbered away, she turned to wave goodbye.

Goodbye to the past.

Hello to the future.

She strained to see the way ahead, her heart pounding out the rhythm of the words as she waved and smiled at those sending them off.

Then they left behind the well-wishers and headed West.

Whatever the future held, it had to be better than the past. Her heart settled into place, feeling more hopeful than it had for so long she couldn't remember the last time.

Nothing would distract her from her plans for a new beginning in Oregon.

Not even her mother.

Chapter Three

The weather was clear, the trail easy. The white-sheeted wagons sailed across the green prairie like ships upon an ocean of green. Purple-and-yellow flowers dotted the landscape.

Mr. Weston called a halt at noon, by which time Abby was more than grateful. She'd tried riding in the wagon, but the hard bench and rough trail combined to make it most uncomfortable. She'd jumped down, preferring to walk. As soon as she vacated the wooden seat Mother left her unsteady chair to sit by Father, using a folded quilt to pad the bench.

Abby had walked almost the whole morning and her feet hurt.

The women immediately got out their cooking utensils and sent children to gather firewood. Father unhitched the oxen but, according to instructions from Ben, left them yoked. The great beasts grazed placidly.

Ben seemed to be everywhere. He rode through the camp calling out instructions or encouragement or, in a case or two, breaking up a fight. Several asked about the robbery. Could the culprit be among them? He tried to assure them there would be guards posted every night.

She turned to preparing a meager meal — all she seemed capable of. She could fry bacon again and eat the biscuits in the package she'd been handed as they left Independence.

She let the word *independence* roll around in her mind. She certainly liked the sound of it.

"Better check your bacon," Sally called.

Abby turned the pieces over. Only the edges were charred. Hopefully they were still edible.

An hour later they were again on their way.

At three o'clock they reached a place Mr. Weston called Elm Grove.

Abby had never thought a few elm trees and some bushes would be so welcome but her blistered feet ached for relief.

Mr. Weston led them into making a circle.

Father followed his instruction and drove the wagon so his front almost met the back of the wagon ahead of him then turned sharply. When the oxen were released, the wagons formed a barricade.

The oxen were set loose outside the circle to graze.

Ben rode around the circle. "Sam says we need to share fires. Soon enough we'll be scrounging for fuel. Three or four families together depending on the size of your family."

Almost before Abby could sort out all the things that had to be done, the others had organized who went with whom.

The Binghams were to be with the Littletons and Ben and his sisters.

Abby went to the back of the wagon as if to pull out something, but everything she needed for the evening was already spread out on the ground in preparation for the night.

The Littletons would be enjoyable people to spend the trip with, but the Hewitts? Why must they be grouped with them? Rachel had made her opinion clear yesterday. She didn't welcome the Binghams on the journey, let alone as their meal companions.

Emma, of course, had been more restrained in her reaction, though that didn't mean she had less of an opinion.

And Ben? What did he think? Was it going

to be awkward? Yes, they had history, but it was ancient history. They'd both moved on. She had no idea what Ben's plans were but seeing as he was obviously still unmarried, likely he would be looking for a suitable wife. One who would prove an asset in the new life they all planned.

She made a sound, half snort, half groan. Ben should enlist help from Abby's mother who thought she had a knack of finding suitable mates.

This time Abby groaned for real. Mother was not going to be happy about this arrangement and if Mother wasn't happy, Abby would have her hands full keeping her mother satisfied.

Oh, God, give me strength and patience.

She held on to the prayer as she returned to the others. She could do this without getting caught up in memories or regrets or guilt.

The men left to tend to the animals.

"Let's divvy up the chores," Rachel said to the women.

The others murmured agreement. All except Mother, who had allowed Father to lift her chair to the ground where she remained seated. Abby understood her mother considered it beneath her station in life to help with mundane chores.

"We'll take turns so no one ends up doing the dishes alone every night."

Again a murmur of agreement at Rachel's suggestion though Abby would have been quite happy doing dishes. It was the one thing she could manage. That and making tea. Both required only that she boil water.

"I'll make tea right away," she offered. "My mother is in need of a drink." Mother was pale, her jaw clenched so hard it would take more than a hot drink to loosen it.

"I'll cook the meat," Sally said.

Emma offered to prepare vegetables and a sweet. Rachel said she'd prepare the beans that had been soaking all day. "That way they'll be ready for dinner tomorrow."

The three women turned to Abby. She swallowed hard knowing they expected her to offer to make something for the supper. Something more than tea. She stifled a giggle. Could she make it through the next few months by making tea at every stop?

"Why don't you make biscuits?" Sally said.

Abby nodded not trusting her voice to speak confidently. She dragged out the reflector oven. She'd practiced setting it up and did so, though she still thought the apparatus was unstable, but others used one so she had to believe it was a suitable means of cooking. She positioned it close to the fire.

Abby measured the flour, lard and other ingredients and mixed them as she had learned at home. She cut them into rounds and placed them on the baking tray. There, she congratulated herself. This was going to turn out just fine.

She put them in the reflector oven, then poured tea for Mother.

Mother pulled her down to whisper in her ear. "I object to sharing meals with . . . with those."

"Mother, be grateful." They'd eat much better for the sharing.

A great clatter and Sally's sharply indrawn breath jerked Abby's attention her way. "Oh, no." The oven had collapsed. The biscuits fallen into a heap.

"I'm sorry," Sally said. She'd been tending Johnny and hadn't noticed where Abby set the oven.

Abby rushed to her side. "Are you okay? You're not burned?"

"No, I'm fine. But the biscuits —"

"They're ruined," Rachel said. Abby knew she wasn't mistaken in thinking Rachel sounded rather pleased about it.

"Why, the oven wasn't even braced. Now all this food is wasted," Rachel continued.

"They can be rescued." Ben had appeared out of nowhere and carefully retrieved the biscuits, then, with gloved hands, set the tin oven back up. He braced it with a branch. "To make sure it doesn't fall again."

Abby nodded, unable to meet his eyes. "Thanks." It was a lesson she wouldn't need repeated. Not repeating harsh lessons was her only triumph. Mr. Littleton returned from taking care of his animals and shot out his hand to Father. "Didn't get a chance to introduce myself earlier. Martin Littleton." He looked about. "So this is our group?"

Ben nodded. "Seems so. These are my sisters."

Rachel and Emma said hello to the man. Father introduced Mother.

Martin looked about. "It's a fine group. I'm sure we'll get on splendidly."

Abby ducked her head. His attitude might not be so accepting once everyone discovered Abby didn't know how to cook a thing.

She could only pray she would survive the trip with her resolve intact.

Ben accepted the plate of food Emma handed him. The Binghams had been placed with the Hewitts because of the proximity of their wagons. It was not a good match.

But what could he do but accept it gracefully? It wasn't like it would change anything. He knew what they thought of him and he, of them. But he would have been happier if he didn't have to share mealtimes with Mrs. Bingham's complaining and Abigail's simpering agreement. Mr. Bingham was okay. He was doing his best to cope in a situation that was completely out of his realm of experience.

Ben sighed. He should do the same.

Mrs. Bingham had been persuaded to pull her chair closer. The rest, including Mr. Bingham, sat in a circle on the ground.

Martin rose to ask the blessing, then they dug in.

Ben guessed by the way everyone tackled their food they were as hungry as he. Except for Mrs. Bingham, who picked at the things on her plate and shot demanding looks at Abby.

Abby seemed unaware of her mother's looks.

Ben kept his attention on Martin as he talked about the excitement of the first day of travel, but in the periphery of his gaze, he observed Abby.

A thought struck him so hard he couldn't swallow. He didn't know how Frank had died. Come to think of it, he didn't know how her twin brother had died, either. She'd always shied away from any questions he asked. All he knew was there had been an accident. Accidents were common. Swamp fever had killed many, as well. Some, like the Littletons, had lost most of their family. Had she lost children? He couldn't imagine the pain. Despite his desire to stay as far away from her as possible, the least he could do was offer his condolences.

Emma carried around a pot of stewed apple dumplings and served generous portions to everyone. Even Mrs. Bingham enjoyed the sweet and managed to lose some of her pinched look.

Abby sat beside Mrs. Littleton — Sally, as she'd asked to be called. Ben studied Abby under the pretext of watching a group of youngsters chasing each other in the middle of the circled wagons. Their excitement remained high after an easy day.

Ben had talked to Sam and learned the days would grow more challenging from here on.

But his thoughts were not on the journey. They detoured stubbornly to Abby and the tightness in her expression.

Sorrow filled her face. She carried much loss. Frank and . . . the same thought surfaced. Had she lost children?

He scrambled to his feet. "I'll check on things." He strode away before he could follow his inclination to ask Abby to walk with him. In the next few days he'd find a chance to ask her more about her life with Frank. But not now. Not today. His feelings were unsettled and he wanted them solid as a rock before he talked to her.

Instead, he turned his attention to the many needs of the emigrants. Guards had been set to watch the livestock and keep them from wandering too far. Each man would take turns at a four-hour shift. It wasn't his turn but even so, he left the wagons and went from one guard to the next. The men were excited tonight and not likely to doze off. Ben knew that it would be harder to stay awake after a few long days on the trail.

He returned to the wagons and moseyed around the circle. It was pleasant to see people in groups, visiting and sharing and learning about each other.

He passed the Jones wagon. Ernie Jones rose to his feet. "You've done made a mistake thinking you can tell me and my son what to do."

Not wanting to get involved in a fracas, Ben would have passed on without answering but several men watched and he knew he must deal with this here and now. "If you care to recall, I had no part in the decision. The committeemen made a ruling." He'd purposely not involved himself except to present his side of the situation.

Young Arty jogged up to stand by his father. "When do I get my gun back?" Belligerence rang in every syllable and showed in the way the boy stood, legs wide, arms akimbo.

"I believe Miles Cavanaugh is responsible for that decision."

Behind him sprightly music caught the attention of many and he turned his back on the troublesome Joneses.

"Skip, skip, skip to my lou."

He recognized the voice and the instrument. Abby and her mandolin. How many times had she entertained him with tunes? And together they had sung song after song. He remembered one particularly pleasant evening. He closed his eyes against the memory but it would not be stopped.

They sat on the porch swing outside her parents' house. Spring had arrived and with it the promise of good things to come. She'd learned a new song, "The Yellow Rose of Texas," and wanted him to learn it, too.

They'd laughed often as he stumbled over the words, happy simply to be with her and able to be outside, away from her mother's constant supervision. How wrong he'd been in thinking Abby shared his feelings.

He escaped the wagons and went out among the cattle. Let people think he was watching them, but in reality he wanted only to forget the bittersweet memory.

But it followed on his heels reminding him how he'd deliberately mixed up the words which sent her into gales of laughter. He'd caught her by the shoulders and shook her a little in mock scolding. Their eyes had locked together. He'd tipped his head low and rested his forehead on hers, breathing in the scent of her. Lavender and things that had no origin in smells but came from a knowledge of her — sweetness, stubbornness, humor, kindness. He'd closed his eyes, thinking how precious she'd grown over the winter months.

It was all a farce. He was only cheap entertainment for the time being.

His stride lengthened as he tried to flee that memory. He forced his thoughts to the ending. Father's successful mercantile business had faltered. He'd suffered under the strain and had a stroke. And Abigail had turned her back on him and married Frank.

His pace slowed. The sound of the mandolin followed him. He loved her music still.

Always would, he supposed, even if the memories were intertwined with pain and regret. It seemed she was still under her mother's watch. How had Frank dealt with that? Not that Ben cared. Not a bit.

Slowly he made his way back to the wagons. Abby's music had enticed some of the men to dance jigs and the children to twirl about.

Then she slowed the tunes and began to sing songs of gladness and hope. The children gathered round her. Men leaned against the wagons and women rocked their little ones.

But Ben remained at the far end, content to watch. He realized he stared at Abby with an intensity that belied how he meant to forget everything about her and he shifted his gaze to take in those around him.

Miles Cavanaugh nodded at him. He remained at his wagon. He traveled alone and perhaps felt as if he wasn't a part of the social gathering. Ben couldn't say, though, as he knew little about the man. He would certainly learn more about him as they traveled together.

A little further along, he detected another lone figure. Clarence Pressman — a smallish man with pale skin like he hadn't spent any time outdoors. Ben had noted the man before and was grateful he'd signed on with the Morrisons. Both parties would benefit from the arrangement.

The Tucker brothers, Amos and Grant — twins, Ben had been told though they didn't look a bit alike — crossed the tongue of a wagon and joined those gathered around Abby. No doubt they'd been out checking on the animals. The pair had joined them part way through the day, driving their oxen at a rate that had the animals sweating and snorting.

Amos introduced them. "We got behind the cattle train by mistake. Took us some hard going to catch up to this group." They'd nudged each other and laughed like the mistake was a huge joke.

Ben couldn't help but like their attitude but he hoped they'd be better at following instructions in the future.

His study brought him back to Abby. And the memory of sitting on the porch swing rushed again to the forefront.

Why must sweet memories be clouded by sorrow?

But they were and he couldn't change that.

He didn't have any doubt that Abby's memories were also clouded with sadness. Oh, not over him. But over the death of her husband.

He ground his fist into the soft spot beneath his ribs but it did nothing to ease the pain lodged there. He didn't wish for anyone to deal with such grief. He'd seen how deeply it had affected Grayson, driving him away from the family.

Ben missed him every day of his absence and anticipated their reunion.

All too soon the mothers called their children to them and prepared them for bed. While Abby had entertained the children, the menfolk had set up tents next to their wagons where their families would sleep.

Emma had prepared the tent she and Rachel would share. He'd sleep under a piece of canvas or just roll up in a bedroll under the wagon.

Abby and her father struggled to put up their tents. It appeared the older Binghams would share one tent and Abby would sleep in another.

After watching their vain attempts for a few minutes, Ben trotted over to assist.

"We can manage just fine, thank you," Mrs. Bingham told him, though she didn't lift a finger to help.

"I can't quite figure it out," Mr. Bingham said as if his wife hadn't uttered a word.

"Here. Take this rope and stake it out there about three feet. Be sure and angle the stake away from the tension so it stays in the ground."

In a few minutes, the tent was up. Mr. Bingham assisted his wife inside. Ben turned to Abby. His first instinct was to offer her help. But the knot in his heart warned him to give her a wide berth.

She grabbed a hammer and stake. "I watched you and Father. I think I can do it."

He'd watch for a moment then leave her be.

She drove in the first stake but when she tried to do the one opposite it, the rope kept escaping her. She laughed. "It's as slippery as a snake!"

How could he walk away from her need? What kind of neighbor would he be if he did? What sort of committeeman? His insides warred between responsibility and a desire to get as far away from this woman as possible.

Duty won out. Duty would always win.

He caught the errant rope and secured it. "It works better with a little help." He had no doubt she'd get the hang of it soon enough. In the meantime, he had no choice but to lend a hand. His gut twisted. How could he put distance between them when they were to share mealtimes and only one wagon separated his from the Binghams?

He straightened and took one step back and then another.

"Thank you for helping," Abby said. "I've been wanting to ask after your father. How is he?"

Ben pulled his thoughts into some semblance of order. "He never recovered." The shock of losing everything had caused him to have a stroke. "He died last year." That said so little of the long years of watching his declining health and how it had impacted all of them. "Emma nursed him."

"I'm sorry." She turned to his sisters who watched the proceedings. "My condolences." She tipped her head to Emma. "I could tell when you helped little Johnny that you are a skilled nurse."

"Thank you," Emma said.

Rachel still looked rather unfriendly.

Abby, to her credit, appeared unaffected by Rachel's expression and spoke to her. "You've grown up since I last saw you. In a very good way."

Rachel gave a half smile.

Abby nodded and bent her attention to the hammer in her hand.

Ben dropped his arms to his sides and

opened his mouth, prepared to scold Rachel for her rudeness but before a word left his mouth, Abby spoke.

"I venture to say we'll all change before this trip is over." She fixed Rachel with one of her piercing looks that he suddenly remembered with startling clarity. Anyone but Rachel would have flinched before those flashing eyes, but Rachel didn't even blink.

"T'would be good if we didn't forget the lessons of the past." No mistaking Rachel's meaning. She'd already made it clear she feared Ben would be hurt again and her words were meant as a warning to him as well as to Abby.

But she needn't worry about Ben. He'd learned his lesson when it came to Abby and he wasn't fool enough to want to repeat it. He might be forced to share their mealtime, even help her with some of the camp chores.

But he would never again be so foolish as to think she could care for him.

CHAPTER FOUR

With a murmured goodnight, Abby slipped into her tent. Her insides coiled with so many thoughts. Ben had never married. His father had passed away. How hard that must be. Ben had always been close to his father and brother. Grayson wasn't in the group. Had he stayed behind? That would be a doubly hard goodbye for Ben.

She tumbled the thoughts and questions round and round in her head in an attempt to ignore Rachel's warning. Her meaning was unmistakable — Don't hurt my brother.

Abby had no intention of doing so. She'd stay as far away from him as possible. She'd burned that bridge six years ago when she informed him she'd chosen Frank over him. Wanting to cut herself from his thoughts, she said Frank had more to offer — possessions, position, power.

She pressed a hand to her stomach as she thought of the cruel, unkind things he'd given instead.

Ben's response had been, "I wish you all the best and I trust your marriage vows will mean more to you than the words you spoke to me."

She knew exactly what he meant. They'd secretly confessed their love to each other. They'd planned to announce it to the world when she turned eighteen. She'd warned him her parents, Mother especially, would object, but had said she wouldn't let those objections change her mind.

But she had. So much guilt had filled her that she was unable to say no to her mother. Not that Mother would have accepted no. Abby would have been forced to follow her parents' wishes. Far better to go freely and of her own will, though every yes was filled with pain and regret.

"I see I was wrong to trust you. Good to know now rather than later." Those were Ben's parting words.

He'd never trust her again. And she couldn't blame him.

She, on the other hand, had learned after the fact how easily trust could be given to the wrong person. She would not trust her heart to any man ever again.

In Oregon, she'd start over. No regrets over anything in her past.

She tried to get comfortable on the ground but the waterproof ground cover rumpled underneath her. She finally pushed it aside and hoped it wouldn't rain.

She'd barely fallen asleep when the sentinels fired their rifles, waking everyone up. They'd been warned they would be called at four in the morning to prepare for departure. Abby hurriedly dressed and rolled up her bedding. She fashioned her hair as best she could then dashed outside.

"Vernon." Mother's voice came from her parents' tent. "I simply cannot survive under these conditions. Why, I don't even have my mirror. Someone stole it right under the nose of that young Hewitt who is supposed to be guarding us."

"Hush, Martha, do you want the whole camp to hear your complaints?"

Abby glanced around. Emma and Rachel were already tending the fire and from the looks on their faces, it was obvious they'd heard every word and did not appreciate Mother badmouthing their brother.

Sally crawled from their tent, baby Johnny cradled in one arm. "My, that was a short night. Johnny wouldn't settle. I did my best to keep him quiet, so he wouldn't wake the whole camp." She rushed on at such a rate that Abby knew she meant to turn attention from Mother's unkind remarks and she silently thanked the woman.

Emma went to Sally's side. "Do you want me to look at his wound?"

Sally unwrapped the baby in the cool pre-dawn.

Abby slipped away, hopefully unnoticed. She stopped at her parents' tent. "Mother, do you need help?" she whispered.

Father ducked out. "See if you can settle her down."

Abby patted his arm. "You look tired."

He nodded. "She fussed half the night."

Abby sucked in steadying air and bent over to enter the tent.

Mother sat atop the mussed covers, her legs out in front of her. She had her corset on but looked about ready to cry as she struggled with her dress.

Abby's heart went out to her. Mother had not welcomed this journey. She didn't see the challenge as something to embrace. But now Abby saw just how difficult it was going to be for her. Mother was no longer young and had never been one to do physical work.

Abby dropped to her knees to assist. "Let me help you." She eased the dress over Mother's head and fastened the buttons. "You'll get used to all this in no time."

"I'll never get used to it." Mother brushed a blade of grass from her skirt. "It's dirty and primitive." She sniffed. "But I don't intend to likewise be uncouth. Fix my hair and then fetch me some water so I can wash properly. And heavens, see that I get some proper food."

Abby spoke soothingly as she did her mother's hair. "Mother, how many times have you told me that a person must set their mind to do what needed to be done and then do it?" Of course, her mother had usually been talking about setting a proper table, or returning an unwelcome visit, but it surely applied here even more.

Mother sniffed. "About as many times as I told you if you made wise choices you wouldn't have to live with unpleasant consequences."

Abby chuckled softly, lest her mother fear she laughed at her. But it was amusing, ironic really, that this was the argument she'd used to convince Abby to marry Frank and the consequences had been horrible.

"This, I fear, is an unwise choice and the consequences will be most unpleasant."

Abby ignored the dire tone of her mother's words and managed not to shiver. If only Mother would stop making it sound as if they would regret this trip. She finished her mother's hair. "Mother, the future beckons. We can make it as good or as awful as we choose."

Abby meant to make the most of it. In Oregon, she would gain her freedom. Somehow she'd convince Mother to let her go so she could follow her heart.

She thought immediately of Ben. But that wasn't what she had in mind. He was of her past and she meant to put her past — all of it — behind her and start fresh. Wouldn't Mother be shocked if she knew the things Abby planned?

She crawled from the tent to get water for Mother.

Rachel frowned at her.

Abby looked about to see the reason. Sally tended a skillet of bacon with little Johnny perched on her hip. The baby sobbed softly. Emma checked the coffeepot. Abby knew from the aroma that it had boiled. Rachel stirred a pot of simmering cornmeal mush. A pitcher of milk perched nearby. Abby wondered who had milked the cow.

Abby's heart sank. She should be helping. Her mother should be helping. Knowing her mother wouldn't meant Abby should be doing enough for both of them. Instead, the others had prepared breakfast while Abby fussed over her mother.

It wouldn't happen again. If she must tend Mother she'd do it before time to prepare food or make her mother wait until after the meal. Abby ducked her head lest anyone think she smiled because she'd arranged to miss breakfast. No, her amusement came from imagining Mother being told to wait to have her needs tended to.

Abby glanced about again. She didn't know how to milk the cow, make the mush or most everything the others did. She vowed she'd learn just as she'd learn to ignore Ben, and the memories that came with his presence.

She looked about, didn't see him and let out a sigh. Easier to ignore him when he wasn't there.

Smiling at her private joke, she hurried to take the water to Mother, then rushed back to offer assistance to the other women. "I'll wash up seeing as I was absent for preparing the meal."

Sally patted her hand. "We work together as best we can."

As best we can. At least Sally seemed to understand.

One glance at Rachel and Abby knew she wouldn't be so accommodating.

"We all need to do our share." Rachel's words shot from her mouth.

Rachel would not hesitate to criticize Abby's failures. Never mind. They'd all learn things on this journey. Even the efficient Miss Hewitt.

Ben stood outside the circle of wagons. He'd been there several minutes. Long enough to hear Abby talking to her mother. The future beckoned. What did she mean? Had she agreed to marry a rich man in Oregon?

He knew such arrangements weren't uncommon. He had to look no further than the letter from Grayson for evidence. Grayson had suggested his widowed neighbor would be a good match for Emma. His three little girls needed a new mother. Emma had nodded when she read the letter. "I could look after them." Emma could do most anything she set her mind to. She'd volunteered at the local orphanage for a time after their father's death and had, according to all reports, been an excellent help with the children. Not that it surprised Ben.

Ben snickered as he recalled Rachel's reaction. "You've spent five years nursing our father. Now you're willing to play nursemaid to a bunch of little girls you don't even know? Emma, when will you stop being so compliant?"

Emma had given one of her sweet, forgiving smiles. "I'm twenty-four years old. I've long ago given up hopes of romance. I'll settle for safety and security."

Ben wished he knew what to say to encourage his beautiful blonde sister.

Rachel had thrown her hands in the air. "I will never settle."

Ben heard Abby speak again, bringing his thoughts back to the present. Did she have a suitor waiting for her in Oregon? Seems like it would explain why they were willing to cross the country.

Martin Littleton joined him. "Smells like breakfast is ready."

"Indeed." Mr. Bingham arrived and they joined the women around the campfire.

Ben stood, hat in hand. "I'll ask the blessing this morning. Then why don't we take turns doing it?"

The men nodded.

"Lord, we thank You for strength, for good weather, for good company and for good food. Keep us safe this day and to our journey's end. Amen."

The others echoed his amen as he sat between his sisters.

The coffee was hot and strong. The biscuits cold and dry. The cornmeal mush filling. The Littletons' cow provided them with fresh milk. But the mood felt strained.

Mrs. Bingham perched on her upright chair and picked at the food. She uttered not a word, but her lengthy sighs said plenty.

Ben had overheard Rachel's comment to Abby and knew she was annoyed. The last thing anyone on this journey needed was friction but there was little he could do about it without adding fuel to the fire. The women would have to sort things out among themselves.

The Littletons passed little Johnny back and forth between them and tried to calm his fussing.

"I simply don't know what's wrong with him." Sally gave the group an apologetic glance. "He's not normally like this."

"Perhaps he's ill," Mrs. Bingham said as matter-of-factly as if she'd mentioned the weather and seemed not to be aware that she'd sent a shock wave around the circle.

Martin grabbed his son and pressed his hand to the little forehead. "He's not fevered."

Sally hovered over the pair. "If he's sick — But Emma looked at his wound and said it was fine."

Abby moved to Sally's side and wrapped an arm around the woman's shoulders. "So many changes are hard to get used to. We're all feeling it." She sent a scolding look toward her mother. "He'll adjust. We all will."

Mollified, Sally sat back and held out her arms to take the baby. "You're right, of course."

Martin patted little Johnny's back.

Ben couldn't take his eyes off Abby. He remembered how kind she was to others back when they were friends. Why should he have thought marrying Frank would change that? But somehow he had.

Rachel nudged him in the ribs. And it made him aware of how long he'd been staring at Abby. He tipped his cup to his mouth for the last drops of coffee and bolted to his feet.

"Time to get ready to leave."

The men brought in the oxen and yoked them to the wagon amid many shouts.

The women cleaned up the foodstuff and packed away the belongings. All but the youngest children ran about helping with the chores.

Ben prepared his own wagon. He'd let Rachel and Emma take turns driving it while he helped keep this company in order. He saddled his horse and rode from wagon to wagon until he was satisfied.

On the other side of the circle, Mr. Bingham tried unsuccessfully to get his oxen in order. Mrs. Bingham's shrill voice reached Ben clear across the enclosure. The oxen stamped and tossed their heads. Between Mr. Bingham's uncertainty and his wife's yammering, they were about to have a wreck.

Martin had his hands full with his own animals so couldn't lend his aid.

Ben spurred his horse into a gallop and reached the Binghams' wagon. He leaped from his saddle and rushed to help with the animals.

"Easy there. Easy, big boy. There you go." He calmed the animal and backed it into place. "The second animal is always harder to yoke into place than the first." He kept his voice low and soothing. "And what's your name, big fella?"

"That one's Bright. His partner is Sunny. The other two are Buck and Liberty," Abby answered.

Ben's gaze bolted to the wagon where Abby sat on the seat, the reins clenched in her white-knuckled hands. Her face seemed rather pale. His heart melted at how frightened she must be with these big animals acting up. What had she said about facing changes? He'd venture a guess she'd never before had any dealings with thousand-pound oxen. They'd all adjust but some had more adjusting to do.

"Liberty? Isn't that a little highfalutin compared to the others?"

She nodded. "Kind of thought so myself. But the man we bought him from said he was born on the fourth of July. What else was he to name him?"

"I guess it's better than Bell." His feeble attempt at humor was rewarded when she laughed.

"Buck and Bell has a certain ominous ring to it."

He chuckled. "We don't want any bucking around here." He helped Mr. Bingham yoke the two remaining animals.

"I fear I'll never get good at this," the man murmured.

Mrs. Bingham poked her head out of the wagon. "I tried to tell you, you weren't the sort to make this kind of journey."

Mr. Bingham sighed softly. "We're going."

Ben patted Mr. Bingham's shoulder. "You'll catch on soon enough."

He spared one more glance in Abby's direction.

"Thank you," she murmured. Her hazel eyes burned a trail through his thoughts.

Leading his horse, he strode away as fast as his legs would carry him. What was wrong with him that he couldn't even look at the woman without his thoughts scrambling like an egg dropped on the ground? Her look had meant nothing but gratitude for his help.

He wasn't about to pick up where they'd left off six years ago. A person could not undo the things that had been done. They couldn't erase the words that had been spoken.

Only the future mattered and that lay in Oregon where he would join Grayson and the two of them would work together again as they had all Ben's life. Like two oxen sharing the load.

He swung into his saddle and turned the horse toward the Hewitt wagon.

Emma and Rachel sat side by side. Rachel's look was sharp with disapproval.

"Already she's got you at her beck and call."

Emma made a quieting motion with her hand. "Rachel, that's not fair. Ben was only doing his duty as one of the committeemen."

"I don't see him helping anyone else."

Which wasn't true, but before Ben could defend himself, Rachel rushed on.

"I see it now. She'll be all sweet with you while she needs your help, but once we get to Oregon, she'll be off in search of better prospects."

"Hush, Rachel." Emma shook her head at Ben. "We all know she would have to search far and wide and still she'd not find anyone better than Ben."

He smiled at his gentle sister. If only everyone thought the same.

"Emma's right. I'm only doing my job." His duty and fulfilling his responsibilities was all he had to cling to. Getting his family to Oregon safe and sound, assisting others on the wagon train, those were the sort of things that made him sit with his shoulders squared.

The bugle sounded to indicate it was time to move out. Ben sat astride his horse, urging each wagon into place. Soon the column was on the move and he leaned back, his heart at ease. This was what mattered — keeping things rolling.

Dust billowed up around each wagon wheel and filled the air. Those in the lead didn't have to breathe in quite so much, but by the end of the column the dust was thick and choking. Soon the wagons fanned out to avoid each other's dust. Still, those at the rear got more than their fair share.

Ben wiped his eyes as he rode past the

final wagons but it did nothing to clear his vision.

Four wagons from the end, he encountered Ernie Jones and his wagon. He couldn't see Arty. Likely the boy had wisely taken to walking far enough from the column to avoid the dust.

Ernie called out to him. "You made sure I rode back here, didn't ya?"

"Everyone will take turns being first or last. Sam Weston ordered it." He made to ride on.

Ernie uttered a rude word. "I'd like to see the day you make that gal friend of yers and her uppity ma and pa ride in the back."

He'd done nothing that would give anyone reason to suspect they had once had an interest in each other. Or so he thought. He snorted. Yet Ernie had seen enough to make his accusation.

Or had he? Ben's thoughts cleared. It seemed Ernie had a knack for creating trouble. That's all it was. No need to get fussed about it.

At the second last wagon, a man signaled for Ben to ride closer. "My missus says her mixing bowl is gone."

Ben had heard such statements before. "Did she leave it behind?"

"Not my missus. Someone's taken it."

82

More suggestion that there was a thief in their midst. "It's easy to lose things in the hustle of moving every day."

"I suppose so." The man seemed ready to accept it was lost. Ben didn't like to think otherwise. He thought of the bank robbery back in Independence but there was no reason to think that person was in the wagon train.

He rode up the column. Many of the women and children walked beside the wagons, far enough away to avoid the dust.

He reached the Hewitt wagon. Emma drove it. He glimpsed Rachel walking in a group of women. Sally Littleton was there, too, carrying little Johnny. She must get weary. She'd tried to carry him in a sling but he'd protested so loudly she'd abandoned the idea.

A familiar figure appeared at Sally's side. Abby. Her bonnet hid her face but he knew her from the way she walked, the way she tilted her head as she talked then she turned to Sally and Ben saw her profile. She smiled at the other woman and held out her arms, offering to take Johnny.

The way Sally's shoulders sagged as she released her baby to Abby's arms indicated how tired she had grown.

Ben smiled and his heart warmed. These

women would soon learn to work together in peace. He dismounted and tied the horse to the back of the wagon then trotted up to the front and swung up beside Emma. "I'll drive for a while. Why don't you join the other ladies?"

"Thanks." Emma barely finished the word before she jumped down.

He grinned as he guided the oxen along. The view was pleasant from up there. Abby did a funny little jiggling walk as she bounced the baby. Her skirt swung from side to side in a way that made her appear almost fluid. The baby caught at her bonnet strings and loosened them allowing it to fall back on her head. Her hair turned golden in the sun. She laughed at little Johnny's antics.

He couldn't hear the sound of her laughter but knew it by heart. Clear and musical as ringing bells. He jerked his attention to the heavy-hipped animals before him. Clumsy looking but they were suited to their task.

And he was suited to his. Just as Abby was suited to hers. He, a simple man. She, a beautiful woman who belonged in a fine parlor surrounded by things money could buy.

Against his better judgment he stole another glance at her. She seemed perfectly at ease with the child.

His heart twisted within him at the realization of why she was good with the baby. If she'd had her own and lost them.

Thankfully no one was about to see him flinch.

CHAPTER FIVE

Abby's arms soon grew weary of carrying little Johnny. He wouldn't settle. But then he hadn't settled for his mama, either, and her arms must be four times as sore as Abby's. Poor little boy was upset about so much change and no doubt suffered pain because of the injury to his side.

Over and over Sally thanked God it wasn't worse. "Just a flesh wound," she said.

"Poor Johnny doesn't know he's fortunate. All he knows is he's hurt." Abby jiggled the baby up and down on her hip. The least she could do was give Sally a break.

Sally had tried to settle him in the wagon, but he refused to let her put him down, and Sally said she got tired of bouncing around.

Emma had joined the others walking along the trail. Rachel was still among the group. That meant — Abby glanced over her shoulder — yes, Ben sat on the seat of their wagon.

And he watched her.

She jerked her head round to face forward. She must be imagining it. Just a trick of the light.

She would not look again though her neck creaked at the effort it cost her.

A horse and rider rode toward them. "We'll be nooning here," the man called.

Thank goodness.

The wagons stopped. The oxen were loosed to graze. The men carried water to them as the women quickly prepared the meal.

Rachel brought out the beans she'd prepared the day before. Sally had leftover biscuits. Emma fetched enough wood to build a small fire to make coffee.

Determined to do her share, Abby added dried apples to the offerings. Yes, she might have thought to make them into a pie the night before. Except she didn't know how to make a pie. Or she might have stewed them.

Watching the others gave her an idea. They used an endless supply of biscuits and bread. Tonight she'd bake up a large batch of biscuits so there would be some for tomorrow.

The men ate and stretched out on the ground and were instantly asleep. Sally nursed Johnny and he settled into her arms for a nap. She laid him on a blanket in the shade and when he didn't stir, she joined the others to clean up.

Abby stopped her. "Why don't you rest with him? I'll do your chores for you."

"That's a good idea," Emma added. "You need to preserve your energy so you can take care of Johnny."

"Thank you." Sally squeezed Abby's hands and stretched out beside the sleeping baby. Soon her gentle snores joined the louder ones of her husband and Abby's father.

Abby stole a glance at Ben lying in the shade of their wagon, his hat pulled over his face. She didn't hear snores from Ben's direction. Did that mean he wasn't asleep? His hat tipped to one side. Was he watching her? Them — she corrected.

Her cheeks grew warmer than they'd been a moment ago. One thought cooled them in an instant. They were no longer children. Both were wiser, more cautious. At least she suspected he would be. She certainly was. In Oregon, she'd find her freedom — from men, from her mother . . . could she possibly ever be free from her promise?

Father God, provide a way. Please.

Mother rose slowly and marched away.

Abby watched her, noting she moved stiffly. Walking would do her good.

She helped Emma and Rachel clean up from the meal, well aware that Rachel sent a frown in Mother's direction.

"I'm sorry," Abby murmured. "Mother has no idea how to help."

Rachel's reply was short. "She might have to learn."

Abby shrugged. "I don't mind doing her share." If she wasn't mistaken, Rachel rolled her eyes before she reached for the last pot to put away.

Yes, Abby had neglected to do her share earlier, let alone Mother's, but she didn't intend for it to happen again.

They were soon on their way. Abby's feet hurt but she would not complain. She went to their wagon. "I'd like to ride for a while. Father, why don't I drive the oxen and you can walk?"

Mother sat upright on the seat, her face pinched.

Father climbed down. "I'll walk beside the beasts."

Abby understood it was to ensure they continued in the right direction, but she didn't mind. To be honest, the big animals made her mouth go dry.

Within minutes she understood why

Mother looked as if she were in constant pain. The wagon jerked and jolted causing the wooden bench to constantly whap Abby's rear. Even with a quilt folded for them to sit on, her bottom hurt almost as much as her feet and her neck ached. How were they going to endure two thousand miles of this? Perhaps Mother was right. The Binghams were too soft for such a challenging journey.

Abby's spine stiffened. Her chin jutted out. Bingham or Black. Rich or poor. She meant to finish this trip. She meant to survive. More than that, she would become strong and capable, because at the end, she saw nothing but freedom. She nodded at the big ox. Liberty was his name. Liberty was her aim.

With every jolt of the long afternoon, her determination grew. When they approached the stopping place, she changed places with Father so he could guide the wagon into the circle.

And if every bone in her body protested, she ignored them. She had things to do. Even before the animals had been set free to graze, she set out to get firewood and returned with an armload in double-quick time. Others had done the same thing so likely no one took note of her actions.

It didn't matter. She had proved to herself she was capable of one thing. Now she meant to prove another and measured out floor, lard and milk. She rolled the dough on the little table Martin set out.

She squinted at the slab of dough. "What is that?" Black dots. She picked one out.

Sally and Emma bent over the dough.

"Did you sift the flour?" Sally asked softly.

"No, I was in hurry."

Sally chuckled. "Sometimes it doesn't pay to be in a hurry. I'm afraid a mouse has been into your flour. Those are mice droppings."

Abby stepped back in horror. "Mice. We'll have to toss out all the flour."

Emma shook her head. "You can sift it out. And likely it's only in one corner. I'll have a look if you like."

Rachel grinned so wide it was a wonder her face didn't crack.

Abby bit back the angry words rushing to her mouth. She grabbed the dough and hurried outside the circled wagons. She reached some bushes and shoved the dough into the branches. Let some hungry animal eat it. Maybe some mice. Let them choke on their own droppings.

She fell on her knees, her breath coming in gasps. Why, oh, why was she so inept?

After a moment, her breathing calmed, although her mind continued to twist and turn. She pushed to her feet and headed back to the camp. This little setback would not deter her. She would learn.

As she approached the wagons, she heard her name and paused to listen. The voice was Rachel's.

"Imagine wasting all those supplies."

Abby edged forward trying to see who Rachel talked to.

Then a man spoke. "Give her a chance."

Ben. She pressed her hand to her throat. She'd know his voice anywhere. He sounded weary. Weary of her failures? She closed her eyes. *Lord, help me. Help me learn what I need to do. Most of all, give me strength to see Ben every day and not be filled with regret at what might have been.*

Again she reminded herself that *what might have been* was a romantic dream. Never again would she trust a man enough to give him the right to own her.

She calmed her heart knowing she didn't make this journey alone. Yes, she had her parents. But she also had God. He'd been her strength and solid rock of refuge for many years. In fact, she remembered clearly when she'd learned to love Him so.

Not ready to rejoin the others, she leaned

against the nearest wagon wheel and let her memories flow. It was at special meetings held in the school. There she also had met Ben. She'd seen him before, but their paths seldom passed until then.

An itinerant preacher held the meetings. He delivered a challenge to the young people to become soldiers of the cross. How his words had fired her soul with resolve. He said as soldiers they needed to prepare for battle and gave such practical steps, each of them relating to soldiers. One of the steps was to learn to wield your sword with skill. There had been a list of Bible verses he'd challenged them to memorize. *And apply with your heart.* She had turned to the young man beside her and said she intended to do exactly that. That was Ben and he said he did, too. They'd spent hours together drilling each other on the list of verses. They had been some of the most pleasant times in her life.

She might have given up her chance to see where her relationship with Ben would go but she would never regret the time they'd spent learning the verses. Again and again, they had been her comfort, especially Isaiah 43:2. *"When thou passest through the waters, I will be with thee; and through the rivers, they shall not overflow thee: when thou* walkest through the fire, thou shalt not be burned; neither shall the flame kindle upon thee."

She'd been through many troubled waters and found God's supply sufficient.

Lifting her head, she looked about her. No water here, just land and lots of it. God would be with her here, too.

A smile on her lips, she stepped back into the circle and went to the fire. "I'm sorry I messed that up. Now tell me what to do to help."

Emma patted her back. "Let's just say that's a lesson you won't have to learn again."

Abby laughed. "No. Once is enough for me, thank you very much. My intention had been to bake enough biscuits for tonight and tomorrow. Can I try again?"

Sally and Emma both nodded. "By all means."

Sally added, "I have a loaf of batter bread baking at the moment. Why not do the biscuits after supper?"

Rachel hung back, her eyes guarded, her expression watchful.

Abby allowed herself one quick glance at Ben, but his attention was on something across the circle.

Well, better disinterest than outright displeasure.

Once is enough for me.

Abby's words echoed through Ben's head. He needed to brand them on the surface of his brain. He'd been hurt by Abby's unfaithfulness once. Once was enough for him.

He'd seen the shock and hurt on her face when she discovered the droppings in the biscuit dough. When she'd rushed from the camp bearing the ruined dough he'd wanted to follow and assure her it wasn't the end of the world. Rachel had stopped him.

"Why do you jump to her aid all the time? You know what will happen when she no longer needs your help." Rachel wasn't about to let him forget that Abby had broken off their relationship. And broken his heart in the process.

Although he knew she spoke only out of concern for his well-being, he had to choke back words of protest. After all, he was a big boy now. He could take care of himself. He'd glanced after Abby, but didn't follow her. Why would he seek to have his scarred heart torn again? Not that Rachel meant to let that happen. She could be very persistent.

Abby returned, a smile upon her lips, and went immediately to Sally and Emma and asked to try again. Her voice revealed nothing but contrite sweetness.

Ben had expected her to be upset. This serenity flummoxed him. He didn't want to look at her but he couldn't stop himself.

She hummed as she helped serve the meal.

When Martin asked the blessing, Ben peeked from under his lashes and stole a look at Abby.

His eyelids jerked up at her posture. She sat on the ground like everyone except her mother. Her hands lay open in her lap, palms upward as if she waited for a gift. Her head was bowed and yet from what he could see of her face he thought she about overflowed with peace.

How could that be? She'd lost her husband and for all he knew, a child or children. She struggled to cope with the chores and trials of this journey and her mother never stopped complaining and yet he knew he was right. All those things had not robbed her of her source of joy.

He recalled the Bible verses they had memorized together and how she vowed to apply them to her life. When she'd chosen to marry a man richer than Ben, he'd decided her determination to live those verses had been as false as her words about caring for him. Perhaps he'd been wrong.

He closed his eyes and added a silent prayer to Martin's. *Lord, she's reminded me that my strength and joy are in You. Help me keep sight of that and forget the petty, confusing things going on about me.* He meant a number of things — Ernie Jones, Mrs. Bingham's litany of complaints, but mostly, he meant his confused feelings regarding Abby. He didn't trust her and never would, yet the memories of the times they'd spent together were rich with sweetness and joy which he wished he could deny.

One thing he wouldn't deny, he was grateful for her reminder to trust God more fully.

She carried a plate of food to her mother.

"I feel dirty all over," the woman whined. "I simply can't do this." She fluttered her hands.

Ben couldn't tell if she meant to include present company or present circumstances but likely both.

Abby smoothed her mother's hair. "Have you forgotten you're a Bingham? Binghams don't let circumstances dictate their behavior."

Beside Ben, Rachel gave a tiny snort.

But the words had the effect Abby no doubt desired and her mother sat up so straight Ben wouldn't have been surprised to see an iron rod along her spine.

"I'll do my best."

Ben released a sigh of relief and heard the others do so, as well. If she would simply accept the circumstances and stop her complaining life would be more pleasant for all of them — herself included.

Abby returned to her spot by her father.

Little Johnny wailed. The child had proven inconsolable all day.

Ben glanced at Emma and they shared their silent concern. It didn't seem normal for the child to be so fussy especially given that both Sally and Martin said it wasn't usual. But then he'd been shot. Ben never had been, so couldn't say how much a flesh wound hurt.

"His wound must be paining him something awful," Emma said. "After supper I'll put something on that might relieve his pain."

"I'd so appreciate it," Sally said, her voice weary.

Over supper, conversation turned to plans for the morrow and various concerns about the animals and the wagons. The meal ended and the women set to work cleaning up.

Martin took Johnny and tried to comfort him while Mr. Bingham set up his tent then helped his wife to it. Seems she meant to retire early. This trip would tax her strength and adaptability.

The animals were grazing under the supervision of others and it wasn't Ben's turn to keep watch though he wondered if he should walk about watching for anything that could lead to trouble. But for a few moments, he'd relax and he lounged back against the rear wheel of his wagon.

Abby measured out flour for another batch of biscuits. She examined the sack of flour carefully then spoke to Sally. "You were right. Only one corner seems to be affected. The rest is okay." She carried the unusable flour outside the camp and disposed of it.

As she worked, she chatted cheerfully with the women. Soon she had Sally and Emma chuckling over some comment.

Ben thought of edging closer so he could share the joke but decided against it. He had no interest in what she said or did.

She rolled the biscuit dough in fluid movements. But then, as he recalled, she'd always had a graceful way about her that made him think of flowers swaying in a gentle breeze.

A picture flashed into his mind. One he'd tried to erase so many times because it made his heart contract with regret and bitterness.

They'd been on a picnic with a group of young people, chaperoned by the pastor and his wife. They'd spread their lunch on a red-checkered cloth in a grassy field outside of town. All around them were blue and red and pink and white wildflowers. Nearby, a lark sat on a branch and sang.

Abby had laughed with utter joy. "It's like God has painted an Audubon picture for us."

That had brought everyone's eyes to her. Some knew of the naturalist but that didn't deter Abby. Her eyes sparkling, she regaled them with stories about John James Audubon. "He set out to paint every bird of the United States. Beautiful pictures. My grandfather subscribed to his series of prints. There were issued every month or so in sets of five. I've never looked at birds or flowers or nature the same since I saw his work." She'd rushed to her feet and run into a patch of flowers, plucking one and dashing back. "This is a common musk mallow. Have you ever noticed the beauty of the pistils and stamens? The heart shape of the leaves? Every detail so amazing." She'd spun away, holding the flower overhead.

She'd been amazing. Maybe still was. Her cheerful countenance certainly brought a smile to his lips even as it had back then.

She pulled a final tray of biscuits from the reflector oven. "Anyone care to test them?"

"I'd like to." Sally took one and buttered it. She laughed. "At least I don't have to churn butter. Just hang the cream on the side of the wagon and it's ready for supper." She took a bite. "Umm, these are good."

Abby passed them around to the others. Martin waved her aside.

"Later," he whispered. Little Johnny slept on Martin's chest.

Ben sat up and took one. He buttered it and bit in.

Abby waited.

He nodded. "It's good. We'll be grateful of them tomorrow."

She smiled. Her eyes sparkled, reminding him yet again of that day in the meadow and her unbridled enjoyment of life.

Rachel broke hers open and carefully examined the inside.

The smile slipped from Abby's lips and she returned to the campfire.

Ben wanted to say something to bring back the sunshine but his throat closed off. What could he say or do to change anything? And he didn't mean only this moment.

Baby Johnny woke up and wailed.

Sally sighed wearily and reached for the child.

"I'll take him for a while," Abby offered, and took the fussy baby. She walked back and forth singing a lullaby. After a few minutes the baby settled to sleep and Abby handed him to Sally.

"I so appreciate your help," the weary mother said. "You're very good with him."

"Thanks."

"Sure would like to hear that mandolin again," Clarence Pressman called across the clearing in a husky voice.

"I'll get it." Abby went to the Bingham wagon and returned with the mandolin and a book. She played and sang several songs. A dozen or more children gathered round to listen and as many grown-ups. When she played hymns, many of the adults sang along.

"She plays beautifully," Rachel murmured, the surprise in her tone conveying her reluctance to admit it.

"Yup." Not only did she play and sing beautifully, she was beautiful in every way. Too bad her unfaithfulness canceled out the fact.

"I've always wanted to play an instrument."

He shifted to look at his sister. "I remember you playing the piano." They'd sold it four years ago to pay a bill.

"Only a little."

His little sister watched Abby with such longing that it tore at Ben's heart. "We should have kept the piano."

She flung about to face him. "That would have been foolish. A piano is nothing but a luxury." Her gaze went back to Abby.

Ben watched her, too. "Say, why don't you ask her to give you lessons?"

Rachel gave him a look fit to cure his hide. "I couldn't do that."

"Why not? She seems to like helping people."

Rachel plucked at a blade of grass. "I haven't exactly been welcoming to her."

"I noticed."

Rachel lifted one shoulder in a dismissive gesture as if that took care of the matter.

Ben studied her a few minutes. "Rachel, don't let pride rob you of the possibility of joy."

Her head jerked up. "I wouldn't do that."

"Good to know." They both settled back. He hoped Rachel would take his words to heart.

After a bit, Abby put the mandolin down. "I thought the children might like a bedtime story."

"Yes, ma'am," a young fella called out.

She began to read. Not only the children listened. Adults hovered by, as well, he as intently as any. Not that the story mattered. It was her voice. The gentle, modulated voice of an educated woman made listening a joy.

He'd always taken pleasure in the sound of her voice and six years' absence, time and losses, not even a world of regrets over how their relationship ended, changed that.

She read only a few minutes. "I can read more tomorrow, if you all like."

Ben chuckled at the enthusiastic response.

She put her mandolin and book back in the wagon. She gasped and he jerked to his feet. But she returned unharmed.

"Mother, look what I found. Your mirror. It must have slipped into the corner when the wheel came off the wagon. At least it wasn't stolen."

Mrs. Bingham took the mirror. "No thanks to anyone here."

Abby patted her mother's shoulder then prepared to pitch her tent.

He waited a moment, so it didn't appear like he rushed to her assistance, then ambled over. "Can I give you a hand?"

She brushed strands of hair from her face. "I will learn to do this." She favored him with a bounteous smile. "But in the hope of getting some sleep tonight I'll gladly accept help . . . again." A tiny sigh escaped.

He chuckled at her wry expression. "I expect you're wore out."

"I'll be glad of a few hours sleep." Not a word of complaint, though her mother could be heard murmuring in her tent about the dust, the crude accommodations and a myriad of nitpicky things.

Abby shook her head as she stared at her parents' tent.

"Martha, hush now and settle down," Mr. Bingham said.

Abby grinned, sending a jolt clear through Ben.

He opened his mouth wanting to ask her so many things.

"Let's get this tent up, so we can all go to bed." His voice carried a sharp note.

She grabbed a rope and jerked it into place, the smile gone from her face.

He wished it could be different. But it was too late for that. Her earlier words blared through his head. *Once is enough for me.*

It was enough for him, too.

CHAPTER SIX

Abby lay in her tent waiting for sleep. Her arms ached from carrying Johnny so many hours. She was such a softy. But she'd made biscuits enough for tomorrow and amused the children with music and story.

The camp quieted around her. From nearby came the sound of snoring. How did anyone sleep through that? Pity the poor man's wife and children. Johnny fussed and Sally shushed him. Poor baby was so uncomfortable.

Abby pulled the covers from her blistered feet. Johnny probably hurt worse than that.

A dog barked. A man ordered him to be quiet. The oxen snorted. The guards called out to one another.

Next thing she heard was the sound of rifles rousing them from their sleep. She groaned, feeling pain in places she hadn't known existed before this journey. But she would not repeat the mistakes of yesterday.

She dressed in record time and hurtled from the tent.

She joined Emma and Rachel at the fire. "I'll make coffee this morning." She'd watched enough times to know she would get it right.

Sally returned from milking the cow.

"How did Johnny sleep?"

"He was restless all night, but I think he's finally settled. I put him in the wagon. Maybe he'll stay asleep after we pull out."

She took care of the milk while the others worked together on the meal.

The men had left to gather the stock and bring the oxen in to harness.

"Abigail." Mother's call came sharp and demanding.

Abby gave the others an apologetic glance. "Excuse me while I help her."

Sally patted her arm. "You go ahead. We each have our own duties to attend to and she's one of yours."

Abby smiled her gratitude, then hurried to help Mother get dressed.

"Am I supposed to wear this dress again?"

"We had to limit how much we brought." Mother knew that and had complained bitterly about it.

She sniffed. "Some people might not object to wearing the same dress day after day, but I was raised better than that."

"Yes, Mother, I know." Abby had learned long ago it was best not to argue. It only added fuel to her mother's opinions. She did her best to hurry her parent but the faster she went the slower her mother went. "Mother, I must do my share." *And yours.*

"I didn't raise you for this kind of life."

"Of course you didn't, but things change." Abby would have given up some of her history and art lessons for cooking and husbandry lessons.

Mother fussed with her hair. "It doesn't feel right."

"It's fine." It would be covered with a bonnet most of the day so what difference did it make?

Mother drew herself upright as far as the low tent allowed. "We might be forced to live with those people." She waved her hand dismissively. "But there is no need to lower our standards."

"Yes, Mother." Not wanting to have to endure a lecture, she managed to keep any hint of disagreement from her voice.

"You must stop encouraging that . . . that Hewitt man."

"I'm sure I don't know what you mean."

"I think you do. You let him help you with your tent. Get Father to help if you must have help. Or Mr. Littleton. I don't want you encouraging him." No matter what Mother thought, Abby wasn't begging for Ben's attention. She had plans in mind that did not involve a man, any man.

Mother poked her finger in Abby's direction. "When we get to Oregon, you will marry someone suitable."

Abby could bear to hear no more. The time would come when she must confront her mother with the fact she had no intention of marrying anyone — suitable in Mother's opinion or otherwise. All she had to do was convince Mother she had fulfilled the spirit of her promise to take care of her parents. Now was not the time or place to deal with her plans. Thankfully, she had finished helping and she backed from the tent.

She turned and looked into the hard eyes of Ben. "I —" She shook her head. What could she say? And what was the point?

Shifting her gaze, she encountered Emma. Her wide eyes and dropped jaw informed Abby that she'd overhead the conversation.

No doubt they all had.

She could either run and hide or —

She followed Mother's example, stiffened her spine and went to the fire to look at the mush simmering. Let them think what they would. She wasn't responsible for Mother's opinions.

But how she wished she could tell them she didn't agree. They were a fine bunch and she was proud to be associated with them.

At that moment, Johnny let out a wail. Poor baby was so tired from crying, he could hardly make himself heard.

"Something's wrong." Sally dashed for the wagon and scrambled in. Three seconds later, she called, "He's burning up. Someone help me."

Emma raced for the wagon, Abby hot on her heels. Her breath caught midway up her chest. She didn't know anything about treating disease, like Emma did. But she knew the fear of someone sick or injured.

Lord, spare us that sorrow on this journey.

Ben struggled to get over the words from the Bingham tent. Mrs. Bingham's opinion had not softened with time. He shook his head so hard he unsettled his hat and jammed it back in place with unusual force.

He already suspected that Abby would be searching for a rich man in Oregon so it shouldn't surprise him.

Nor did it. No, it wasn't surprise so much as shock that everyone had heard Mrs. Bingham's comments. And . . .

He couldn't think what to call this feeling except it caused a burning taste in the back of his throat. Reminiscent of how he'd felt six years back when Abby and her mother had told him the truth about how they saw him. It hadn't bothered him to hear the harsh words from Mrs. Bingham, but to hear Abby inform him he wasn't suitable had shaken him to his core. Left him with feelings of uncertainty. It had taken him a long time to realize their opinion — Abby's opinion — did not define who he was. From that moment he had sought to develop strengths that came from within. No one could take that from him.

Not even cruel, unkind comments from the Bingham tent. He would simply consider the source.

At Sally's cry for help, Emma rushed to the Littletons' wagon and jerked Ben from his troubled thoughts.

Martin had been tending his oxen and returned in time to see Emma clamber under the canvas.

"Johnny?" Forgetting the animals, he ran to his wagon. "Is he . . ."

Ben dragged his feet after the man. His chest felt heavy. *Please, God, don't let Johnny die. The Littletons have already lost three*

111

children. Of course, God knew that and didn't need reminding. Ben couldn't think how they'd endure the loss of their baby, as well. He'd watched Grayson struggle when Suzanne had died delivering their firstborn. For a time, he worried his brother might not ever be the same and despite knowing he'd miss him like crazy, he'd been glad when Grayson said he was going to Oregon. It would provide a new start.

Which is exactly what Ben hoped for. He filled his lungs with a mighty gulp. The future still beckoned. He had only to endure the days of crossing.

Abby scurried past him to the wagon.

He forced his feet onward until he reached the tailgate. "Is he . . . ?" The word stuck on his tongue.

Abby answered him as she jumped from the wagon and scurried away. "Fevered. I have to take water to sponge him." She filled a basin from the barrel of water, grabbed a cloth and slowed her steps to carry the water without spilling it.

"Infection?" From the beginning Emma had been concerned about the flesh wound, saying she hadn't treated it as aggressively as she normally would because of the pain she'd have to inflict on the baby. She would never forgive herself if her concern resulted in something far worse than temporary pain.

Abby kept her attention on the basin and spoke without glancing at him. "Emma is looking at him now."

She reached the wagon and handed the basin inside.

Ben stepped to her side, resisting the urge to reach for her hand and grip it, offering his strength and encouragement. She'd already grown fond of the child. And if she'd lost her own children, this little one's illness would be a sharp and painful reminder.

He looked into the crowded wagon. "Emma, what's wrong with him?" he asked his sister who knelt by the baby. All Johnny wore was his white diaper.

"I can't see any sign of infection." She spoke calmly so as to not alarm the baby's parents, but Ben knew her well enough to hear the note of alarm in her voice.

Rachel hurried up. "What's going on? What did I miss?"

Ben filled her in.

"What can I do?" she asked, ignoring Abby at her side.

There was not room inside for another person. Emma and Sally both hovered at the baby's side. Sally sponged the baby while Emma studied him. Her shoulders rose and sank just once. "We're doing all we can. Go ahead with the chores."

"Look after Brownie for me, will ya?" Sally called.

Abby spun away first and marched toward the cow. She stopped two feet away and stared at the animal, then slowly turned away. "I'll see to the dishes."

Rachel glanced at Ben, but at least she had the good grace to keep her opinion of Abby to herself.

A person isn't born knowing everything, he wanted to shout at her.

Sam rode to them. "What's the holdup here?"

Ben jerked around. He'd forgotten his duties. "The baby is sick."

"Sorry to hear that, but we have to keep moving. We're already behind schedule with spring so late."

Ben knew what he wasn't saying. They had to cross the mountains before winter. He clapped Martin on the shoulder. "I'll yoke your oxen for you."

Martin slowly eased away from watching his little son. "I'll do it. Sally and the boy will be fine in the wagon. I'll get on with the business of the day."

Rachel and Abby scurried about cleaning up the camp. Mr. Bingham folded away the tents and moved his wife's chair into the wagon while Ben backed his oxen into place.

Rachel climbed to the bench and took the reins. The Bingham wagon was ahead of them and Mr. Bingham had not yet yoked his animals.

Rachel sighed. "You better go help him. Or maybe we should just leave them behind."

Abby came around the back of their wagon in time to overhear Rachel's comments.

Ben gave his younger sister a scolding look. "I know you don't mean that."

Rachel shrugged.

Ben turned to apologize to Abby but she was gone.

"Rachel, you were raised better'n that."

She had the grace to look contrite.

Martin saw Mr. Bingham's struggles and hurried to help him.

The wagons had begun to move and Ben swung into his saddle. He'd neglected to check on things last night and rode up and down now. The few cattle — assorted milk cows mostly — and spare horses were guided along by young men.

Jed Henshaw herded several animals in the right direction only to have them snort and veer away. Jed couldn't see what frightened them but Ben did. Arty Jones had pelted the lead animals with rocks.

Ben rode up behind Arty. "Having fun?"

Arty jerked about, surprised at being discovered. "Don't know whatcha mean."

"Go find something useful to do." Ben reined about and headed back to the wagons. Something hit him in the back. Arty had taken to throwing rocks at a human target. Ben didn't turn around. He knew Arty was the sort to find pleasure in getting negative attention and he didn't mean to give it. He rode onward and chuckled when Arty uttered an angry grunt just like a frustrated child.

All morning he mulled over how to deal with Rachel's unkind remarks. Should he simply apologize to Abby and say none of them thought they should leave the Binghams behind? But of course, he couldn't speak for all of them. Only himself.

He didn't want to leave them behind. Didn't want them to give up and head back to Independence and that bothered him. They had every right to be among the emigrants but that wasn't what he meant. His heart was closed to her but somehow or other, he still cared if she succeeded or failed in her endeavors. Seeing her daily constituted both torture and delight. For now, one balanced the other. The good part would come to a sudden and painful end when they reached Oregon.

He'd ridden full circle back to his own wagon. He passed it, passed the Bingham wagon where Abby's parents perched on the bench, and slowed at the Littleton wagon. Abby walked beside it.

"Any change," he called as if talking to Emma or Sally but his gaze met and held Abby's concerned eyes.

Emma climbed from the back of the wagon and withdrew several yards from it. She waved Ben to follow. Abby, too.

He dismounted and faced Emma. His nerves jangled at Abby's nearness. She smelled of campfire and something sweet and familiar.

Remembrance rushed over him. Sitting next to her on the porch swing or on a church pew, lounging on a blanket at a picnic or walking her home after a meeting. At each and every occasion he'd inhaled the same sweet scent.

He closed his eyes and pushed away the memories.

"Johnny has a high fever," Emma said. "It doesn't want to break." She brushed strands of hair off her forehead. "His wound doesn't appear to be infected. What if — ?" She swallowed loudly and couldn't go on.

Ben pressed his hand to her shoulder. No words were necessary between them.

She slowly sucked in air. "What if his insides were damaged?" A shudder shook her.

"Emma, you can only do what is humanly possible."

"I know." Her shoulders slumped. "If only I knew what was wrong with him."

She trudged back to the wagon and climbed inside.

Ben stared after her, troubled by her concerns. "I can't imagine how difficult it will be if the Littletons have to face the death of their only surviving child." As soon as the words were out he wished he'd not spoken.

"I can't, either. We must pray for Johnny to get better."

He faced her squarely. "Our prayers are not always answered the way we want."

Her gaze was steady. "No, they're not. Do you remember the verses we memorized back —" A heartbeat of silence. "Back then?"

He remembered many of the verses. Mostly he recalled how much he enjoyed her company as they drilled each other.

She continued. " 'When I am afraid, I will

trust in thee.' I take that to mean when it's hard to understand God's ways."

"Psalm fifty-six verse three." He contemplated the words of scripture and hers. "It's easier to trust when things go as we want."

"But what is the need of trust in such a situation? It's in the hard times we learn the true meaning of trust. Like now." She trotted after the slow-moving wagons and spoke to those inside the Littleton wagon.

He stared after her. He should have asked her what hard times she meant. Did she refer to Frank's death? Had she suffered the loss of children? His stomach constricted so hard he tasted bile in the back of his throat. He must find the courage to ask if only so he could offer his condolences.

He rode up to his wagon and took Rachel's place. She climbed down and walked.

Driving the oxen didn't require much of his attention, giving him plenty of time to think.

Unfortunately he did not like the direction his thoughts took. Seeing Abby again, watching her around others, triggered many memories that he'd hoped he'd buried deep enough they'd never resurrect.

But they proved to be too stubborn to die peacefully. Why must he remember her struggling to get the verses word perfect and

laughing at her mistakes? Or see her helping one of their friends who had married
and had a new baby? She'd taken the baby
and looked into the solemn little face then
lifted her eyes to Ben. Eyes so full of awe
and hope that to this day his throat drew in
tight. He'd thought . . . hoped even . . . that
they might one day gaze so adoringly at
their own child.

He groaned and forced his mind back to
the here and now.

He was on his way to Oregon and a new
beginning. He'd have to endure Abby's
presence for several weeks. Indeed, several
months. He would not, however, forget the
vast gulf between them. Not if he meant to
keep his sanity and his heart safe.

"We're nooning here," Sam called, riding
back to inform the other wagons.

Grateful for the diversion Ben jumped
down and released the oxen to graze.

Emma edged to his side. "I think I know
what's wrong with Johnny." Her voice
trembled informing Ben that she did not
have good news.

CHAPTER SEVEN

"It's measles," Emma whispered, her voice strained.

Abby stood where she could hear and understood Emma's distress. The disease would spread through the camp like wildfire.

"I'm certain," Emma said. "He has the spots inside his cheeks."

Abby looked at the wagons on one side to those on the other. All those wagons. All those people. Now exposed to the disease. It wasn't like they could hope the others hadn't somehow been in contact with the Littletons.

Emma said the same thing. "Think how so many hovered over Sally and Johnny after he was shot." Shock filled her eyes. "Maymie Patton was right there and she's expecting a baby."

Abby knew from the expression on Emma's face that was bad. "What will happen?"

Emma rocked her head back and forth. "If she gets them, she might lose the baby."

"Oh, no."

Ben pushed his hat back on his head and wiped a hand across his eyes. "I'd hide this news if I thought it would protect the Littletons. But even if I could, there's no point. I'll have to inform the other committeemen." He strode away and returned sometime later to join them for dinner.

"There'll be a meeting in fifteen minutes. All the men should attend." He wolfed down his food. "Emma, perhaps you should come and explain what needs to be done."

"I don't think there's anything I can say."

Rachel gave her sister a little push. "Go. You can't always hide."

Emma slanted a look of denial at Rachel then trotted after Ben.

Rachel chuckled. "She prefers to remain in the background."

Abby smiled as Rachel included her in her look.

Martin and Father strode to where the men had congregated.

Sally peeked out of their wagon. "Will they make us leave the wagon?"

"I don't see any call for that," Abby and

Rachel said in unison and then chuckled.

Mother had been disapprovingly silent until now. "You and your husband and little boy should go back. We should all go back. This trip is cursed. We're all going to perish out here. Our bones will bleach in the sun." Her voice grew higher with every word.

Abby tucked away her sigh. She grew weary of Mother's complaints and dire predictions. But if she said anything Mother would only become more verbal. She hurried to Mother's side with more tea. "Mother, people are upset enough already."

"Apparently not enough. If any of them had an ounce of sense they would abandon this foolish notion."

The noise from the gathered men grew loud.

Emma left the crowd and hurried across the clearing. "Everyone is upset. The committeemen are trying to come to a consensus."

"This is all our fault." Sally ducked into the wagon where soft cries could be heard.

Abby hurried after her. "Sally, it isn't anyone's fault." She opened her arms to the woman and Sally laid her head on her shoulder. "It's just life. No guarantees. 'Yea, though I walk through the valley of the shadow of death, I will fear no evil: for thy rod and thy staff they comfort me.' "

Sally sniffed and sat up. "You are right."
She touched Johnny's forehead. "At least
he's sleeping for now."

Emma peered in the back. "If he gets hot
again he'll need to be sponged. Fever is the
worst enemy at this point."

"I know." Sally sat back.

Abby didn't ask what would happen.
She'd been sheltered from the harsh reali-
ties of life, but a kindly maid when Abby
was mistress of her own house had often
chattered to Abby. "Fever done took his
brain," she'd said, talking about the child of
a former employer. "T'would have been a
mercy if the little one 'ad died. Seen others
go blind, too."

The men returned. Sam Weston led the
committeemen. "We must go on. The way I
see it, you folks have two choices. You can
either drop out, return to Independence if
you choose, or try and catch up later. Or
you can tend the sick while we travel."

Miles Cavanaugh spoke for the others.
"Each family is to make their own choice.
But those going on will depart in twenty
minutes."

After they left, Abby joined her parents.
"What are we going to do?"

"I want to go back. I was never in favor of

124

this journey in the first place. I think we need to heed this as a warning." Mother crossed her arms and stared straight ahead as if the decision had been made.

Father turned to study the oxen as they grazed beyond the wagon. Slowly he brought his attention back to Abby and Mother who waited his decision. "I can't go back. There is nothing for me to go back to."

Abby moved to his side. "We can do this, Father. Together, and with God's help, we can face whatever lies ahead."

Father draped his arm across her shoulders and pulled her close. "You're a good daughter and always have been."

His approval eased the tension that had gripped her insides since Emma's announcement of measles in the camp.

Mother's hands twisted in her lap. "So long as our good daughter remembers she will see we are advanced in Oregon."

It was on the tip of Abby's tongue to say she had other plans, but with no desire to engage in such a discussion, she held her tongue. She took courage from Father's gentle hug.

"Then let's get ready to travel." She put away the last of the dinner supplies, smiling that her biscuits had been enjoyed despite the worry that consumed them all.

Glancing back at the line of wagons, she saw no one had turned around.

She lifted her head, silently praying for each wagon she could see, especially the Littletons. *Help Johnny get better. Protect others from disease and danger.*

Her gaze came finally to the Hewitt wagon. Ben stood by his oxen. His eyes were hidden under the shadow of his hat but she was certain he looked directly at her. His mouth lay flat, revealing nothing. She felt a jolt clear through her body.

She jerked away.

It wasn't her imagination that he'd been studying her. Did he like what he saw? She closed her eyes against the painful truth. What he saw was a woman who had scorned him in favor of a man a fraction of his worth. A woman who owed such a debt to her parents she could only dream of ever being free.

But she'd start afresh. She would. She'd allow nothing from her past to hinder her. Somehow she'd even put aside regrets over Andy's death and her feelings for Ben . . . feelings that should have died six years ago. Feelings she would not heed nor trust. All she wanted for herself was independence. She smiled. She'd left Independence, Missouri, on a journey she hoped would lead to independence for Abigail Black.

Ben forced his attention from Abby. Why should the words of the overheard conversation with her mother sting like angry insects? It was exactly as he'd expected. But for a moment, as she spoke fine words of courage about facing the trials ahead, he'd dared dream she would stand up to her mother's control.

But when Mrs. Bingham alluded to the promise of a good marriage, Abby had turned into the dutiful daughter. Not that he, or anyone, would object to her doing her duty. Except in this case, her compliance went beyond duty. He had never understood it and didn't even now. Abby wasn't a weak, wish-washy sort of person and yet her mother exerted such control over her.

Well, never mind. He had a trip to complete and two sisters to see safely across the country. And now a wagon train that must deal with a measles outbreak.

Indeed by evening, six other children were irritable and fussy. Signs, Emma said, that came before the rash. She suggested all those who appeared sick should avoid direct light and ride in their wagons with the canvas pulled tight.

Fussy children did not care to be shut up in a hot wagon.

Sally had her hands full caring for Johnny that evening.

Between them, Emma and Abby helped Sally and the other families with sick children. Both had the illness previously so were at no risk.

Rachel prepared the meal on her own.

"I'm sorry," Abby said, rushing back to help, though it was well under control. "I intend to do our share."

Rachel stood with a big stirring spoon in hand. "You're helping the sick. That's important, too. I'm afraid I'm not much good around the ill."

Mrs. Bingham sat stiff and upright, her expression pinched with disapproval.

Ben's insides coiled at the sight of her. He turned away. Although he burst to ask why she controlled Abby so tightly, he doubted she would answer him. Besides, if Abby wanted to be free of it, she'd have to find a way.

"I'll fetch some more wood," Abby said, and hurried to collect it outside the camp.

"A Bingham should not be scrounging for firewood." Mrs. Bingham spit out each word.

Ben tried to catch Rachel's gaze and signal her not to respond but Rachel avoided looking at him.

She poured a cup of tea and took it to Mrs. Bingham. "You'll feel better after you drink this."

Mrs. Bingham looked carefully into the contents. "Did you put something in this?"

It so accurately echoed Ben's concern that he choked back a laugh.

Rachel faced Mrs. Bingham. "Just tea and hot water and a touch of sugar. Just as you like it."

Mrs. Bingham took a delicate sip. "It's fine."

No *thank-you* or any sign of gratitude.

Ben held his breath waiting for his volatile sister to react.

She shrugged and turned away. Out of the corner of her mouth, she murmured, "Now why didn't I think to put something else in it?"

Ben turned his back to Mrs. Bingham so she wouldn't overhear them. "Because you're a nice person."

"Sometimes it's very difficult to be so." Rachel grinned.

Abby returned with firewood and Emma crossed to the campfire and gratefully took the offered food.

It was Martin's turn to ask the blessing. "Father God, bless our food. Thank you for providing our needs. I beseech You —" His voice cracked as he finished. "Spare our son. Amen."

A hush fell on those gathered round. "Amen," Ben whispered. *Spare us all from danger.*

"The good news is many of the children and a good deal of the adults have already had measles." Emma spoke calmly as if she wanted everyone to think she wasn't worried.

Ben knew better. He looked around their little gathering. "How many of this group has had them?"

"Our family all did," Emma said. "Remember. You and I and Grayson had them the same time. I was only four so you two would be six and eight. Rachel got them when she was two." She laughed.

Ben was relieved to hear the note of joy in her voice. "She was so cranky she makes Johnny look like an angel." All heads turned toward the Littleton wagon where Sally tended the baby.

Rachel chuckled. "I hope you all gave me plenty of attention."

Emma smiled adoringly at Rachel. "Father was so worried he barely left your side."

The three of them shared a moment of sadness.

Emma sighed and pulled herself back to the here and now. "Abby, have you had measles?"

Abby nodded. "When I was little."

Mother quickly added, "You and Andrew had them at the same time when you were four." Each word came out in quick, harsh succession. "Of course you got over them quickly. We worried about Andrew for weeks."

"Andrew?" Rachel, God bless her, couldn't constrain her curiosity.

"Her brother. Her twin brother." The woman's words carried a harsh note. "He died."

Mr. Bingham caught his wife's hand. "That's over, my dear. We need to let it go."

"I'm sorry," Emma said softly.

Ben knew she'd had a twin brother but that's all except that he'd died a couple years before he and Abby met at the meetings. She'd never wanted to talk about it and he'd respected her wishes. Now he wished he'd asked what happened.

They finished their meal and Emma went to relieve Sally so she could eat and stretch her legs.

Clarence Pressman called across the clearing. "Didn't Mrs. Black promise us more music and reading?"

Abby didn't appear to hear.

"Abby?" Ben's voice made her startle. She must have been lost in her thoughts. "Would you play the mandolin again, please?"

"Of course." She hurried to get it from the wagon.

He stared after her. Did her steps seem jerky? Was she tired from all that walking? Likely her feet were blistered. He'd mention it to Emma. Perhaps she could suggest something to ease the pain.

Abby again played and sang, then read. Her voice filled him with such sweet peace.

Ignoring the dangerous thought, he leaned back and relaxed.

Knowing four in the morning would come far too soon, she ended after only a few minutes. Already many had withdrawn to their tents or unrolled their bedding under their wagon, too tired to bother with a tent.

Emma and Rachel put up a tent without a problem, but then there were two of them.

Abby struggled to secure the ropes on hers.

Rachel and Emma glanced her way.

"She needs help," Emma said softly, giving Ben a look that plainly said a gentleman would not let a lady struggle on her own.

"I will learn to do this," she said through gritted teeth.

Even though he longed to jump up and help immediately, he took his time. He didn't want the others on the wagon train thinking he gave her special attention. Then he thought of all the things he'd observed her do — how she helped her father with the oxen, how she'd learned to use the reflector oven, how she willingly and efficiently helped Emma, how she walked many miles every day — "I think you'll do just about anything you set your mind to. Are your feet hurting?"

She jerked back to stare at him. "What are you suggesting? That I'm unfit for this trek?"

"Of course not. Didn't I just say you could do anything you set your mind to? But I noticed you walked like your feet hurt. I expect a lot of the emigrants have blisters."

She lowered her accusing gaze. "I'm sorry to fly off the handle at you. But —" She shrugged and didn't finish.

The last rope tightened under his hands, but he didn't immediately leave.

She slowly brought her attention to him. "Yes?"

"I enjoy hearing you sing." His tongue grew heavy. "I appreciate the way you help

Emma with the sick ones." So many things sprang to his mind. How patient she was with her demanding mother —

A mother who exerted such tight control over Abby. That was her problem and he did not intend to let it become his.

"Thank you." She seemed uncertain as to how to respond.

He had run out of things to say. Or at least, things he thought he could safely say. "Well, then, good night."

"Good night to you and thanks again for your help."

He strode back to the Hewitt wagon as if a wild animal was on his tail.

Emma and Rachel poked their heads out of their tent. "Everything okay?"

"Fine. Just fine. I think Abby could use something for blisters."

"Of course. I've been busy with the sick children but I should have thought to take her something." Emma backed out with her satchel of remedies and went to Abby's tent to softly call her name.

Rachel remained at the tent flap. "Ben, my big lunk of a brother, I'm worried about you. I don't want to see you hurt." She thankfully kept her voice low enough the others wouldn't overhear her.

He wished he could pretend he didn't

know what she was talking about. "I'm fine. Just fine."

All he had to do was endure miles and months of traveling in Abby's company. But whatever errant thoughts sprang to his mind or memories of a sweet time shared with her, he would never ever let himself forget what really mattered to Abigail Bingham Black.

It wasn't love. It wasn't even truthfulness.

It was advancement, high society acceptance and a life possible only to the wealthy. Her goals were firmly supported by her mother.

If he ever forgot the hard lesson he'd learned about caring for Abby, he had only to look at Mrs. Bingham, see the disapproval on her face, and he'd be reminded.

There was no future possible between himself and Abby.

And he was okay with that. But an ache as deep as an ocean filled his heart.

CHAPTER EIGHT

The next day, Abby helped Emma tend the children who had come down with measles. Emma never pointed out her mistakes, but gently taught her how to check each child's fever and what instructions to give the parents caring for their sick little ones.

One wagon was home to six children and their parents — the Jensen family. Two girls, Annie, aged nine, and Betty, eight, bustled about taking care of chores as best they could while their mother tended two little ones, a boy of two and a girl of four.

"We had the measles two years ago," Annie said, "So we ain't gonna get them."

They were nooning near a cluster of bushes. Abby glanced back to the Bingham wagon. She should hurry back and help with dinner, but Emma had asked her to check on this family. She handed a container of water to Mrs. Jensen who poked her head out from the back of the wagon where the canvas had been drawn tight to keep out as much light as possible.

"Where are the twins?" she asked the older girls.

Abby stiffened. Twins. Would she ever hear the word without her insides stinging?

A girl's little face peeked around the wagon wheel. "We're here, Ma."

A boy joined the first child, his eyes big with curiosity at this stranger at their wagon.

Abby squatted to speak to them. "I'm Mrs. Black. I came to help your ma with the little ones. How old are you?"

"Five," they chorused together.

"And what's your names?"

The little girl answered first. "I'm Cat. He's Dog."

The boy shoved her. "I am not. Don't listen to her. She's Cathy. I'm Donny."

Cathy scrambled back to her brother's side.

Abby studied the pair. Both blond-haired and blue-eyed. They measured her, assessing whether she was someone they could trust. They stood shoulder to shoulder, one against any threat.

Just as she and Andy had been.

Tears clogged the back of her throat. She'd thought she was defending him against the mocking of some no-matter girl.

Instead, she should have been watching out for his well-being.

She smiled past her tears. "Have you two had measles?"

Both shrugged solemnly.

She straightened and turned back to the wagon. "Is there anything you need, Mrs. Jensen?"

"Would you mind helping the girls with the meal?"

"Not at all, but I warn you, they likely know more than I do."

Laughing, Mrs. Jensen poked her head out again. "Another pair of hands can't go wrong. I'd feel better simply knowing there is an adult present."

"Of course." She was an adult and she knew how to boil water.

"I gots wood," Betty said. "So we can have a fire and make Ma some tea. Can you help us start the fire?"

"I can do that." She soon had the fire going and water boiling. Annie and Betty pulled out biscuits and beans from their food box. Mr. Jensen returned just as Abby made the tea.

"You're welcome to join us," he said.

"Thank you but I need to see to my mother's needs." Besides, she had no wish to eat from their supplies.

Bidding them goodbye, she made her way to her parents. She'd gone but three steps when Ben rode to her side and dismounted. "Emma sent me to see if you needed help."

"How sweet of Emma." Would he have come on his own? "I wanted to make sure the Jensens could manage. The two older girls are trying to take the place of their mother who is nursing the two little ones." She sucked in air and rushed on. "There are five-year-old twins — Cathy and Donny." She told him how Cathy had said they were called Cat and Dog and laughed though her voice felt strangled. Hopefully, Ben wouldn't notice it.

"I suppose it reminded you of yourself and Andy."

She nodded, surprised Ben remembered his name.

He opened his mouth likely with the intent of asking what happened to him. Six years ago, with his death still raw in her mind, her guilt almost overpowering, she had refused to discuss Andy.

She increased the pace of her steps. She still had no desire to talk about Andy or explain how he'd died.

They reached the campfire and she hurried to Mother's side, her guilt and regret more raw than it had been in some time.

Someone had already given Mother a cup of tea.

"I'm sorry I wasn't here to help."

Emma gave a dismissive wave. "Everyone knew you were helping the Jensens. How are they?"

"Only the two little ones have the measles, though the twins weren't certain if they'd had them." She barely got the word out. Why should it be so important to her that they were twins?

She let out a quiet sigh. Because the children were a reminder of her and Andy.

Father rose to ask the blessing, then they ate a hurried meal. At least Mother had begun to eat better, likely out of desperation, and she didn't find fault quite so vehemently. Was it because she was too weary? Although Abby was grateful for less complaining, she had no desire to have Mother ill. She would keep a closer eye on her.

Abby felt Ben studying her and kept her attention elsewhere. No doubt he wondered at how she'd rushed away rather than talk about Andy. Well, let him wonder. She wanted to put it behind her. This whole trip was meant to help her put the pain and guilt of Andy's death behind her. Instead, the Jensen twins had refreshed the memory.

She remembered when Andy had called her silly names, too. Sometimes Gabby Abby, or Babby. She'd enjoyed the way he teased her. Never enough to make her cry, only enough to make her laugh.

Would the hole in her heart from losing him ever go away?

She'd planned to leave memories of Ben behind her, too. That was proving impossible with him riding in the same wagon train. Why couldn't the Hewitts have stayed behind?

"How is Johnny?" Emma called to Sally who remained in the wagon with him.

"Much better. No fever at all today." Sally appeared at the back of the wagon. "How many days must we stay shut in here?"

Emma considered her answer. "Until his rash is gone, his eyes are clear and his nose stops running."

Sally groaned. "He's not going to be happy stuck in here."

"Nor are you." Martin sounded sympathetic.

"Better to deal with that now than complications later," Emma said.

Abby listened intently to Emma, finding it was easier to ignore the past if she focused on the present.

She'd like to also dream of the future but

she now felt less certain of what she'd do when she reached Oregon and how she'd deal with her mother. She stiffened her resolve. She would find a way.

They soon finished the meal and hurriedly cleaned up as the men again put the oxen on the wagons.

No new measles had been reported over the noon break and everyone seemed settled as they moved on. Emma climbed up beside Ben on the wagon seat.

Abby walked beside the wagons. How was she going to put the past behind her when it kept following on her heels?

How was she going to get her mother to release her from her promise so she could find a new future in Oregon?

Ben smiled at Emma sitting next to him on the wagon seat. It had been a few days since brother and sister had time to be together alone. "How are you holding up?"

She shrugged. "Fine. If measles is the worst we have to deal with, I shall fall on my knees and thank God with my whole heart."

He didn't know if he should laugh or scold her. "Don't you start sounding like Mrs. Bingham. She never stops saying this trip is cursed."

Emma patted his arm. "I don't believe that. This is an adventure but as all adventures are, it is fraught with dangers and surprises."

"Good surprises, I trust." Something about the words stirred his heart. It took only seconds for the memory to surface. He'd accidently run into Abby one day when they were still spending time together and his appearance had startled her. Funny how thinking of that could still bring a smile to his lips.

Emma tipped her head to consider him. "Speaking of surprises, is discovering the Binghams are our traveling companions a good or bad one?"

He should say it was not good and yet he couldn't force the words to his mouth.

She didn't wait for him to answer. "Never mind." She patted his arm again. "I trust God has His hand on our journey and will guide us safely over, though I am not so naive as to expect that means none of us will face difficult times. Or that we won't encounter deaths."

He nodded. "Death is as much a part of life as is birth." He needed to apply the thought to his regrets over Abby. Yes, he'd once cared. That was over. Dead.

"I know." Emma sounded sad.

He wondered if she thought of their father, or mother or even Suzanne, Grayson's wife who had died in childbirth along with the girl baby.

Emma continued. "You know the most pleasant surprise so far is watching Abby. She's changed. Or maybe I simply didn't have a chance to see her like this before." She paused as if to contemplate. "Somehow, I expected her to act more like her mother. But she's a valuable asset to the company. She is wonderful with the sick, so kind and gentle, and she cheers and comforts the whole camp with her music and reading."

Ben didn't respond. What could he say? That he'd noticed even though he'd tried not to? That he'd seen this side of her before she chose to marry Frank? And yet it wasn't enough to enable her to choose a financially struggling young man over a well-heeled one.

Emma studied him. "Did she ever say how Frank died?"

He shook his head.

"You haven't asked her?"

He slowly brought his gaze to hers. "See no need to."

Finally Emma turned aside from studying him and gave a little shrug. "All I'm saying is she is not what I expected."

"I heard you the first time."

She chuckled a little. "Don't get all touchy now."

"I'm not." Though truth be told, it did feel like she'd poked at a bruise.

In the periphery of his vision, he saw Abby marching along. There were others walking, too, but she seemed alone. Emma had pointed out Abby's value, yet he wondered if Abby was aware of what she contributed. He'd often seen her frown as she watched the other women preparing stew or a sweet. Frank had been a rich man. There would have been servants to do the menial chores, so she likely had never learned practical things that would enable her to help around the camp.

It would be nice if someone would teach her, but Emma had her hands full tending the sick and Rachel made it plain she had no patience with Abby and her complaining mother. Sally would be a kind teacher, but she had Johnny to take care of.

One of the many verses he'd memorized with Abby sprang to mind. Strange how many of them he recalled lately even though he hadn't given them a lot of thought over the years. Philippians chapter four: verse nineteen. *"But my God shall supply all your need according to his riches in glory by Christ*

Jesus." He didn't know if it was a need or a want but he'd sure like to see someone help Abby — one of the women, of course. It would be thought strange for him to try and teach her how to cook a meal. Besides, his skills were limited to beans and bacon.

He handed the reins to Emma. "I think I'll walk for a bit."

"Uh-huh." She sounded so pleased with herself that he paused to add, "I'm just going to walk."

"You go right ahead." She looked forward but didn't succeed in hiding a little smile.

He shook his head. Sometimes his quiet little sister surprised him. He walked beside the wagon but the dust soon drove him to move further away.

Abby walked a little to one side, away from the others and he fell in step with her.

She jerked about, startled by his appearance.

He grinned to himself. "Sorry, didn't mean to interrupt your thoughts. Just stretching my legs."

"Feel free."

Did she mean feel free to stretch his legs or to walk at her side? He'd believe both. That made it easier to stay there.

"Emma was saying how much she appreciates your help."

She ground to a halt. "Me? I'm not much help to anyone."

He'd been right in thinking she wished she could do more. "Emma says you are a great comfort to the mothers caring for their sick children."

"Oh, that. I just take them water and get whatever they need. Anyone could do that."

"I suppose anyone could play the mandolin and sing, too. And read a story."

"Anyone who had as many lessons as I have could do it."

Her attitude annoyed him. "Why are you determined to believe you can't do anything of value?"

"Who said I am? I can make tea and biscuits."

He laughed at the challenge in her voice. "All you need is a few lessons and you can do anything."

"Seems we left the teachers back in Missouri."

"I hope we left lots of things back there."

She glanced at him. "What are you leaving behind?"

"Memories."

"Me, too."

They sighed in unison which made her laugh.

"I've been meaning to ask you about

Frank. How did he die?"

She walked faster but he had no trouble keeping pace.

"I'm sorry. I don't mean to upset you."

"He was killed in a buggy accident." Her voice was strangely devoid of emotion.

"I'm sorry. I know how hard it is to lose those you love. I've lost my mother and father." And Abby, though he wasn't about to say so. "And I watched Grayson's grief when his wife and baby died. Losing children is perhaps the hardest."

"I wouldn't know. I never had a child."

Ben opened his mouth and closed it without speaking. What did one say to that? Was not having children another loss she had faced? He opened his mouth again. Snapped it shut. He had no idea what to say.

She surveyed him out of the corner of her eye. "Don't look so concerned. I've dealt with Frank's death." Why did she never mention Andy's death?

"Good to know." What else was he supposed to say? But his mind raced with questions. Did she mean she was looking to the future?

Humph. What difference did that make to him? He already knew what her plans looked like. Her mother had made certain they all knew she was to marry well again. That left out a poor mercantile owner.

"So what's ahead for you in Oregon?" Would she provide a name? Or specifics enough to make him see her as belonging to another?

They walked on in silence for the space of near ten minutes. He assumed she hadn't heard him or wasn't prepared to answer. In either case, he wouldn't ask again. He had his own future to deal with though, at the moment, partnership with Grayson sounded lonely.

"I hope —" She spoke so softly he had to bend his ear to her. "The future will be full of hope and joy."

"Me, too." But seeing Abby again made him wonder if he'd ever again find what he'd had with her. They'd shared something he'd found sadly lacking in the young women he'd courted in the intervening years. Seems they were either too serious or not serious enough. He'd not been able to find any with the balance he'd seen in Abby. Too bad it hadn't been wedded to commitment and honesty.

"Anyway, I just thought you should know what Emma had to say about you." He purposely gave her a challenging look to see if she would deny she had anything of value to offer.

She smiled, though only with her lips. "Thank you."

He returned to the wagon and climbed up.

Emma and Rachel had traded places so Emma now walked and Rachel drove the oxen. He took the reins from her.

"Did you have a nice visit with Abby? What did you talk about?"

Of course she'd seen. Anyone who cared to look would have. Even Mrs. Bingham. Wonder what she'd have to say to Abby tonight that they'd all get to hear?

Rachel elbowed him in the ribs. "I asked you a question."

"I merely told her how Emma appreciated her help."

"I see."

"She didn't believe it at first."

Rachel looked at Abby then back to Ben. "How do you know that?"

"She said so. She thinks she is useless because she can't cook." She hadn't said those exact words but he knew she meant that. And likely more.

"Tsk. Anyone can learn to cook."

"I told her that."

They rode on in silence.

"She just needs some lessons," he added.

"I suppose so." After a bit, Rachel climbed down and joined Emma who walked at Abby's side. If his sisters would take Abby under their wings . . .

Seems he would simply have to let things work out on their own in God's good time and loving way. He smiled as another verse sprang to mind. Ecclesiastes three, verse one. *"To every thing there is a season, and a time to every purpose under the heaven."* He tried to trust God in everything, but sometimes it was hard. *"A time to weep, and a time to laugh; a time to mourn, and a time to dance."* He would sure welcome a time of laughing and dancing.

The long, dusty afternoon trudged on. The oxen were slow creatures. Those walking had no trouble keeping pace. Ben leaned his elbows on his knees. Bouncing along behind these creatures gave a man far too much time to think. Far too many opportunities to glance at Abby and his sisters. He sat up and stared at the spot where they'd been just moments ago. They were gone. He looked up and down the trail, but as far as he could see through the dust, he couldn't spot them.

He leaned far to the right. Then far to the left. Where were they? Not that he was disappointed not to see Abby. Why, that wouldn't make a lick of sense.

There was no need to worry. Both Emma and Rachel knew how to take care of themselves.

Unless they encountered Indians. "Friendly for the most part," Sam had said. "They'll likely remain that way if they're treated fairly."

It was the *for the most part* that concerned Ben.

With no one to drive his wagon, he couldn't search for them. He sank back, trying to relax but every five minutes he looked about hoping to spot them.

When Sam called for the wagons to circle he still hadn't seen hide nor hair of them and his head echoed with every sound from the wagon train.

He pulled in behind the Littleton wagon and leaped down to unhitch the oxen and turn them out to graze. Once his urgent chores were done, he jogged toward his horse, ready to ride out and find the missing girls, when he spotted them approaching, laughing together, their arms full of wood and each with a bouquet of flowers.

With a groan he turned back to his chores. They'd been picking flowers while he worried himself into a frenzy.

If it wasn't so funny, he'd be angry. He

chuckled softly as he sauntered over to help Mr. Bingham with his animals.

The girls chattered away as they built a fire and started to prepare a meal. Emma took her medicine satchel and went to check on the sick, glancing back over her shoulder as if she regretted leaving the other two.

Rachel handed a stack of ingredients to Abby who set them on the little table they'd put out. "Batter bread is easy," Rachel said. "You put in —"

Ben ducked outside the circle but stayed near the wagon where he could overhear Rachel and Abby. At first, he thought he must be mistaken but after a few minutes he knew Rachel was teaching Abby to cook.

"Better sift the flour," Rachel said.

Ben held his breath. Did she mean to remind Abby of her failures?

When Abby laughed, his lungs relaxed.

"You surely won't complain if there's a little color in your bread."

Rachel laughed. "Yes, I think I might."

"Where's Miss Hewitt?" The tone of voice calling across the camp sent steel into Ben's spine. Something was wrong.

He jumped across the tongue of the wagon. "Which Miss Hewitt?"

"The one with the doctor's bag." It was Mr. Morrison. "Young Clarence has hurt himself. Where's your sister?"

"Emma." He roared her name, then ran after Mr. Morrison.

She jumped down from the back of a wagon. "What's wrong?"

He slowed his feet so she could catch up. "Clarence Pressman is hurt. Don't know where or how bad but Mr. Morrison is certainly concerned."

They crossed to the wagon and joined the dozen men and women crowded around Clarence. He sat on the ground, pale as a sheet.

"Leave me be. I don't need any help." Young Clarence never spoke above a gruff murmur. Even now.

Ernie Jones threw up his hands at Ben's and Emma's approach. "He's too stubborn for his own good."

"You're hurt," Mrs. Morrison said, reaching toward the young man. "Someone needs to look at that cut."

He shifted away. "I'm okay. Go away and leave me alone." But he held his left arm as if it hurt.

Emma edged around to the man's back. She raised her eyes to Ben and he read her concern. Slowly, not wanting to further alarm the young man, he edged around to stand at her side.

The man's shirt was torn across the shoulders and a cut bled profusely, soaking his shirt.

Emma pulled a clean cloth from her bag and stepped to the man's back to press it to the wound.

Clarence jerked away, eyes wide.

Ben studied the man. What reason did he have to be so afraid? Unless he had something to hide. Perhaps the items that kept mysteriously disappearing.

"This will stop the blood." Emma spoke gently, calmingly and moved closer. "Why don't the rest of you leave and I'll take care of this?"

The others hesitated but Ben knew she was right. Clarence might let her clean his wound if he didn't have an audience, and he herded away the onlookers. He stopped on the far side of the wagon. He wouldn't be leaving his sister unchaperoned with a single young man even if he was hurt.

"How did this happen?" Emma asked.

Ben could imagine her bending over the man to better look at the wound. Their heads would be very close. He didn't care for the idea.

"Fell and caught it on that hook."

"Ouch. It's awfully deep. I'll clean it good, then dress it. You need to get out of this blood-soaked shirt, though."

Did Ben hear Emma gasp? He jerked about, meaning to rescue her. Save her reputation.

"No need for you to worry," Emma said. "I'll take care of it."

Ben settled back. Pressmen must have gasped. For a few minutes, he couldn't hear their murmured words even though he strained to catch every sound. Unfortunately the camp was noisy enough to drown out the voices on the other side of the wagon.

A few minutes later, Emma reached into the back of the Morrison wagon.

Ben leaned forward to catch her attention.

She jumped in surprise. "I didn't know you were there."

"Did you think I'd leave you alone with a man?"

"No, I suppose not."

Did he detect pink creeping up her cheeks? "Emma, I can go with you."

She waved him away. "No. No need." Did her hands tremble? "I'll just take him a clean shirt." She pulled one from the valise she located in the wagon and darted away without another word.

He stared after her. Odd behavior for his normally calm sister. Surely she wasn't attracted to that man? Why she'd grown up with big strong brothers and father. Of course she would see how weak and puny Clarence was.

She returned in a few minutes. "He'll be okay."

He knew he didn't imagine that she avoided looking directly at him as she spoke.

He rubbed a weary hand across his forehead. This trip was getting more and more complicated. He needed to avoid Abby as much as he could and now he needed to keep a sharp eye on Clarence in order to protect Emma.

CHAPTER NINE

Abby watched Emma and Ben walk back. The news had quickly circulated through the camp that Clarence Pressman had injured himself and refused treatment until Emma took things into her own hands and insisted everyone else must leave.

But the scowl on Ben's face informed one and all that he wasn't exactly pleased about something. Abby couldn't say if he was worried about Clarence or Emma's reputation. But knowing Ben, she could assume both.

Knowing Ben? What did she know about him? Now all she knew was he'd never married, his father had died and he and his sisters were going to Oregon to join their brother. She didn't know what he thought or felt or dreamed or wished for.

She snapped shut a door in her mind. She no longer had the right to such intimate knowledge of him.

"How does this look?" she asked Rachel.

Rachel looked at the beans and bacon. "You're a fast learner."

"Or maybe you're a good teacher. Thank you for offering to help me." She couldn't have been more surprised when Rachel came to her side during the afternoon walk and said she would teach Abby to cook and do the practical chores. Rachel only wanted music lessons in exchange.

"You might not be so grateful when you try and teach me to play the mandolin."

They laughed together as Ben and Emma joined them.

Ben's eyes widened as he shot a look from one to the other.

Rachel bumped shoulders with Abby. "I love surprising my big brother."

Ben swallowed loudly then smoothed his expression. "I don't know what you mean."

Abby chuckled. "Too late. Your expression already gave you away."

He grinned. "At least it's a good surprise."

His gaze held hers, burning away every defense. Did he mean to remind her of another time when they'd had a similar discussion?

She'd gone to his father's store on the pretext of needing a new pen nib. But Ben wasn't there. Only Grayson and the elder Mr. Hewitt. Grayson didn't know where

Ben had gone. Disappointed, she'd left the store and with no destination in mind, had wandered along the street. At the corner, Ben had stepped in front of her. She'd been so startled she'd pressed her hand to her throat to calm her racing pulses. "You surprised me," she'd gasped.

"At least it's a good surprise," he'd said, laughing, obviously glad to see her.

She shook her head. The past had no part in the present.

"Abby made the bean stew and the bread," Rachel announced, with so much pleasure it brought a sting of heat to Abby's cheeks.

Father patted Abby's shoulder. "Good for you."

Against her better judgment, Abby glanced toward her mother. Would she show the least sign of approval?

No. She shook her head and her expression showed nothing but disappointment.

Abby knew better than to expect otherwise and yet she kept hoping. She quickly dismissed the longing and helped serve up the simple meal. The pride she felt in her part in preparing the food far exceeded any reasonable boundaries.

Emma went to watch Johnny so Sally could enjoy her meal and a break from the confines of the wagon.

A few minutes later, Mr. Jensen called out a request for Abby to play her music so she got her mandolin and book from the wagon and sat down on the grass by the wheel to play.

Ben rested a few feet away. It surprised her no end that he hung about when she played and sang. He'd always claimed to enjoy her music. For some reason she thought that would be reason for him to avoid listening.

Did his hovering nearby suggest he still had some feelings for her? She dismissed the idea. He only meant to enjoy the music. Her choice six years ago had sealed her fate in more ways than one. It had given her a husband who was cruel and reckless, it ended any possibility of a relationship with Ben and it had left her a much wiser woman.

She ducked her head over the instrument and played jolly, cheerful tunes while inside, pain twisted into a horrible knot. Her wisdom had come on the heels of sorrow and regret.

It was time to read and she opened the book to where she'd ended yesterday. Two children crowded to her side. Cathy and Donny. She smiled at them and read past the lump in her throat.

A few minutes later, she closed the book. "That's enough for tonight."

The other children scampered off to join their parents and prepare for the night. But the twins didn't move.

"Mama says we have to let Annie and Betty put us to bed tonight." Donny sounded mournful.

"I'd sooner have Mama." Cathy's tone matched her brother's.

"You would, too, wouldn't you?" Donny regarded Abby solemnly.

She wondered what they would say if she told them that a governess had put her to bed. Her insides ached. Not once could she remember Mother tucking her in.

"Would you like me to do it tonight if it's okay with your mama and papa and your big sisters?"

Two little heads bobbed in unison. "They won't mind," Cathy said. "They say we're a nuisance."

She guessed they referred to their big sisters. "I don't expect they really mean it."

"I guess they were just mad because we spilled the water and made a mess."

"We was just trying to help."

Laughing at the pair, Abby pulled them to their feet and took them back to their wagon.

Both Mr. and Mrs. Jensen looked relieved when she offered to put the twins to bed.

"They sleep in the tent with the girls. Their nightclothes are there." Mrs. Jensen indicated the two nightshirts.

Abby supervised the twins washing and added a swipe or two of her own to complete the job. They folded their clothes into a neat pile and put them into a corner of the tent.

"You have to come in and listen to our prayers." Donny had retreated into the tent after his sister and turned to indicate Abby should follow.

She crawled into the small space. Four children crowded into the same size tent as the one she had to herself. She would have gladly shared hers with a sibling.

They said their prayers, interrupting each other, so that it became a joint prayer. It had often been the same with her and Andy — finishing each other's sentences, even their thoughts. Often speaking in unison.

She rode the pain, knowing it would subside in a moment.

"Good night." She backed out of the tent.

Feeling too raw to rejoin the others, she stepped over the wagon tongue and out into the dusk. The sounds of camp were muted as people bedded down for the night.

The aroma of bacon and smoke wrapped

about her. The oxen grazed placidly. A sentinel nodded from his nearby post.

She fixed her eyes on the western horizon now aflame with orange and pink. The beauty of the sunset calmed her soul. God was with them. Their times were in His hands.

Ben strode toward her.

She kept her eyes on the sky, doing her best to ignore the way her heart leaped at his presence.

" 'From the rising of the sun unto the going down of the same, the Lord's name is to be praised.' "

She jerked about to stare at him. "Psalms one hundred and thirteen, verse three."

A smile creased the corner of his eyes. "I think I remember every verse we memorized."

"Me, too." Just as she remembered every sweet moment, every gentle touch, every brimming smile and joy-filled laugh. She tried to put a stop in the flow of her thoughts, but found herself unable. Something in his look drew her along paths of tender remembrance.

Deep inside her, something wrenched. A sensation of both pleasure and pain. Hope and regret.

"I remember a lot of things." His voice

was husky as if he too had been drawn back to the time when their relationship was tender and trusting.

A nearby animal coughed, breaking the spell.

Out of breath, Abby turned her attention back to the setting sun.

"I couldn't help but notice you with the Jensen twins. They are attracted to you."

"They're feeling out of sorts because their mother doesn't have time for them at the moment." Delores Jensen hated to let the twins out of her sight even though she was busy with the sick babies.

If Abby was ever a mother, she would not let others raise her children. She'd devote complete attention to them. They'd know they were loved and valued.

"You're so good with children. I guess I thought —"

"Thought what?" she prodded when he didn't finish his sentence.

"Until you said otherwise, I thought you must have had children."

When she turned to object, wondering if he thought she'd left them behind, he held up a hand to stop her and rushed on.

"It hurt me to think you'd had children and lost them like the Littletons did. That's all I meant." He turned away as if seeking escape in studying the horizon.

It afforded her a chance to study him without meeting his gaze. He'd been hurt by the thought? Because he didn't want to think of her pain? Or simply because the death of a child was tragic and sorrowful? But why did it matter? She turned back to the sunset which was now only a hint of orange.

"It will soon be dark." Ben sounded regretful.

Or else she only transferred her emotions to him. "Time to bed down." Still neither of them moved.

"I'm glad Rachel is helping you."

"Oh, no." She covered her mouth. "I promised to give her mandolin lessons. I completely forgot."

Ben planted a big, warm hand on her shoulder. "You'll get plenty of opportunity. We have months of travel ahead of us."

"Months and miles." Again their gazes locked.

"Anything can happen." His words were soft. Full of promise?

She knew the only promise he would offer was to help guide them across the wide, lonesome plains safely to their new future.

Try as she might, she could not quench the longing within that wished he could guide her heart back to his. Back to a shared future. Back to belief in a loving relationship between a man and a woman.

Pain and regret tore at her soul and she jerked away from his watchful gaze. "Good night," she called as she hurried to the camp.

She paused to apologize to Rachel and promise a lesson the next day, then crawled into her tent that Rachel had helped her put up earlier.

She fell on her knees, bending low to the ground. *Lord, help me guard my heart.* Another of the verses she and Ben had so diligently memorized sprang to her mind.

"Guard thy heart with all vigilance."

But even the scriptures were intertwined with memories of Ben. How they had laughed together as they drilled each other. How they had shared their thoughts on each verse and spoken of how their future would be built on the solid ground of God's Word.

She'd clung to her faith throughout the trials of the past six years. Indeed, without it, Frank would have destroyed her just as he intended to.

But she feared she faced an even greater trial in the months ahead. How would she survive when her memories haunted her?

She took three slow breaths. Memories

were part of the past. She had a future to pursue. Nothing could be allowed to divert her.

The next day Ben did his best to pretend he didn't see or hear Abby. Last night had been a mistake. He should never have followed her outside the camp. His only excuse was he meant to see that she was okay. But that excuse sounded weak even as he thought it. Then he'd gone and confessed it hurt him to think she might have lost children.

He groaned. What had he been thinking? Obviously his brain had stopped working for an hour or so.

It wouldn't happen again.

Ignoring her would have been easier if she and Rachel hadn't crawled in the back of the wagon for a music lesson. How could he not hear every word, every laugh? And why must they laugh so often? It made him want to join them. Listening but not being included was sweet agony.

Thankfully, the lesson ended and the girls got out to walk.

Must they stay within his sight? Was she purposely tormenting him? Yet if they disappeared, as they had yesterday, he would be concerned.

Dinner provided no relief.

While Emma went off to check on the ill and injured, Rachel and Abby chattered like spring birds as they prepared the meal.

Johnny fussed.

Sally sat at the back of the wagon trying to console the little one. "He doesn't like being so cooped up all the time."

"Maybe he's well enough to be out." Rachel looked up and down the line for Emma. "I wonder what's keeping her."

Ben jerked to attention. He'd been so distracted by his own internal struggle that he'd forgotten his responsibilities. He couldn't allow that to continue and trotted off in search of Emma. He made a beeline toward the Morrison wagon. He knew, though he couldn't say how, she was there.

Indeed, she and young Pressman had withdrawn several hundred yards. They talked a lot as she checked his wound. What would Emma have to say to a man like that?

She finished the dressing, but did she leave? No, she sat beside Clarence and they continued to chat like old friends. Emma could do far better than that. Tristan McCullough, for example. Grayson had written a glowing letter about the man who expressed an interest in marrying Emma.

"Emma, we're waiting to eat," he called.

The pair bolted to their feet and rushed back to the camp.

Clarence ducked his head, unwilling to meet Ben's challenging gaze.

Ben fell into step at Emma's side. "How's his wound?"

"Oh. It's fine. I just need to make sure it doesn't get infected. You know with all this dust, it's always a risk. And he can't reach it to clean on his own."

This rushed burst of words from his sister set his teeth on edge. "Mrs. Morrison could do it for him."

"Clarence is kind of funny about people getting too close to him."

"Except for you, I notice." They'd reached the others, but he wasn't done. All kinds of romances might bloom and blossom on a trip that forced them together for several months, but he wouldn't allow this one. "Emma, watch yourself. He's not the sort for you."

Emma ducked her head and hurried over to the far side of the cooking fire.

Rachel, however, planted herself directly in front of him. He tried to sidestep her, but she wouldn't allow it. She jammed her hands to her hips.

He sighed, knowing she would have her say before she was done. Might as well get it over with. "What?" The word contained a world of impatience and frustration though much of it was directed at himself, not his sister.

Rachel scowled at him. "When does Emma get to decide what she wants instead of being told by her brothers? Who are you —" she jabbed her finger into his chest "— to make her decisions for her? Can't you see she's smart enough to know what she wants and what's best for her?"

He caught her hand and squeezed it. Not enough to hurt. Only enough to signal he didn't care for her questions. Not that she'd ever let that stop her.

"You and Grayson decide she should marry this widower friend of Grayson's. How nice for all of you. But what does Emma truly want?"

He glanced at Emma. She sat staring at her hands. "Seems it's up to Emma to speak up if she doesn't like things the way they are."

"She cares too much about what you think." Rachel tossed her hands upward to show her frustration. "You don't even approve of a friendship with Clarence Pressman. What do you have against the poor man?"

"Nothing. But Emma deserves better."

Rachel rumbled her lips. "Only Emma knows what she wants and deserves. Let her decide." She stomped away.

Abby hurriedly served up the cold beans and biscuits. Her eyes darted past Ben as if afraid to become part of his argument with Rachel.

"I'm sorry." He spoke to the entire group. "We shouldn't have aired our family disagreement in public."

Abby rolled her eyes. "Yes, you should have done it in the privacy of the wagon so none of us could hear."

It took a minute for everyone to realize how impossible privacy was and to recognize Abby meant to joke about it.

Rachel was the first to laugh, but only seconds before Ben and soon everyone joined in. Well, except for Mrs. Bingham, who, so far as Ben could recall, laughed at nothing.

They ate dinner in a jolly mood and were soon on their way again.

Feeling considerably better, Ben left Emma and Rachel in charge of the wagon and rode his horse from wagon to wagon checking on each family.

Several more children and one adult had come down with the measles. So far, thank God, none of those afflicted had suffered too badly. Emma had said Johnny could leave the confines of the wagon. Ben wasn't sure who was happier, Johnny or Sally.

His thoughts shifted to a problem that hadn't been resolved. Several of the committeemen complained of missing items and were convinced there was a robber in their midst.

Sally eagerly joined those walking and the others took turns carrying the baby until he grew tired and settled in the wagon for a nap.

Ben completed his rounds, checking on the travelers and returned to the Hewitt wagon. Sam had warned them they would reach the Kansas River today. Ben did not like river crossings and the dangers they posed, but there was no other way to cross the Great Plains.

The lead wagons had reached the banks of the river and Ben rode ahead to assist in the crossing.

The river was too high to ford. He and the other committeemen gathered to consider their options. A Frenchman named Papin had a crude ferry and they approached him to ask if he could take the wagons across, but after some wrangling they could not come to an agreement on a reasonable price, so they decided to build their own ferry.

Ben watched Sam and knew he was concerned with the delay required to make a suitable conveyance.

But what choice did they have? Most of those present would lack the funds Papin had demanded. So Ben joined those selecting two trees to cut down and make into canoes. He spent the rest of the afternoon helping hollow out one of the trees while several others tackled the second one. He stopped only to eat hurriedly.

Martin sidled up to him. "There's some unrest. Some of the families are willing to pay Papin to cross. They aren't happy with the delay."

Ben downed a dipper full of water. "Our ferry will be ready by this time tomorrow."

"How many wagons could be across in that time?"

"Are you among those wanting to pay Papin?"

Martin chuckled. "Even if I had the funds, I don't much care for the man's attitude. Even worse, I had a look at his ferry. I have my doubts it's as good as he claims."

"I agree. Why don't you go up and down and tell the others of your observations. I'd do it, but I need to see to the building of the ferry."

"I'll do my best."

Ben grabbed another biscuit.

Abby watched him. He allowed himself to meet her gaze.

"Be safe," she murmured.

He nodded, unable to find his tongue to respond.

Rachel played with Johnny. The baby gurgled, bringing Ben's attention to him. Freeing him from the power Abby held over him with her steady gaze.

"Thanks. I plan to be." He hurried back to his task unreasonably buoyed by Abby's words.

He worked until dark. Then they lit bonfires and continued. The men took turns, spelling others so they could each catch a little sleep.

By morning, the canoes were ready and the men began adding planks to make the platform. By noon, it was ready to go.

A crowd gathered on the bank of the river as they launched the ferry. It teetered to one side then righted itself and floated.

A cheer went up.

"Who's to be first?" Sam Weston called.

The crowd grew silent then a low rumble came from them.

Ernie Jones glowered at Ben. "Seems no

one wanted to be the first on an untried ferry."

"I will." Miles Cavanaugh volunteered and drove his wagon onto the floating platform.

With men poling it to keep it straight, they made it safely to the other side. Now everyone vied for a place.

"We'll go in an orderly fashion," Ben said.

Again a grumble of complaint. Then a number of wagons pulled out.

"They've made an arrangement with Papin," Martin said.

"I wish them well." Ben had too much to do guiding wagons and animals and people over to try and dissuade them.

Sam Weston watched. "The faster we get this bunch over, the sooner we can be on our way."

Ben couldn't argue with that. He only hoped they'd be safe.

Martin informed him the Jensen family had joined the exodus to the Papin ferry.

Ben paused to look for Abby. She'd sat on the bank all afternoon watching. He'd been aware of her gaze even when he was otherwise occupied. *Be safe.* Her words made him both cautious and bold in his actions.

Abby looked up the bank toward the other ferry. "I pray they'll be okay."

Likely she felt a strong connection to them

because of the twins.

He wasn't surprised when she headed toward the other ferry to watch. At least she would be safe on the bank watching them.

His insides knotted as she hurried away. He'd feel better if she stayed back with his sisters where he could see her.

Only because he wanted to make sure she was safe . . . that all of them were safe.

His concern was unfounded. Nothing could happen to a spectator. He turned his attention back to the next wagon and did his best not to glance in the direction of the other ferry every ten seconds.

CHAPTER TEN

Before they even began the journey, Abby feared one thing more than any other. River crossings. There'd been no end of tales of people drowning in the treacherous rivers.

She stood on the banks of the Kansas River running full and turbulent. She shivered at the rushing roar of the water. Her only consolation came from the knowledge that Ben had overseen every step of the construction of the ferry. Miles Cavanaugh had been the first to use it and showed no fear. Since then many more had crossed.

Yes, it looked frightening, especially when the current caught the ferry and threatened to take the whole affair downstream. But the men seemed to know what they were doing.

Once the ferry had tipped dangerously as it twisted in the river but Ben had managed to steer it right. Her attention had been glued to the bulge and swell of his muscled arms, clearly visible with his wet shirt plastered to his skin. He was one of the bigger men on this trip and put his size to good use in the river.

Watching him, she'd pressed a hand to her heart feeling it thud with a combination of excitement and —

Something she would avoid admitting but the word could not be refused. A claiming sort of admiration. As if she had some right to admire him.

She didn't. It was foolish to think otherwise. So she welcomed the diversion of following the wagons that had opted to use this Papin fellow's ferry.

Not that escaping the necessity of watching Ben was the only reason. She wouldn't feel at ease until she saw the Jensen family had crossed safely. It didn't make sense, but she felt a strong need to protect the twins. Perhaps knowing they were safe would somehow ease the loss of her twin. No one would understand her way of thinking. She wasn't even sure she did.

She reached the other ferry just as the Jensen wagon boarded and she waved to the twins who peered out the back of the wagon. The older girls each clutched one of the little ones and peered out the front. Mrs. Jensen held the reins while Mr. Jensen stood beside the oxen, holding them so they wouldn't bolt.

The ferry left the shore, floating like an ark upon the waters. The twins continued to wave.

The current caught the vessel and twisted it about.

Abby caught her breath. But she'd seen this happen before and the men had turned it right.

This time, despite the frantic efforts of the men, this ferry did not turn. Water came up over one corner. Her lungs locked tight.

Mrs. Jensen yelled at the animals. They strained toward the highest corner. But it was too late. The wagon tipped.

The twins slipped out the back and into the river as the wagon slid into the water. She blinked. It had all happened so suddenly she could almost believe she'd imagined it.

"No," she wailed, her voice lost in the hubbub of men rushing to save the wagon. She glimpsed Annie, her face white as flour then she strained to see where the twins were.

She could taste the fear in her heartbeat as she searched for them. They weren't in the river. Someone must have plucked them to safety. But no one held either of the twins.

Where are you? Whether or not she called aloud, she couldn't say and it wouldn't have made any difference. No one would have heard her above the shouting.

There. She saw a little blond head bobbing downstream and raced down the bank.

There was the other. *Oh, thank God. Please don't let them drown.* A wooden yoke floated by.

"Grab it." She'd never yelled so loud in all her life. Whether or not the children heard her, they grabbed the wood and hung on as the current dragged them onward.

Abby raced up the bank until she caught up to them. "Swim for shore."

They thrashed about, putting them in danger of drowning but made no progress toward the bank. The current held them in its grip.

"I'll get you." She dived into the river. The cold water stole her breath. The current was fierce, but she used it to her advantage and swam after the children. She caught up to them and grabbed the yoke, taking a minute to catch her breath.

Tears streamed down Cathy's face. "I'm scared."

Donny's eyes were wide enough to swallow his face.

"You'll be okay. I'll take you to shore."

181

She tried pushing the yoke as the children clung to it but the unwieldy wood refused to leave the current. She was a strong swimmer but she fought the river and the weight of her sodden layers of clothes.

She glanced toward the bank. Why had no one else come to help? A look over her shoulder gave her the answer. Everyone continued to help with the Jensen's wagon. Had no one else seen the twins fall into the river?

Please help me. Please give me strength. She'd need one arm free to swim. That meant she could only take one child at a time. Every heartbeat seared her veins. How would she choose?

Cathy sank lower in the water.

Abby grabbed her. "Hang on." Donny had his arms over the yoke. Hating to pick one over the other, yet knowing Donny had a better hold on the yoke, she grabbed Cathy under her arms. "Relax and let me pull you along."

Her gaze lingered a painful moment on Donny. "You hang on and I'll be back to get you." She turned toward the bank, paddling against the current but the shore did not get any closer. She was being sucked under. From deep inside, she found the strength to fight but all she could do was keep herself and Cathy's heads above water. "Help. Help." Where was everyone? Where was Donny? He and the wooden yoke had disappeared, swept away by the rushing waters.

"Lord, save us."

"Ben!" The urgency in Rachel's voice jerked his attention to her so fast he almost lost his footing on the wet wood of the ferry as it approached the bank of the river.

"What's wrong?"

"The Jensen twins are missing and so is Abby."

He clambered from the water, alarm burning through his veins at the tone of her voice. "What do you mean? How can anyone be missing? Surely they're just off exploring." Maybe away from the noise and confusion of this place. Perhaps they'd stopped to pick flowers.

In hurried tones she explained how the Jensen wagon had ended up in the river.

His whipped about to look at the turbulent waters. "Then what happened?"

"I didn't see it but I did notice Abby dash along the riverbank. I wondered where she was going in such a hurry." She grabbed Ben's elbow. "Then we noticed the twins were missing. Annie said Abby saw them fall into the river. If she thought they were in danger —"

Her concern echoed his own. He raced along the riverbank. "Abby," he called. The current was swift. The water cold. How long since she'd hurried after the twins? Had she jumped in to rescue them?

Without a doubt, he knew she would. How well could she swim? Why didn't he know? After all, they'd had a couple of outings to a lake when they were spending time together. Only their interest had not been in the water. Or swimming.

"There." He didn't know if Rachel had followed or kept up but ahead he made out two blond heads in the river. One an adult, the other a child. Abby and Cathy. Where was Donny?

The pair disappeared under water. He waited for them to resurface, his heartbeat thundering inside his head, his lungs drawing in so fiercely it was impossible to pull in strengthening air.

They didn't come up. They were drowning. His heart exploded with a rush of hot blood. Not if he could do anything about it.

He dove into the river and swam to where he'd last seen them. Filling his lungs, he pushed under water. Where were they? He swam underwater until he had to surface for air.

"Abby," he roared. Not that he expected an answer. He simply had to express the fear that threatened to overwhelm him. "God, help me."

He dove back under the water twisting and turning like an overwrought fish, hoping . . . praying he'd find her. Did he see something? Was that — ? Yes. Fabric. He swam that direction. *Abby. Oh, Abby. Don't die.* Her arm clutched Cathy to her.

Don't either of you die. Not now. Please not now. Help me, God. Help me.

He grabbed her. His lungs cried out for air. He surfaced and swam toward shore with his heavy load.

Hands reached out and drew Abby and Cathy to the bank. More hands pulled him safely to dry ground. He lay on his back, exhausted and out of breath. But in ten seconds he forced his trembling limbs to act and staggered to where Rachel pressed on Cathy's back.

She shook her head.

No, God. Don't let her die.

Where was Abby? There. Mr. Henshaw pumped on her back, expelling water from her lungs.

Ben fell on his knees at her side. "Abby,

don't you die." He wanted to say so much more but he didn't have the right. "Don't you die." He could not think beyond those words, the alternative too overwhelming to contemplate. *Don't die. Don't die. God, don't let her die.* The words wailed through him in an endless litany.

She coughed and water spewed from her mouth.

Ben helped Mr. Henshaw sit her up. She coughed again and again. And sucked in air. Her color slowly returned.

She saw Ben and grabbed his hand. "Cathy and Donny?"

He looked toward Cathy where Rachel still pumped on her back.

Abby sobbed into her hand. "Is she . . . ?"

Mr. Henshaw left Abby and shifted to Cathy's side. "I have an idea. Let's sit her up." He rolled her over and he and Rachel sat her upright.

Ben shuddered. She already had the waxen look he associated with death.

Mr. Henshaw lifted Cathy's arms over her head and lowered them again. Over and over.

Ben had forgotten to breathe until his lungs ached and he released the tension locking them. Someone had brought blankets and draped one over his shoulders and another over Abby's. He tightened the blanket under her chin and pulled her into his arms. It would have taken an ox pulling on each arm to release his hold. Everyone would credit him with trying to get her warm.

Cathy coughed, the sound shattering the sorrowful silence.

Rachel laughed. "She's breathing. She's okay."

Abby burst into tears. She leaned her head on Ben's shoulder and sobbed as if her heart had split in two.

He held her tight. "She's okay," he murmured over and over.

She sniffed. "Where's Donny?" Her voice shivered past her teeth.

"They're looking for him now."

She pushed away and attempted to get to her feet but her legs refused to hold her. "I must find him." She tried standing again without success.

"Abby, you're too weak. Let the others look." He caught the edges of the blanket to pull her back to his arms.

She waved him aside. "He can't die. He can't. I won't let him."

She got her feet under her and staggered along the bank.

It would take only one misstep for her to

fall into the river again. Ben rushed after
her. He had no intention of letting her
drown.

"Abby, stop. There's nothing you can do."

But she hurried on as fast as her weak legs
would take her.

He followed after, his arms out to catch
her if she fell.

CHAPTER ELEVEN

Abby's insides had turned to ice and not solely from being in the river. Far worse was the fear that Donny had drowned. Was she to be responsible for the death of two twin brothers?

Over and over she shrieked a single word. *No. No. No.* If she could go back in time and stop Andy, she would. She'd trade her life for his if she could.

This time she had at least tried to save both twins, but she should never have left Donny. Should have dragged both children to shore. Never mind that she couldn't manage to save one on her own.

Did she dream it or had Ben pulled her from the icy water?

Never mind. No time to think about that now. Must find Donny. He couldn't die.

She staggered along the bank. The searchers were ahead of her now, milling around. Why weren't they looking in the water instead of standing there?

The only reason for it shuddered through her. Her legs threatened to unravel beneath her.

Ben grabbed her hand and stopped her ragged flight. "Abby, look."

An Indian on horseback. The first one she'd seen. Any other time she would have been curious and fascinated. Not now. "I have to find Donny. He can't die."

Ben wouldn't let her pull away. "Look closer."

He caught her chin and turned her attention to the stranger in their midst.

She blinked. The Indian held something in his arms. A body with blond hair. Donny? Had he — ? Was he — ? She tore from Ben and raced toward the mounted native.

Donny turned his head, saw her and flashed a bright smile.

He was alive. She laughed. *Thank You, God. Thank You.*

"Boy brave." The mounted man handed Donny to her. Her legs melted beneath her and she sank to the ground holding him. Ben knelt beside her, his arms encircling them both.

"You're safe. You're safe. Thank God." She murmured the words over and over, each one choking past her tear-clogged throat.

"And the Indian," Donny said. "He was nice to me."

Of course. She looked up at the man. "Thank you. Thank you."

Mr. Weston rode up and spoke to the rescuer. He chuckled. "Our friend says Donny was hanging on to a piece of wood. Wasn't about to let it go."

Mr. and Mrs. Jensen raced up to them, Mrs. Jensen crying out her children's names. She scooped Cathy into her arms and her husband took Donny. They huddled together, sheltering the children between them and kissed and hugged them.

"Thank you. Thank you." Mrs. Jensen sobbed.

Mr. Jensen held a hand out to the Indian and they shook then the mounted man reined about and rode away.

Amid much chatter, the crowd made its way upstream.

But Abby didn't move. Her limbs were rubbery. More than that, she couldn't think why she should leave the warming shelter of Ben's arms. If only she could stay here. Belong here.

She shuddered.

"You're cold."

"No more so than you." But their bodies created warmth in their shared coverings.

"We should return." But he didn't release her. Nor did she make any effort to get to her feet.

Just a little longer until her insides stopped quaking.

"I'm so glad Donny and Cathy are both safe." Her voice broke at how close it had been.

"Thanks to you. From what Rachel said, it seems you were the only one who realized they needed help. I suppose everyone else thought the next person had reached out and grabbed them."

"I'm so glad I could do something."

"Abigail. Abigail." Father rushed toward them.

Ben let her blanket fall to her shoulders and pushed to his feet. He held out a hand to pull her up.

She didn't want to leave this moment. This connection with Ben. She wanted to pretend they belonged together. She closed her eyes as if she could shut out the truth. This moment had only been about saving the twins. It had to be enough to satisfy her.

If only she could silence the lonely wail of her heart she might believe it.

Father reached her side. "Are you okay? I heard you about drowned." He pulled the blanket tighter under her chin and put an

192

arm around her shoulders. "You're freezing. We need to get you back so you can get into dry clothes."

He held her close as he hurried her back to the camp. "Our wagon is already across."

Emma and Rachel waved from the other side.

Ben grunted. "Ours is over safely, too."

A wagon perched on the ferry. Clarence sat on the bench ready to take the Morrison wagon over.

"We'll ride across, too," Ben said, and jumped to the ferry.

Clarence spared them a defensive look as if to inform them he could handle this on his own.

Ben ignored him and held out his hand to assist Abby.

She clung to Father. The ferry looked small and insignificant. It hardly seemed enough to keep them afloat. She glanced over her shoulder. For the first time since they'd departed she considered going back.

Father must have understood her confusion. "Abigail, there is nothing for us back there. Our best hope is to get to Oregon. A new beginning, remember?" He gently urged her forward.

" 'The Lord is my shepherd. He leadeth me beside the still waters.' " The verse ran through Abby's mind. But the waters were not still. They rushed and roared and sucked one downward. Oh, for some still, calm waters.

She faced the ferry but could not force her feet to step forward and commit herself to the insignificant bit of wood.

Ben leaned forward and took her hand. "I've got you."

His hand steadied her. His words comforted and she took a step and then another until she stood at his side.

Father jumped aboard and again wrapped his arm about her shoulders.

The ferry moved away from the shore. It floated free, shifting with the current.

She closed her eyes and bit her bottom lip until she tasted blood.

"You're safe," Ben murmured, his voice close to her ear.

That's when she realized he pressed to her side and she gripped his hand hard enough to numb the fingers of a smaller hand.

The ferry bumped. She squealed.

"We're safe on the other side."

They had to wait for the wagon to offload before she scrambled to solid ground.

Emma and Rachel rushed to her holding blankets. Emma rubbed her wet hair. "You need to get into dry clothes," she murmured, and led her to the Bingham wagon.

"I can manage," she said when it appeared they would climb inside with her.

Mother perched on her high-backed chair. "What were you thinking?" Her harsh whispered words were like wooden bullets piercing Abby's brain.

"I was thinking I didn't want the twins to drown." She pulled her dry clothes from her bag and turned her back to her mother to work her way out of the waterlogged outfit.

"Have you forgotten your duty to us? Your promise?"

If she ever did, her mother would certainly remind her. She had made a promise. Yes, she hoped she would be freed of it but until that happened . . .

In the meantime, she was more than aware of the command to honor her parents. "I've not forgotten, nor have I forgotten how it feels to lose a twin brother."

"Drowning yourself in the river won't bring Andy back."

"I know that, Mother."

"If only you had been as concerned about saving your brother as you were about saving strangers Andrew would still be with us."

If only. If only. The words battered the inside of her heart.

Mother talked as Abby changed her clothes, pointing out the risks and dangers of the journey they'd undertaken. "A journey of death."

Abby couldn't listen to another word about dying and hurriedly buttoned the bodice of her dress. Despite Mother's objections, she'd left her fine silks and satins behind and brought only practical, simple cotton frocks.

Mother had been quite dismissive of Abby's choice. "Next you'll be making your own gowns from sacks."

Abby climbed from the wagon with Mother's warnings following her.

Rachel pulled her toward the fire and urged her to sit down on a quilt she'd spread on the ground. She and Emma took the few remaining pins from her hair and brushed it before the warm flames. They talked softly and soothingly as they worked.

Abby had never had sisters to fuss over her. Her nurses hadn't been unkind but their attention had never felt this way — warm, embracing. Again *if onlys* filled her thoughts. If only her mother had shown this kind of love. If only Abby had been able to prevent Andy's death.

A silent moan ripped through her body. She hadn't even tried to stop Andy. Rather, she'd encouraged him. She'd always been so proud of his boldness and quick wits.

She'd never be free of the past. Even if she could be free of the promise she'd given, she could not follow her heart.

At this fragile moment she wanted to have Ben hold her and protect her. But that wasn't what she really wanted. She wanted independence, not belonging to another man.

Maybe he's different, a tiny voice whispered inside her head.

Maybe he was, she argued back. *And maybe he wasn't.* She could be friends with him but nothing more. Never again would she risk being owned by a man, subject to his moods and meanness.

Not that she'd been offered anything but his concern. The same concern he'd have shown to anyone else.

That, she assured herself, suited her just fine.

And if she shivered it was only because of the cold dunking she'd taken. Certainly not because her heart had turned to ice.

Ben had changed his clothes. He needed to return to the river and help ferry wagons over, but not until he made certain Abby was okay. Of course, Emma and Rachel could look after her, but until his mind was at ease he posed a distracted risk at the crossing.

Abby sat with her head bowed as his sisters tended her hair.

He'd never before seen her blond mane loose and falling down her back. Thick and luxuriant, it mirrored the sun's rays. He curled his fingers against an urge to edge closer and run them through it.

Instead, he studied her posture. He'd like to believe she looked relaxed, but couldn't convince himself it was so. Her shoulders slumped so much he wanted to hug her and comfort her. Everyone had overheard Mrs. Bingham's comments. Like Abby had jokingly pointed out, there was little hope for privacy with only a canvas barrier. He wondered if Mrs. Bingham cared whether others heard her. In her opinion, they were of little note.

Why did she seem to blame Abby for her brother's death? How unfair. Near as he could recall, Abby would have been about fourteen at the time. How could she possibly be held responsible even if she'd been the cause of an accident? Accidents happened no matter how careful a person was.

He took a step closer and halted. What could he do? He didn't have the right to hold her. Nor to say the words he longed to say.

His sisters continued to fuss over her hair and talk to her.

Her head came up. The strain around her eyes eased, but the sunshine of her smile was absent.

He took another step. The least he could do was say something. Perhaps not the words welling up inside him, yet other words of comfort and encouragement might help.

At that moment, the entire Jensen family made their noisy way over.

The twins, now dry and back to normal, rushed to Abby. She opened her arms and welcomed them, kissing each on the top of the head.

"I'm so glad to see you're okay."

Mrs. Jensen handed the littlest baby to one of the bigger girls and knelt before Abby. She reached around the twins and enfolded all three into a hug.

"You saved my children. I will never forget it." She drew back and wiped her eyes.

"It wasn't me."

"Mostly, it was," Mrs. Jensen said.

Abby squeezed her hand. "I'm glad everyone is safe."

Mr. Jensen reached for Abby's other hand and pumped it up and down. "We're so grateful."

The older girls murmured their thanks, as well.

"Sit down and visit a spell," Emma said as Rachel prepared tea. "Mr. Jensen?" she offered him a cupful.

"Alvin, please, and my wife's name is Delores." They took the offered tea. The children sat back quietly as the adults visited.

Sally joined them, leaving Johnny with the Jensen girls. Mr. Bingham and Martin remained at the banks of the river.

Where Ben should be, he thought with a guilty glance that direction. Soon.

Emma offered him tea and he joined the group.

Abby's eyes darkened as if something troubled her as she looked from Alvin to Delores. "Last I saw, your wagon was in the river. Did you, is it — ?"

Alvin answered her faltering question. "Our wagon made it across in one piece."

Ben heard the note in his voice that said it wasn't entirely good news. "Did you lose much?"

Alvin and Delores exchanged glances.

"Some." The word was spoken cautiously.

Ben felt their pride but pride wouldn't feed and care for six children and their parents. "Can you be more specific?"

Again the Jensens shared a look. Alvin nodded. "We have one sack of flour that didn't get ruined. We saved a lot of our things. We have our milk cow and Mr. Weston assures me we can hope to find game."

"We'd all be glad of some fresh meat." Ben understood what they didn't say . . . they'd lost more than they cared to admit.

"Well, we best be on our way." The Jensens gathered up their children and departed.

Ben looked about at his sisters and friends and saw his concern mirrored. "I'll check with Sam to see exactly how much they lost." He strode back to the river and found the wagon master.

The news wasn't good.

"I saw a lot of stuff floating downstream. And much of what stayed in the wagon was water soaked."

"We'll all share with them." Ben passed the word along and by suppertime, numerous gifts had been left for the Jensens.

"We'll share, too," he said to Emma. "We can surely spare something."

"Of course we can." Both sisters hurried

to the wagon.

"We'll send over something, as well," Abby said. "We've got more sugar than we need." She went to their wagon.

Mrs. Bingham spoke loudly. "We will not sacrifice because of someone else's foolishness."

"It wasn't foolishness, Mother. It was an accident."

"I've said from the first that this trip is doomed for failure." Her voice grew louder, sharper.

Around them, people stopped and stared in her direction.

Mr. Bingham strode in from wherever he'd been and went directly to the wagon. "Hush, Martha. This kind of talk serves no good purpose."

Mrs. Bingham's voice rose even louder. "People should not be encouraged to take such rash actions. Abigail, put that sugar back. We'll starve to death and it will be your fault."

"Abigail," her father sounded firm and tired. "Take what you think we can spare. Now, Martha, why don't you come with me and we'll go for a little stroll. You need to stretch your legs."

Abby slipped away with the sugar and crossed to the Jensen wagon without looking to the right or left. Her cheeks shone a rosy pink.

Some muttering and muffled words came from the Bingham wagon and then Mr. Bingham alighted, reached up to assist his wife and the two of them walked away from the stunned listeners.

Ben stood rooted to the ground. What was wrong with that woman that she blamed Abby for things beyond her control? That she saw nothing but doom and disaster?

He watched for Abby to return. Mrs. Jensen sat beside their wagon, surrounded by the many generous gifts. She wiped her eyes.

The twins chased each other across the grass. The older girls played with the babies.

Where was Abby?

He looked farther afield. Was that her hurrying past a wagon several hundred yards away? A smile tugged at his lips. He'd know her graceful way of moving amid a thousand women dressed alike. Concern erased his smile. Why was she going the wrong direction?

He jogged after her, not wanting to overtake her immediately lest she protest.

She hurried on past the last wagon and onward. Not until the commotion of emigrants and their animals had faded to a dull hum did she slow her steps. She stared to the west then to the river. What was she thinking? Then she sank to the ground overlooking the river.

He stood still but he must have made some sound because she turned and saw him.

She considered him with wide hazel eyes then turned to again stare at the river.

Assuring himself she would have said something if she didn't care to have him join her, he closed the distance and sank to her side, far enough away not to make her uneasy, but close enough he could enjoy her sweet scent.

He didn't speak. He didn't feel the need, nor did he have any idea what to say.

The silence went on and on for about ten minutes then she released her breath in a loud gust.

"Mother did not want to make this trip."

That was clearly evident to one and all.

"Father wants to start a new business where the economy is flourishing."

Ben continued to listen.

"Why did I think anything would change?" She cranked around and stared at him.

He swallowed hard and thought fast. "Your circumstances are surely going to change."

She quirked an eyebrow as if to tell him his answer was far from adequate. "People don't change." She resumed staring at the river. Or at least in that direction. He couldn't say if she actually saw the water or something deep inside her own thoughts.

"Sometimes they do," he ventured.

"You've seen it for yourself, or you're just making it up?"

"Seen it for myself. Pa changed after Ma died."

"For the better or worse?"

He had to think about that a moment. "Neither. He just changed. I guess having four children to care for on his own made him more serious, more cautious and maybe even more loving."

"He's the only one you can think of? And it hardly counts, because his circumstances and responsibilities forced him to make changes. Yet, I expect he was still the same sort of man."

She had a point, yet it annoyed him that she ignored his argument. "I still say people change. I'm sure you've changed since . . . well, since you were young . . . younger," he quickly corrected himself.

She appeared to consider the possibility. "I think you'd be surprised at how little I've changed." She pushed to her feet and hurried toward the wagons.

He stared after her. Then jerked up and rushed after her. "How can you say that? You lost your husband. You're headed West with your parents. Those things must have changed you. Changed your views. Changed your feelings. Something."

"I suppose you're right." She marched onward.

He didn't follow. She obviously didn't agree despite her words. But what did she mean? What hadn't changed?

Could she possibly mean her feelings toward him hadn't changed? But that simply wasn't possible.

Was it?

And what if it were true? His heart flew to the top of his mouth and as quickly fell toward his feet. He turned back to the river.

Things could never be the same between them as they had been. He, for one, was not as eager to give his heart to anyone. Least of all, someone who had treated it so poorly.

He didn't always agree with Rachel, but this time her words served as a guide. Abby would only use him while it suited her.

He knew it and knew enough to guard his heart.

CHAPTER TWELVE

Abby managed to avoid Ben the rest of the evening. She didn't even play her mandolin or read, explaining she was simply too tired, which elicited unwelcome sympathy from those around her. She didn't want it — didn't deserve it.

She retired to bed early, but despite her fatigue, sleep didn't come easily. She'd said too much to Ben. Hinted that she still had the same feelings for him she'd had six years earlier.

Only her fright of almost drowning and the comfort he'd offered after rescuing her had emboldened her to say as much as she did.

Thankfully, he hadn't understood what she meant.

Now she must get her feelings back under control. But how could she forget how tenderly he'd held her? Especially when she owed her life to him. Rachel had explained how Ben had dived into the river without a thought and stayed underwater long enough to make Rachel think he'd drowned.

"He said he wouldn't have given up until he found you."

She'd shrugged it off. "He'd do that for anyone. After all, he's got the responsibility of being a committeeman."

Rachel's eyebrows had gone up at Abby's denial, then she shrugged. "I expect you're right. Ben takes his responsibilities rather seriously."

Abby smiled, thinking how he'd wrapped a blanket about her and held her close. Despite the cold that sucked at the marrow of her bones, her heart had warmed at his attention.

But she could not, would not, believe it meant anything more. What if it did? Could he possibly have any sweet regard for her after the way she'd treated him?

Not very likely. She flipped to her side. Even if he did, she knew better than to trust her feelings, much less to trust how a man acted. They could be one thing in public, quite another behind closed doors.

She wakened the next morning with a smile on her lips and her arms hugging herself like Ben's had.

She jerked her arms to her sides. She must

not think along those lines. She hurried to help Mother dress.

"I'm going to stay in bed today," Mother said, waving Abby's help away. It would take more than one day to get the wagons all across so they wouldn't move today.

"Mother, why would you do that?"

"I'm already wore out and we've only been gone a week. I'll never survive the weeks ahead." Mother groaned.

A thread of concern wove through Abby's thoughts. Was there something wrong? She sat at her mother's side. "Are you ill?"

"I truly do not see how I can be expected to endure this day after day."

Abby sighed. Her mother had always complained about things — the temperature of the food, the dust she thought she saw on a table, the wrinkled apron a maid wore. Abby had always ignored it or laughed it off as inconsequential. Now it grated on her nerves. The constantness of it. The pettiness of it.

"Mother, have you forgotten you're a Bingham? Haven't you always told me a Bingham rises above circumstances?"

"You know I wasn't referring to things such as this." She waved her hand around to indicate the tent, but Abby knew she meant everything about this trip.

"You should walk more. It's preferable to the bouncing on the wagon seat."

Mother sniffed. "Ladies don't walk all the way to Oregon."

There was no point in arguing and Abby slipped out to help prepare breakfast. She glanced about to see where Ben was. When she didn't see him, she tried to tell herself she was relieved. So much easier to put him from her mind if he wasn't in her sight.

Sally returned with fresh milk, Johnny perched on her hip.

"It amazes me how you do everything while carrying him," Abby said, and held out her hands to take the little guy so Sally could use two hands to strain the milk.

Johnny came readily. Seems he was prepared to accept their group as his family.

She rumbled her lips at him, earning a jolly chuckle.

Father and Martin returned together, talking about how the oxen were enjoying the chance to rest.

Breakfast was ready. But where was Ben?

She moved to the back of the wagon as if needing something from within and while there, she glanced toward the river. The ferry was on the other side and there was Ben, taller and broader than most of the other men. He stood with his feet apart, his hands on his hips looking like he was content to rule his world. The sun poking over the horizon silhouetted him in golden light.

Men and women crowded around him. She was too far to make out any words but something about the way they talked made her catch her breath. She tipped her head trying to hear the sounds from across the river but the camp on this side drowned out any possibility.

Mr. Weston stepped to Ben's side and held up his hand to silence the crowd. They appeared to stop talking, but their expressions plainly said they didn't want to.

A few seconds later, the crowd dispersed and Ben crossed the river on his horse.

Abby scurried away, not wanting him to find her watching.

Even more, not wanting to admit to herself she had been. She wasn't so naive as to think he could ever again regard her as he had six years ago. Not when she'd made her rejection as harsh as she could bring herself to. Over the years, especially when Frank had made her cry, she'd consoled herself that Ben had likely married a suitable, hardworking woman and was supremely happy. She'd taken a tiny bit of comfort in believing at least one of them had found happiness.

Seems he'd been too busy with his family responsibilities to take on a wife. But the words she'd spoken had ensured he would never have any feelings for her.

"A wise woman looks to the future," she'd said. She'd even tipped her nose a little exactly as her mother had done when she'd spoken the words to Abby. "I feel I deserve more than a struggling existence, which is all you can give me." She'd had to be cruel. Had to convince him this choice was entirely hers. She'd said more. So much more.

She pressed her hands to her stomach. Every word had cut her deep. The wounds had never healed.

She'd continued to think of Ben as a kind, generous man but the things she'd said were not forgivable.

He rode to the first wagon and spoke to the group without dismounting. He rode from wagon to wagon. Obviously, he delivered a message. He approached their group.

Abby sat by the fire, curious as to what he had to say, but intent on revealing no special interest in his return.

"It's Sunday, and because of that, some of the families are refusing to move. Sam says we can't afford to delay for any reason. Winter will catch us soon enough. Rev. Pettygrove says he's prepared to conduct a service."

The reverend and his wife were still on the other side. Did he expect they'd all go back over the river? Abby shuddered at the thought.

"We're to put it to a vote. We'll meet at the edge of the river."

Murmurs followed Ben's departure. They swelled as he delivered his message. The men hurried to the meeting spot.

Abby and Rachel crept closer to listen to the discussion.

Ben spoke first. "Sam says winter will be upon us before we cross the mountains if we delay."

One man spoke up loudly. "One of the Ten Commandments is 'Remember the Sabbath day, to keep it holy.' I don't see that we get to pick and choose which commandments we're going to keep or when."

The argument sank heavy in Abby's thoughts. The next commandment was "Honor thy father and thy mother." Because of those words she would not break her promise to her mother. She prayed the trip would change Mother enough for her to release her.

So far she'd seen no hint of change.

Voices rose defending each side of the

question. Across the river, another commit-teeman held a similar discussion while Mr. Weston stood by waiting.

It must surely be difficult for him to let these people decide on such a question. They didn't know what lay ahead of them but he did. Shouldn't that make his opinion the only one that counted?

Ben held up a hand to signal quiet. "You've all had your chance to speak and you bring up valid points. Remember how our Lord was challenged by the Pharisees for healing a sick man on the Sabbath?"

Heads nodded.

"Do you recall His response to them? He asked if they had an ox that fell into a pit, would they leave him there? Isn't our situation similar? We have many oxen, plus women and children to get safely across this great, empty land and then across the mountains. Would God be honored if we kept the Sabbath but caused needless deaths on the trail because of our delay? Bear in mind, it isn't just one day, but one day every week, for up to six months. That's a lot of delay." As the crowd started to murmur again, he held up his hand. They grew silent. "What I suggest is each group take the time to read from the Scriptures on Sunday morning and thus honor God that way.

214

Now let's vote. Who believes we should make use of every good day, Sunday or otherwise?"

Most hands went up. Others slowly joined them. Only a few crossed their arms and refused to agree.

"The majority votes to continue." Ben shouted the decision across the river.

"Same here," came the reply.

Abby kept her attention on those across the river so no one would notice how she blinked away tears. Ben was a man among men. Good, wise, noble. She was proud to know him. And to have counted him as a special friend at one time.

She and Rachel hurried back to the campfire to complete breakfast preparations.

Ben joined them for the meal. "We'll have time to take care of other business while the rest of the wagons cross. Use it wisely."

Emma handed him a Bible. "Read a chapter."

Ben took the Bible and held it reverently. Then he chuckled. "I suggest we read from Exodus." He read a chapter. "I'm off to help get the wagons across the river."

Abby had been studiously avoiding looking directly at him until now. She pretended to glance at something off to his right. She felt his waiting and allowed her gaze to shift.

He looked directly at her. The morning sun filled his blue-gray eyes with a piercing look that erased all her fine intentions of acting like she didn't care. Time ceased. Camp sounds silenced. Nothing existed but the two of them, locked in solitude. His look went on and on, searching her thoughts, probing her dreams and wishes.

Someone rode up. "Come on, Ben."

He blinked, jerked away and swung into his saddle.

She ducked her head as the world resumed turning and pressed her hand to her heart in silent consternation. Had she imagined it? Surely it was only her own impossible yearnings that made her think he had any interest in her.

Delores wandered over and spoke, snapping Abby back to her surroundings.

"I regret my children will have to miss church all these months. I don't want them to forget what's important."

Her words gave Abby an idea. "I could have a kind of pretend church with the children if you like. We could sing hymns and —" She thought of how she treasured the Word that she had hidden in her heart. "I could help them memorize Bible verses."

Delores squeezed Abby's hand. "That would be wonderful. Do you mind if I let the other mothers know?"

"Not at all." She'd enjoy spending time with the children. It would give her something to do beside wonder about Ben and look for excuses to wander down by the river so she could watch him. That was an interest she did not intend to pursue. Independence was all she cared about.

Thirty minutes later, she sat on a grassy spot, surrounded by a group of eager children. She played her mandolin and taught them hymns. Some of the mothers sat nearby and joined in the singing. Clarence Pressman watched from a distance then hurried away before she could invite him to join them, though a lone man would surely feel out of place among women and children.

"I want to tell you one of my favorite things from church. Something that means more to me now than it did when it happened. Who wants to know what it is?"

Little hands went into the air.

She leaned forward as if sharing a secret. "I found a treasure and I buried it." She looked about like she didn't want anyone to hear her.

Eyes widened and the children waited for her to continue.

"Do you want me to tell you where I

buried it?"

The children nodded. Some whispered, "Yes."

She pressed her hand to her chest. "Here. In my heart."

Confusion and surprise filled the children's faces. She told them of how she had memorized verses and they had been such a treasure for her. She selected a verse and taught it by putting it to music and by having the children play a recitation game. By the time she dismissed them, many of them were chanting, "Psalm one hundred nineteen, verse eleven. 'Thy word have I hid in mine heart, that I might not sin against Thee.' "

The mothers gathered round her to thank her then she watched them depart.

It had been fun. She liked teaching. Maybe when they reached Oregon, she'd become a teacher. She could just imagine how her mother would react if she suggested it. *Please, God. Free me from my promise. I know You have the power to do this.*

She edged around the nearest wagon and watched the ferry crossing again. Ben rode along as guide.

In her thoughts she considered him noble and kind.

Her heart seized within her. Too heavy

with fear to beat. She ordered it to beat again even though she knew it would bleed sorrow into every vein.

Frank had not appeared to be a bad man when she married him. She hadn't loved him, but he didn't seem to care. All he wanted was a woman he could control . . . a wife to do his bidding in and out of bed. Was he any different than other men? When Father spoke firmly to Mother, she obeyed. And he was but a soft-spoken banker.

A big, strong, bold man like Ben would expect even more compliance. She rubbed at her breastbone, willing away the pain, the regret, the sorrow that held her heart like a vise.

She'd once dreamed of being a wife and mother. But that dream had died at Frank's hands. She'd lament it to her dying day but she didn't plan to go through that misery again. God willing, she'd find contentment teaching, running a boardinghouse or any of the other things she'd considered. Most of all, she'd find the independence she sought.

She turned away, unable to look at Ben any longer. Every look tore at her insides with regret over her dead dreams. She realized she had wrapped her arms over each other, again imitating the way Ben had held her, warmed her, comforted her.

If only she could hope for more. But it was impossible.

How would she endure this trip?

Ben knew the exact moment Abby stepped around the wagon to look his direction. He could explain her presence by saying she was interested in watching the ferry crossings as many were. He could also say he hadn't been watching for her. But both would be half-truths.

He didn't even need to see her to know she was nearby. He felt it in the way his heart rate picked up.

Then she'd spun around and run away.

He could think of a dozen reasons for her sudden departure. Her mother had called. Or Sally or Emma or Rachel. Or she might have heard a baby cry and gone to investigate. Or a sudden urge to attend to one of the camp chores had come over her.

But he knew in the depths of his heart that she had run from him. Just as she had in the past.

He hardened his heart against the regard he had for her. Yes, she seemed sweet and helpful. But as Rachel had once or twice pointed out, it suited Abby to use Ben while traveling. And perhaps suited her mother for the time being though she showed no hint of gratitude. Once they reached Oregon, the whole group knew Mrs. Bingham's plans for her daughter did not include Ben. As she'd told him six years before, Abby could do better. Much better. She could marry a man with social status and a generous bank account.

He wasn't about to stick his hand to the fire a second time. Except — he sighed and bent his back to the pole lest anyone overhear him. Except he'd never backed away from the fire. He'd never stopped caring despite his best intentions. Even though he knew she would use him and discard him, he still couldn't stop caring.

Rescuing her from the waters of the river, holding her to warm her afterward had served to fan the live coals into a blazing fire.

His mind whirled. They had four months, maybe as long as six, before they reached Oregon. He had tried to harden his heart against her. Had tried valiantly to push her from his thoughts. Still tried. But she was everywhere . . . at the meals, walking beside the wagons during the day, circling the camp at evening, playing her music. Even at night, he heard her tossing and turning.

How could he possibly pretend she didn't exist?

He stood a good chance of getting his heart broken again. But he'd survived it once, knew he could survive it again if it came to that.

He knew she would reject him as a suitor. Her mother would not allow it. But he could hardly blame her mother that Abby had chosen Frank. She'd made it abundantly clear that it was what she wanted — a man with more promise than Ben.

Yet the thought didn't stop him from glancing after her. Perhaps he should nail a big sign to his chest reading, Proceed with Caution.

He jogged to their wagon and jumped over the tongue and skidded to a halt. There she sat laughing with Sally.

Sally held Johnny before her, steadying him on his two little feet. Abby held out her arms and the baby toddled unsteadily to her.

Abby caught him, and hugged him, laughing. "Look at you walk."

Martin hurried up to his wife. "Get him to walk to me."

Abby turned Johnny toward his father and steadied him. He clung to her fingers. She eased from his grasp. The little guy's legs bent. Abby reached for him but he stayed upright without her assistance.

"Come to Papa," Martin called.

Johnny took one step and then another straight into his father's arms.

Martin swung him overhead, laughing.

Little Johnny crowed with delight.

Abby scrambled to her feet and as she turned, saw Ben. She blinked, looked away.

He wanted to open his arms to her and have her run to him like Johnny had gone to his father, in complete trust and acceptance. He pressed down a thousand desires equally as foolish and impossible. Trust went both ways and he would never trust her again.

Her gaze slowly came back to his. She pressed her lips together. Pink stole up her cheeks.

He stared. Despite his resolve, his longings swelled to impossible proportions. They'd shared something when he pulled her from the river. She'd leaned into his arms when he warmed her. Had she felt the same hope and promise he'd felt?

Her eyes darkened.

He didn't know what it meant.

His ma's words tracked through his thoughts. *There was still day by day.* She'd said it often when one of the Hewitt children got looking too far into the future. For the days and weeks of their crossing, he must guard his heart and his thoughts. Even his glances at her.

What they had shared in the past was over and he wasn't foolish enough to think it could be resurrected. Nor foolish enough to think she had changed.

"Dinner is ready," Emma called, and he turned his attention to the food. He listened to the conversation and did his best not to watch Abby. But again and again his gaze found her and darted away before she noticed.

He had time to relax a little while others took over the ferry. He meant to put it to good use and lounged against the nearest wagon wheel nursing a cup of coffee long past the time it normally took to drink it.

Martin had stretched out for a nap with Johnny asleep at his side.

Mr. Bingham had found an old friend in another wagon and gone to visit him. Mrs. Bingham must be roasting in her tent but refused to come out except for meals. Sally, Abby and his sisters sat together, working on quilt squares. From the conversation, he knew they were giving Abby a lesson in sewing.

"Ben, what do you think of this?" Rachel

224

held up a square. It was a dark piece of fabric with a white-canvassed wagon, and a field of flowers.

He wasn't sure what he was expected to say. "It looks nice."

"It was Abby's idea to make quilt blocks to tell of our journey."

He shifted his gaze to Abby. "Are you going to do one of the river crossing?"

She nodded, her eyes wide and questioning.

Would she show a man and a woman wrapped together in a blanket? He swallowed hard. "That should be interesting."

Sally threaded a needle and bent her head over her piece of fabric. "Abby is such an asset to our group. To the whole wagon train."

Ben tried to think how to respond.

"Yes, indeed," Sally continued. "I was so impressed with how you took over the children this morning."

Ben cast a questioning look at Abby. She shied away from his glance, took the quilt block from Rachel and poked her needle through the fabric with such concentration, he knew she was self-conscious.

"What did she do?" he asked Emma, knowing she would be the most forthcoming.

"She played hymns for us and taught the children a Bible verse."

"I would have never thought to turn it into a song or a speaking game for them," Sally said with much admiration.

"We really appreciate your work," Emma added.

Ben studied the women. Emma gently appreciative. Sally enthused. Rachel's face full of uncertainty. He guessed he felt a little like she did. Abby was different than he expected, reminiscent of the Abby he'd known and cared for in the past. He was impressed with how quickly she adjusted to life on the trail.

Which Abby was the real one? The one sitting before him? The one he remembered from six years ago? Or the one who chose a man for the size of his purse?

"It wasn't anything special," Abby murmured, glancing toward her mother's tent.

And that glance said it all. Abby was strong and helpful and everything a man might hope except in this one thing — her mother controlled her in what he considered an unnatural way.

Again the question. Who was the real Abby?

"I best get back to work." He nodded goodbye to the women in general, letting

226

his gaze rest on Abby just a second longer than the rest. She kept her head down.

He glanced toward the Bingham tent. Was it because of her mother? Did she fear to have their conversation overheard? He shook his head. It didn't matter. His heart was safely locked away from her charms.

He returned to the ferry and crossed to the other side to help another wagon. It took a long time to take so many wagons over one by one. He was anxious to be moving as were all of them. But they had to move with caution and wisdom.

A good principle to apply to his life, as well. Strengthened by the thought, he was about to guide the next wagon to the ferry, when Sam rode up with a stranger at his side. "Ben, you need to get the committeemen together. Something's come up."

That didn't sound good. Nor did the look on the stranger's face provide any reassurance. Ben turned to the wagon driver.

"Get your wagon on board." He looked about for someone to guide the ferry across. Arty and Ernie Jones stood nearby and had the size to do it, but could they be trusted? "You men, come over here." He signaled to them.

Scowling darkly they ambled over, in no haste to answer his call. He hoped he wasn't making a mistake.

"Think you can guide this ferry across the river?"

Ernie stared at him. "You asking or telling?"

"Asking."

Ernie shrugged. "I'll consider it."

"I need someone big and strong. You were my first choice."

"That so?" Both chests swelled. "Guess we can do that." Ernie jumped to the ferry and Arty followed. They grabbed the poles and shoved off.

Ben grinned. The pair might be belligerent and troublesome, but he figured they'd do a good job just to prove they could.

He hurried away, calling the other committeemen who were all on this side of the river to help control the impatient travelers. Seems everyone thought they should be next.

They joined Sam and the visitor and withdrew so they could speak privately.

"This here is James Stillwell," Sam said. "He's got something to say."

James stepped forward. Ben thought he might be of a similar age. Not as tall but broad shouldered. He took off his hat and set it carefully on his saddle horn and rubbed his hand over his hair as if to settle it in place.

Ben grinned. The man looked as though he'd recently had his black hair cut. Everything about him spoke of special care of his looks. Then the man crossed his arms and peered around the small group of men, his dark eyes intense beneath bushy eyebrows.

"I'm the agent for the Thayer and Edwards safe company. It was one of our safes that was robbed in Independence."

Ben nodded as did the other men. They'd heard about the robbery on the day of their departure. But what did that have to do with the wagon train?

"I followed the trail of the thief to the Plante farm. Their wagon had been stolen. They had just arrived home from purchasing enough supplies to last them the summer and the wagon was still hitched up to oxen. I suspect the thief used it for escape. I lost the trail in the many wagon tracks of this wagon train. At first I thought it was a clever ruse to hide the tracks, but after a few days of searching I could find no sign of a missing wagon or the money. My conclusion is the thief is in this party."

Miles said what Ben and likely all the committeemen were thinking. "That would mean a late arrival." There had been several who'd straggled after them for various

229

reasons . . . something broken, a missing ox, or just plain disorganization but none that raised any suspicions.

James listened to the explanation then nodded understanding. "It's impossible to tell who might be the guilty party. I will need to search every wagon until I find the missing fifteen thousand dollars."

The men gasped at the thought there might be that much money in one of the wagons.

Sam stepped forward. "That's not possible. The wagons on this side must cross as quickly as possible and then we must keep moving. Any delay might be costly."

James gave Sam a hard look. "More costly than losing fifteen thousand dollars?"

Sam held his ground. "More costly in the way of lives."

James sighed. "Of course. I would never put money ahead of people. But my integrity is on the line if I don't return that money to the shipping company."

Ben admired the man's honor. "Why don't you join the wagon train? That way you could do some investigation while we continue moving."

James considered the suggestion for a moment then nodded. "That might work. Do all of you approve?"

The men nodded.

James seemed to mull the idea over further then spoke. "It will work best if no one knows my real reason for being here."

Miles Cavanaugh stepped forward. "I've got my hands full traveling on my own. Why don't you sign up with me?"

James nodded. "Agreed."

The men clustered about, asking James all sorts of questions. He had a few of his own. Had they noticed anyone acting strangely? Perhaps not joining in the social activities as much as they might.

Ben knew of one such person. Clarence Pressman. The young man had little to do with his fellow travelers, although he'd allowed Emma to continue to tend his wound. The two of them spent too much time a far distance from the camp for Ben's liking. Rachel had accused him of interfering in Emma's life. But there was something about young Pressman that seemed odd. He'd keep an eye on Clarence and share his concerns with James in private. No need to stir up things until he had at least a shred of proof. But he'd watch and see what Clarence did while the others gathered around socializing in the evening.

"There have been rumblings about items lost or stolen," Miles pointed out.

James looked thoughtful. "Could be our culprit isn't happy with the money from the robbery. If we could catch him in the act it would give us a reason to search his wagon." He looked around the circle of men. "We need to be more vigilant in watching without raising suspicions, it might allow us to find this person. Perhaps if we all took turns walking about after we stop. Keeping it innocent looking, of course."

One of the men said he'd take his young sons out for a walk. Another said he'd welcome a chance to stretch his legs after riding on the wagon all day. "But I don't want to draw attention to myself."

"Why not ask your neighbor to walk with you?" James suggested.

Miles turned to Ben. "You've got the perfect arrangement."

Ben stared at the man. He wasn't sure his sisters would want to walk with him. Seems they deserved time to spend as they liked.

Miles continued. "Ask Mrs. Black to walk with you. Can you think of a better reason than to be courting a pretty young woman?"

Ben's mouth fell open. Courting? He couldn't pretend something he wanted to avoid at all costs.

"Why that's perfect," James said. "You'll do it?"

"Of course he will." Miles clapped him on the back.

Ben managed to close his mouth and nod, feeling very much like he'd been railroaded into something he didn't want to do. Yet he couldn't deny a certain anticipation.

That night he returned to their camp with his thoughts tangled on a dozen different things. The crossing was going well. They'd soon be on their way again. A walk about the camp would enable him to watch young Pressman. And if it meant spending time with Abby, it was for a good cause.

Shouldn't he be a little more concerned about taking this step?

Yet he wasn't. He could do it and still guard his heart, he assured himself.

The women worked together over the fire — with the exception of Mrs. Bingham who perched in her chair waiting to be served. The way Abby laughed with the others brought his gaze to her often. As he'd observed earlier, she had adjusted to the rugged life in a way that belied her upbringing.

"Abigail." Her mother's voice edged with disapproval. "I'm waiting for my tea."

Abby hurried to her mother's side with a cup of tea. A china cup and saucer. How long before it got broken or chipped? Would

Mrs. Bingham blame Abby?

The other women exchanged sympathetic looks as if they felt sorry for Abby having to wait on her mother. Or — he saw with startling clarity — it was more than that. Waiting on a parent who needed it would be perfectly natural. But Mrs. Bingham seemed perfectly healthy and moreover, she was demanding and ungrateful.

Perhaps Abby would welcome an excuse to escape her mother in favor of accompanying him on a walk after supper. But what could he use as an enticement? He wasn't ready to risk her saying no by simply asking her to walk with him. He needed a reason.

He mulled over the possibilities as he ate supper. Beans, bacon and biscuits again. Sam had mentioned the possibility of encountering buffalo and Ben looked forward to the promise of fresh meat.

The meal ended and the women did dishes. Sally put Johnny down for the night. A sense of peace settled over the others.

But for Ben, his tension increased. He'd yet to find a way to invite Abby to join him. But the committeemen had agreed to keep a closer eye on the goings-on of the camp. Ben planned to walk around the circle with a particular interest in Clarence Pressman's activities.

He could no longer neglect his duties and pushed to his feet. "I thought I'd stroll about the wagons and see how everyone is faring. Anyone want to accompany me?" Before either of his sisters could offer, he looked directly at Abby. "Would you care to come?" He spoke casually as if he asked out of courtesy, and not because he wanted it so bad he could barely get the words out.

Perhaps she'd refuse. He half hoped she would.

Yet he held his breath waiting for her answer.

CHAPTER THIRTEEN

He asked her to walk with him? Abby couldn't think what it meant. Perhaps only a desire for company. Or maybe he thought she wanted to see how the others were doing though Emma had said the measles outbreak had subsided. Only two new cases in the past two days, and those who had it were well on their way to recovery, without any of the dreaded side effects.

Emma still accepted her help with the sick travelers. Except for Clarence Pressman. "He's embarrassed about his accident," Emma had explained. "I promised him I would treat him alone." It seemed a little strange, yet under the circumstances strange things became ordinary and ordinary things impossible.

Thinking that helped her make up her mind. Did it matter what reason Ben had for asking her to accompany him? She'd welcome some time away from Mother. She glanced toward the tent where her mother had already withdrawn.

No doubt she overheard this conversation. Unless she'd fallen asleep. If only Abby could hope that was the case. Otherwise Mother would clutch Abby's arm and remind her of her promise, and of the opportunities for advancement in Oregon. Abby had had to bite her tongue several times in the past few days to keep from asking advancement for whom? Besides, she knew the answer. Mother might think it was for Abby's sake but in reality, it was for Mother's. She wanted to be assured she could live in the style she preferred even if Father's business struggled or failed.

"I wouldn't mind stretching my legs. I was getting rather used to all the walking and today we've not walked a mile. My legs are restless." She realized she babbled nonsense and forced herself to clamp her mouth shut.

She followed Ben as he stepped over the wagon tongue and held his hand out to assist her across. She couldn't refuse without appearing rude and risking falling on her face should her skirts catch on the wood. But she'd had her hand in his just a day ago and knew the touch would set her nerves to dancing and threaten her resolve.

She wished to be free, to find independence so neither her parents nor a husband could decide her daily activities and the shape of her future.

Please, God, make it possible.

As she placed her hand in his work-roughened, big-palmed one her heart caught against her ribs. As soon as both her feet were on solid ground, she withdrew and pressed her hand to her waist.

The ground might be solid beneath her feet but not beneath her heart. She drew in a deep breath forcing herself to remember her goals.

They turned to the right.

"We'll finish crossing the river by noon tomorrow, God willing. Sam says we'll need to move after our noon break. He's worried about every delay. He often says, 'Travel, travel, travel. Nothing else will get you safely to the end of your journey. Nothing is wise that causes even a moment's delay.' "

She heard the tension in his voice. "You sound concerned."

"I want to make sure I get my sisters safely to Oregon. And all these others too, of course."

"But it isn't entirely your responsibility." She'd noticed he took his duties seriously. Always had, which was one of the things she'd admired about him.

"The other committeemen are very caring and knowledgeable and Sam is committed to getting us safely across the mountains."

She chuckled. "Shouldn't that comfort you?"

He slowed his steps and came round to face her. "I try not to worry, but sometimes there are reasons." He grew thoughtful . . . opened his mouth. Closed it again without speaking. "I simply can't afford to let down my guard."

Did he mean to warn her that he would be on guard around her? But that would presuppose he still had feelings for her and she'd made sure that would never be a possibility.

They reached the Morrison wagon, where Clarence leaned against a wheel. His bedroll was spread under the wagon. He glanced up at their approach then lowered his gaze, suddenly interested in one of his thumbnails.

Ben stopped. "How is your wound?"

"Fine." The man never spoke in much more than a hoarse rumble. Although Rachel defended Emma's friendship with Clarence, Abby wondered what she saw in the man. He was slightly built and so shy it hurt to talk to him.

"Good to hear." They moved on.

"What do you think of Clarence Press-man?" Ben asked.

She measured her words. "He's not the sort I would expect to join a wagon train. He seems better suited to entering numbers in a ledger. But Emma says his only living relative is a sister in Oregon and he plans to join her."

Grant and Amos Tucker jogged up to them. Their hair was wet.

"We had a nice swim," Grant said. "Very refreshing."

Amos gave his brother a playful punch on the shoulder. "Fess up. Tell them I had to dare you to jump in."

The pair laughed.

"Say, you gonna give us some more music tonight?" Amos asked.

Abby smiled. This pair was always up to something. Chasing each other or one of the children. Running to help some woman lift her kettle of water. A jolly couple of men. "I'll play my mandolin later if people want me to."

"Oh, they will." The men moved on. They jumped across a wagon tongue, greeted the owners cheerfully and continued on their way.

Ben and Abby resumed their walk. She noticed that he paused at each wagon and observed it a moment.

"Are you looking for something or some-one?"

"Just checking on things."

"Good to know." She couldn't keep the amusement from her voice.

He grabbed the wheel of the next wagon and shook it. "A loose wheel can be very dangerous." He faced her. "But I suppose you know that better than most."

She sprang to her father's defense. "Father had tightened the bolts on his wheel. He simply didn't know how tight they had to be. I daresay there were others in the same situation."

He drew back. "Your father? I wasn't referring to him. I meant Frank. Didn't you say he died in a buggy accident? I thought —"

"His wheel didn't come loose. He was drunk and going too fast." She wondered if her eyes were as wide and shocked as his. She had not meant to reveal the truth.

"Drunk?"

"Frank was drunk a lot."

"Frank? I thought he was a pillar of the community, a virtue of sobriety and the kind of man high society people value."

She heard his thinly-veiled sarcasm but continued all the same. "Frank was not what people thought. Especially behind closed doors."

Ben's expression went from shock to suspicion in a flash. He caught her upper arms, holding her fast without hurting her.

In fact, his touch made her feel safe.

"Abby, did he hurt you?" He pulled her to within a breath of his broad warm chest. She could feel the heat from his body. Or was she only remembering the way he'd held her and warmed her after pulling her from the river?

"Tell me the truth." His voice sounded rough as if he forced the words through a grater.

"I —"

"Hello. Mind if I join you?"

Ben dropped his hands and put a discreet twenty inches between them. "Of course not." He waited for the other man to reach them. "Abby, this is James Stillwell. James, this is Mrs. Black. James caught up to us this afternoon and has joined Miles Cavanaugh."

"Pleased to meet you, Mrs. Black. I've introduced myself to many of the men, but I haven't had the pleasure of meeting your husband."

"There is no Mr. Black." Was that thin voice hers? "I'm traveling with my parents, the Binghams."

"I believe I met your father. No Mr. Black? I'm sorry." He didn't sound as sorry as he might, but then, she wasn't sorry, either.

They moseyed onward and she found herself between the two men.

She'd been saved from making the confession that burdened her heart. How Frank had been so cruel to her. A pillar of the community! Nothing could be further from the truth.

No one had ever heard the real story of her marriage and she'd almost blurted it out to Ben.

Thankfully James had come along before she could.

She owed the man her thanks.

Except . . .

Except it wasn't gratitude she felt.

Why did her heart ache with regret?

Ben had no need to resent James's intrusion. They had the same thought in mind — keep an eye on the travelers and take note of anything out of the ordinary. Likely James wanted to familiarize himself with the many emigrants.

Yet he wished James hadn't come along when he did.

Abby had been about to tell him about Frank. He was sure of it. Had Frank hurt her? He curled his fists. His insides burned. He wasn't good enough for Abby. Both she and her mother had made that clear. But he would never have hurt her.

Seemed like an awful price to pay for the privilege of marrying someone of class.

He faltered. Frank was supposedly wealthy. Why hadn't Abby rescued her father's business? Or did her money provide the chance to start over in a more prosperous part of the country?

His insides burned. Was it still about money and who had the most?

James asked Abby about her plans for the future and Ben listened carefully.

"I hope I can start a new life," she said.

"What would that look like?" James asked the question that Ben didn't dare.

The lowering sun caught Abby's eyes, filling them with golden light. "I hope . . ." She spoke softly. "With God's blessing, I can become a free woman."

Her words set him back on his heels. That did not sound like a woman agreeing to marry a man of her mother's choosing. Or any other man, for that matter.

Abigail Bingham Black was turning out to be a very complicated woman.

They made their way back to the Hewitt wagon and bid James goodnight.

Ben was in no hurry to return to the campfire and share his time with others. But how could he persuade her to linger? How could he persuade her to explain the questions she'd raised in his mind?

"Perhaps we can do this again?" It was the plan, wasn't it? Though she didn't know his reason for asking.

Her raised eyebrows informed him she wasn't certain what he meant.

"Go for a walk."

She smiled. "I'd like that." Then she hurried to the back of the Bingham wagon and retrieved her mandolin and the book.

He sat by the wagon and watched and listened, his heart hoarding the many questions he yearned to ask her. Had Frank hurt her? Did her freedom mean she wasn't planning to follow her mother's wishes? Had she or would she change her mind about thinking Ben had nothing to offer her?

That was rather a large leap in the logic of his thinking. He wasn't exactly penniless, but neither was he rich. He didn't want her to see him that way.

Ben sank into relief when, as predicted, they were on their way after dinner the next day and made good time in the afternoon.

Sam's dour expression grew less fearsome. "Travel is good," he said several times.

James laughed at him. "You're going to wear those words out before we get where we're going."

Sam spared a smile. "So long as we get where we're going." He rode on ahead to scout out a stopping place for the night.

When they stopped for the day, the travelers were more energetic than usual having only spent half a day on the move. Amos and Grant seemed to be in especially high spirits as they drew their wagon into place. Their laughing and good-natured joking could be heard above the normal sounds of the camp settling in.

The pair took their time about unyoking their animals then wandered away to see to watering them before they turned them out to graze. If they followed their normal routine, they would wander around the camp greeting everyone they encountered, eagerly jumping to lend a hand should they see a need.

Ben suspected they looked for opportunities to help others in exchange for a meal. As bachelors they likely didn't have much in the way of cooking skills. By all reports the pair were big eaters and Grant, especially, favored sweets.

He helped Mr. Bingham who still struggled with his oxen and then took care of his own animals. James came alongside with Miles's animals.

"How do you think the day went?" James asked.

"Fine. We made a good distance for only half a day. I've not seen any unusual activity. But I've been thinking. Wouldn't the thief be the most invisible if he didn't do anything to draw attention to himself?"

"True. But I find most thieves are brazen. They like the challenge of the steal. They like outwitting their prey. Didn't you say there have been minor incidents reported?"

"Little things missing. I've put it down to dropping them or misplacing them. I've backtracked a few times to retrieve several items that were dropped or left behind." He didn't like to think someone in their midst was stealing, but the evidence was growing too strong to dismiss. Again his suspicions went to Clarence. Yet, to be honest, he'd never seen anything that would support his misgivings. Only his feeling that the man hid something. He meant to keep a sharp eye on Clarence and watch the actions of the campers.

"Mrs. Black and the Binghams seem ill-suited for the journey."

Ben bristled at the comments then smoothed his feelings. The man was only making observations. Wasn't he? Or was he interested in Abby? "They're adjusting." He didn't intend to say more than that.

"Let me know if they need help. I wouldn't mind lending a hand."

I don't suppose you would. "The Hewitts and Littletons provide the help they need."

"Good to know."

"How did you enjoy your first day traveling with the wagon train?"

"It's beastly slow. And dusty enough to choke both man and beast."

Ben laughed. "I saw you begging Miles to take over the wagon so you could ride your horse. You had the misfortune of having to ride toward the back today. Tomorrow you'll get a turn to ride closer to the front. It won't be so bad."

James grew serious. "Oh, but I wasn't trying to escape the dust. I needed to check on the various groups. Look for anything that would indicate the Plante wagon."

Ben raised his eyebrows. Seems James was a bit too serious. "Oh, of course you did."

The skin around James's eyes crinkled, then he tipped his head back and let out a roar of laughter. When he could speak, he said, "It was a very welcome excuse."

Ben chuckled along with him as they returned to their respective wagons. He was still chuckling when he joined the others for supper, the late day meal.

Rachel stuck her face close to his. "What's so funny, big brother?"

He opened his mouth then closed it. He couldn't reveal why James was riding with them. "I'm just enjoying the day," he murmured.

He felt the others studying him. "What? Can't a man enjoy a private joke?"

"Seems rather selfish not to share," Rachel murmured.

"Especially when the day has been so hot and dusty," Abby said with sorrow.

Emma sighed softly. "I bounced along on the wagon seat all afternoon with the only interesting thing the swing of the oxen tails before me."

Ben laughed. "My, my, aren't we a sorry bunch?"

The girls had the good grace to laugh.

Mrs. Bingham's scowl was enough to make the sun run and hide, but the sun continued to shine blissfully.

Ben shrugged. He'd give the woman the same amount of concern. No need for everyone to be miserable because she was determined to be so.

Over the meal they shared observations of their day. The crows that had scolded them as they passed. Three of the dogs fighting over a bone they found. Emma reported no new measles cases.

"Those who were exposed here won't show any signs for a week or two."

Ben continued to sit and visit as the girls washed the few dishes.

"Abigail." Mrs. Bingham made her name sound like an order and Abby jumped like an obedient soldier. "I need help preparing for bed."

"Coming, Mother." Abby hustled away.

Ben sighed to himself. Or so he thought until he felt his sisters watching him. He gave them a challenging look, silently informing them he didn't want to hear their opinions.

Rachel turned to Emma and whispered, "I don't know whether to admire Abby's patience with her mother or pity her for being under such strict control."

Emma hushed her.

Not that Abby would have been able to hear over her mother's complaints. A repeat of what she said every night. The trail was dusty and rough. The food unpalatable. The company beneath her dignity and the entire journey doomed.

Abby emerged a few minutes later, her expression tight.

Ben's heart went out to her. Caring for her mother had to be a trial. He pushed to his feet. "I'm going to check on things. Abby, would you care to go for a walk?"

Her eyes drawn at the corners, she nodded agreement.

He wanted nothing more than to pull her to his chest and assure her everything would work out. If freedom was what she craved, then he hoped she'd achieve it, even though the idea pinched his heart.

They crossed to the outside of the circle and set a leisurely pace. He had to remind himself he meant to watch for any clues as to the thief and any suspicious activity, but his attention kept wandering to Abby.

"You look upset," he said after they moved away from the hearing of the others.

She shrugged. "It's nothing."

He wanted to assure her if it upset her it was not unimportant. "You're concerned about your mother." She had every right to be. It was only natural. Except in Abby's case there was something not quite normal.

Again she shrugged. "She can't help being the way she is."

"You don't think she can change?"

She gave a sound of half amusement, half

251

exasperation. "She would laugh at any suggestion she should."

He tried to think how to respond. "You are very patient with her."

"She's my mother." A beat of silence. "I owe it to her."

Odd how she'd connected the two thoughts . . . as if they were two separate things. He understood fidelity to one's parents. "I promised my father I'd make sure our family was reunited by taking my sisters to Oregon."

"Then you understand."

"I suppose. But it wasn't a promise I made reluctantly. I was eager to move on. Start a new life." Except his old life had followed him on the journey. What was God trying to teach him? Hadn't he learned his lesson well enough? *Don't be giving your heart to a fickle woman.*

James unwound from the side of the Cavanaugh wagon and trotted out to join them. "Evening Ben, Mrs. Black." He touched the brim of his hat in a respectful way.

Ben darted a look at Abby to see how she responded to this man.

She murmured, "Good evening." Dare he hope she looked as disappointed by the man's appearance as he?

"Mind if I walk along with you?" James asked.

What could Ben say? It was a free country. "Sure, why not?"

They walked the distance of two wagons, slowing their steps at each as both James and Ben glanced over the wagons and the travelers.

"Wait up." Miles Cavanaugh trotted after them. "Can I speak to you men?"

"Excuse us." Both Ben and James murmured apologies to Abby and turned aside to join Miles.

Miles spoke softly. "I thought we had a plan. It looks perfectly innocent for Ben to be out walking with Abby. No one would suspect he is looking for a thief. James, I thought the plan was for you and I to walk together."

"You're suggesting I wait until later to take a walk?" He shrugged. "Seems reasonable I could walk with anyone and not raise suspicion." James's voice remained neutral. "But if you think otherwise . . ." He saluted a goodbye to Ben and spoke to Abby. "Miles needs my help. I'll see you later."

"Good night," she said.

Ben watched the pair walk away with decided relief. Now he'd get a chance to ask Abby how Frank had treated her.

They walked on past two more wagons. He gave each careful study, but again saw nothing to indicate a stolen wagon, stolen money or a guilty thief. The vast majority of these people were simply hardworking folk looking for a fresh start.

He slowed his pace. "You were telling me about Frank before we were interrupted last night."

"Was I?"

He stopped to face her. "Abby, my mind has been in turmoil since you said he was different at home. Please tell me the truth. Did he hurt you?"

CHAPTER FOURTEEN

Abby forced herself to inhale and exhale calmly. Something she'd learned in her marriage to Frank that helped control her emotions. Part of her cried out to tell Ben all the details. But pride held her words back. Her marriage had been a failure beyond anything she could ever have imagined possible.

Ben again caught her arms.

His touch ignited painful, fearful memories of Frank hurting her. Surely he must feel her trembling.

He lifted one hand and caught her chin, tipping her face up.

She waited for the pain she'd come to expect. Instead, his hands were gentle and warm on her arm filling her with a fearsome ache for more of the same.

She knew she should close her eyes and shut him out, clamp down on her weak, needy feelings, but she lacked the strength and looked into his eyes. In the lengthening rays of the sun, they appeared almost black. And brimmed with concern.

That look loosened her tongue.

"He was a cruel, vindictive man." Each word was bitter gall on her tongue.

His palms pressed against her shoulders in a way that felt like a hug, that rooted her in an invisible embrace. She felt safe. A foolishness she would deal with later.

He didn't say a word. But his mouth pulled into a hard line. It further opened her heart to release more details.

"He delighted in tormenting me. He'd mock my desires. If I wanted something, he would deliberately withhold it. He'd take away anything he thought I valued." Her lungs felt like Frank held them in his fists. "I had a little dog, Perky, who gave me so much comfort." She shuddered as the memory flooded her mind . . . pictures she'd tried unsuccessfully to erase from her thoughts. "Frank killed her."

Ben rubbed his hands along her arms.

She leaned her head against his chest. Her hands clenched together between them.

"Did he — ?" Ben coughed. "Did he hurt you?"

"Not at first."

She felt him stiffen. "But when he realized

he could no longer hurt me by taking things away, he found other ways of hurting me."

His hands pressed to her back but she flinched at his touch, remembering instead Frank's cruel hands.

"I'm sorry," he murmured, and pulled his hand back to her shoulders.

She continued to rest her forehead on his chest.

"Why didn't you leave him?"

She shuddered. "Where would I go? Mother saw him as the man who would save the Bingham family. Father's business had already begun to falter because of the depression."

"I would have thought your father would take you away, never mind the money."

"They never knew. Still don't."

He wrapped his arms around her and held her tight.

She stiffened for a second then allowed him to hold her, finding sweet comfort in telling him, certain he would not hurt. Not now. Not here. Perhaps never? "The irony of it is, Frank had no money. He'd lost it in foolish investments. His life was nothing but show. Three days after he was buried, officers showed up on my doorstep and told me I must leave. I took only what I could carry. The rest belonged to the creditors."

She exhaled until her lungs protested. She felt a sense of release from that part of her past by telling Ben.

He had always been a kind, generous man who offered sympathy out of the goodness of his heart. But she knew better than to trust a man's embrace to remain gentle.

She eased back.

At first he resisted her effort to escape his hold and then he dropped his arms and allowed her to step away. She put six inches between them but couldn't force herself to do more. "I've never told anyone about Frank. I wouldn't want my parents to know." She studied her entwined fingers, not wanting to look at him and see pity and worse, condemnation. He could ask if marrying for money and status had been worth it.

And if he did, she would have crumpled to the ground in a weeping mess. No, it wasn't worth it.

Would marrying for love be any different? The only way to find out would be to enter into a binding relationship she could not escape. She shuddered. It wasn't a risk she would take.

She didn't need marriage again. All she needed was to find a way to take back her promise so she could live a life of independence. *Oh, Lord, change Mother so she'll be more concerned with my happiness than status.*

Ben curled his finger and caught her chin to bring her attention to him.

Rather than accusation or pity, his eyes revealed only concern. "I wish I'd known," he said.

"What would you have done?" She knew she sounded surprised and annoyed at the same time. No one could help. Marriage gave Frank the right to do as he pleased with his wife.

His expression grew fierce. "I would have taught Frank not to hurt you."

That brought a smile to her face as she imagined Ben riding up on a big white horse and frightening Frank so bad he ran away. Her smile departed. Frank would not have left. He would not have learned a lesson. "I'm ashamed to say I was relieved when he died. I didn't even care I was left penniless. I'd sooner have my freedom any day."

"And you believe you have that?"

"What do you mean?" She could guess but she had to make sure.

"Do you have your freedom? I'm not criticizing but it appears that your Mother controls you."

"I wish that weren't true." She stepped

aside and continued their journey around the wagons. *How I wish it weren't true.*

Ben walked at her side. "As I recall, she's always had this control over you."

Of course he would remember it that way. He'd met her after Andy's death. After she'd promised she'd do anything Mother said in order to make up for it. If Mother knew all the details, she would be even more demanding, though perhaps that wasn't possible.

It was her guilt as well as her promise that made Mother's control possible. She hoped to gain her freedom from the latter but would never escape the former.

"She didn't always." Only perhaps she had and it had only intensified after Andy's death.

"Then why now?"

"Things happen. Things change." She could say no more though she felt his demanding look upon her.

It wasn't as though she owed him anything just because he'd heard her confession about Frank and comforted her.

Nor did she owe him anything because of their past. She'd ended that with complete finality.

Frank had been cruel to her. Ben ground

his teeth together. He realized his fists were squeezed so tight his knuckles protested, and forced himself to relax.

Abby had paid an awful price for what she'd deemed to be social status and financial gain. Instead, she'd ended up with nothing and was back home with a mother who had an unnatural control over her.

It hadn't always been. Things happen. Things change. What could she possibly mean? It didn't make sense.

"Abby, what happened?"

"To Frank? He was thrown from his buggy when it overturned."

"I'm sorry that a man died, but not that Frank is gone. But that isn't what I mean. What happened between you and your mother to make her so overbearing?"

Abby stared straight ahead and walked on at a furious pace.

He didn't intend to be ignored and stayed in step with her. "You said things happen. Things change. What did you mean?"

"It's just a manner of speaking." Her voice was cool, dismissive.

He knew it wasn't the truth. "Abby, can you look me in the face and say that?" He stepped in front of her forcing her to stop.

She lifted her head, but her gaze went past him as if he wasn't there. He caught her shoulders. Wanted to shake the truth from her but at the way she trembled beneath his palms, he stopped himself. Whatever had happened held her in the grip of some dark emotion. He had no desire to make it worse.

"Never mind." Why did it matter to him? Yes, he felt terrible that Frank had been so cruel. No one deserved that. Yet she planned to marry again for advancement if what her mother said day after day meant anything. No wonder she talked about freedom and independence. Would her mother ever allow it?

He wanted to comfort her, remove that fear from her eyes when he touched her. He wanted to understand why she allowed her mother to control her.

But he did not mean to go beyond that. She would never see him as anything but a convenience and he didn't intend to be hurt again.

He thought of something that might turn her mind from the darkness of her past and again fell in at her side. "Do you recall the time we decided to visit old Mrs. Gunther?"

"Of course. Pastor Macleod had been challenging us to put the verses we learned into practice. 'Be ye doers of the word and not hearers only.' " He could hear the smile in her voice and congratulated himself on achieving that victory.

She continued. "We decided to follow the verse just below that. 'Visit the fatherless and widows in their tribulation.' Mrs. Gunther was the poorest widow we could think of."

"And the crankiest."

She chuckled. "Nothing like a good challenge."

Her laugh was better than a drink of cold water on a hot, dusty day. "As I recall she didn't exactly welcome our visit."

"No, she said, 'Ain't you got nothing better to do than go around bothering an old lady?' I was about ready to turn around and run but you were behind me, so I couldn't."

At the time he had been prepared to always be behind her to protect her. When she'd chosen Frank over him, he had expected Frank to take care of her. He knew it didn't make sense, but he felt he had somehow failed in fulfilling his duty to Abby.

He shook his head to chase away the thought.

She continued to recall the event. "I remember what you said. 'We don't mean to bother you, but we brought you these flowers.' " They'd picked a large bouquet from Abby's mother's garden. Abby had thrust them toward Mrs. Gunther.

The woman had stared at the flowers and then at Abby and Ben. "What good are flowers?"

"They're nice to look at." Ben had stepped forward with a box of cookies. "And these are nice to eat. God bless."

They'd turned and hurried away, but once outside the gate had paused to glance back.

"When Mrs. Gunther thought we were gone, she buried her face in the flowers and smiled."

Ben and Abby looked at each other and smiled too, the shared memory sweet and happy.

"Mother was not pleased when she discovered I'd picked half her flowers and taken them to Mrs. Gunther."

Back to her mother. The woman didn't appear to have a generous bone in her body.

The look in Abby's face revealed her regret. "I told Mother that good things should be shared."

"What did she say?"

Abby's expression closed off but he waited, hoping she'd answer. "Mother thought I should be more concerned with my own mother than a cranky widow."

Ben sighed. Would he ever learn why Mrs. Bingham had such a strong hold over her daughter? Would Abby ever be free of whatever it was?

They returned to the campfire and Abby played her mandolin and sang then read. Miles and James wandered past and waved.

They fell into a routine in the following days. Rise at four, start the day's travel at seven. Noon at a place Sam chose. In the evening, circle the wagons and take care of the animals.

After supper, he asked Abby to walk with him. Every time he expected her to refuse. He considered whether or not he tell her the real reason for their walks if he needed to persuade her . . . that she was his excuse for moseying around the wagons watching for suspicious behavior.

So far he'd never had to convince her to join him.

It had saved him from facing the truth — he looked forward to this time they spent together for reasons that had nothing to do with watching for a thief.

They talked as they walked. Mostly they talked about young Johnny who did his part to keep them entertained. Or they talked about the cow that had balked at having to spend another day walking. Or Abby would tell about the Jensen twins who spent a great deal of time with her during the day. It didn't matter what they discussed. Ben enjoyed spending time with her, sharing a chuckle over events, learning to know her again.

In the back of his mind lay the warning that he must guard his heart. Surely he could do that yet enjoy some pleasant diversion.

At the moment, they traveled onward. He drove the oxen that led his wagon to the West. Abby walked far enough away to avoid the ever-present dust. The twins had been with her a few minutes ago, but had run ahead to join their mother.

Ben signaled to Emma to take over the wagon and when she did, he jumped down to join Abby.

"Hot today." The sun showed them no mercy.

She nodded. "The dust is fearsome, too."

He could think of nothing more to say although his mind was crowded with questions. None of which he felt free to ask at the moment.

Bushes filled a little hollow not far to their right. He pointed. "Let's see if there are any berries."

"Wouldn't that be a nice treat?" She grabbed a basket from the back of the wagon and then they hurried toward the hollow and found scratchy raspberry bushes tangled in the silver willow bushes and set upon them eagerly. Others had found the same enjoyment along the draw, but Abby and Ben were alone in this particular patch.

He stayed at her side. "Look at this big one." He showed her. "Open your mouth." She did so and he popped it in, his fingers brushing her lips, sending sweet nectar straight to his heart.

She closed her eyes. "Umm. Good."

He swallowed hard, his lungs clenching with expectation and a dozen unfulfilled wishes. With supreme effort he pulled his hand to his side and turned about lest she read the strength of his emotion in his eyes. He pushed aside the forbidden rush of pleasure, purposely replaced it with the reminder of how she'd dismissed him to marry Frank. His thoughts under control, he moved on.

They foraged deeper into the bush. The bushes caught at their clothes, the prickly raspberry canes scratched.

"Ben!"

He was several feet ahead of her and jerked about at the tension in her voice, every nerve on alert. A sweeping glance revealed no imminent danger.

"I'm caught and I don't want to tear my dress." She tugged at her skirt but it wouldn't come loose and she couldn't turn to free herself without getting scratched on the bushes.

"Hang on." He pushed his way past her, giving the thorns little concern though they tore at his hands. He knelt behind her. "I'll have you free in a minute." He eased the fabric from the tangled branches. "There you go."

She stepped to the nearby grass and turned. "Thank you."

He pushed through the bushes and joined her. "Are you okay?"

"I'm fine." Her gaze went to his hands and she gasped. "You're bleeding."

"It's only a few scratches."

"A few? You look like you barely survived a fight with a wildcat." She grabbed his hand, dug a hankie from the depths of her pocket and pressed it to his flesh.

He stared at her small, long, beautifully-shaped fingers on his hand. His mother had once remarked on a friend's fingers. Called them musician's hands. The description fit Abby perfectly.

She lifted the now soiled fabric and peered underneath. "It's a nasty mess. I'm afraid Emma will have plenty to say when she sees this." She blew on his scratches. "Does that feel better?"

Better? Yes if she meant did his heart race, did his lungs forget to work, did his brain simmer like a kettle about to boil?

When he didn't answer, she lifted concerned eyes to him. Hazel, someone had said of their color. But hazel didn't begin to describe the flecks of gold and brown that gave them a distinctive color.

"Does it still hurt?" She blew again.

He closed his eyes against the sweet torture.

She lifted the hankie and fanned it over his hand. "I expect Emma will have some ointment that will help. Do you want to go back now and see?"

"No." The word scraped past his teeth. No. He didn't want to end this afternoon.

She raised her eyebrows. "You seem rather certain."

He'd never been more certain of anything in his entire life. Not his name. Not his age. Not where he was going. Nothing. "I want to find more berries."

She grinned. "Me, too. They're delicious." Spying some plump red berries to her right, she moved away.

He was rooted to the spot. Berries? Who cared about berries? He wanted to catch her by the hands and swing her around in a do-si-do. Catch her around the waist and lift her clean off her feet.

She glanced over her shoulder and saw him lingering. She straightened and studied him long and hard. Her gaze probed his. Did she see all he felt? For he had no barriers in place at the moment.

"I thought you wanted to pick berries?"

No wonder she sounded confused. He hadn't moved a muscle since she'd walked away.

"Yes, berries. I'm coming." He forced his feet to move and plucked a ripe berry. Its sweetness jolted his brain into motion. Well, almost. He got as far as thinking this was a very pleasant way to spend an afternoon.

Abby straightened. "Listen. Did you hear that?"

His brain instantly forgot its fanciful dreams and focused. Wasn't he supposed to be paying attention to their surroundings? What if a wild animal or a hostile band of wanderers stalked them?

Gobble, gobble, gobble.

Turkeys. He pressed his finger to his mouth to signal silence and eased his way through the bushes doing his best to be silent. He peered through the leaves. A big tom turkey. Wouldn't that make a tasty meal? Moving slowly and quietly he edged closer. The bushes ended. The turkey was ten feet away gobbling and strutting.

Two leaps and he'd have the best dinner they'd had in many days. Ben tensed his muscles and sprang forward.

The turkey flapped away amid much gobbling protest.

Ben chased him, determined to have this meal.

He sprang forward, caught the turkey by one foot and hung on despite the battering of wings and the scratching of the free foot complete with a very sharp dewclaw.

"Ouch. Ouch." He tried to subdue the bird, but for an animal a fraction of Ben's size the bird put up a valiant fight.

Over the ruckus of the angry turkey came Abby's ringing laughter.

He cranked his head around.

She stood in the dappled shadows, a ray of sunshine pooling on the top of her head turned her hair into mirrored gold.

He stared and almost lost his hold on the turkey.

"Don't let him get away," Abby called.

"Never." He renewed his efforts to get control of the bird and finally was able to succeed. He held the heavy creature up proudly. "Dinner."

She grinned. "Fresh meat. I can hardly wait."

He carried the bird as they made their way back to the wagons. They'd be a distance behind the Hewitt and Bingham wagons by now, but it wouldn't take long to catch up at the slow pace of the oxen.

He led them at an angled direction that gave the shortest route to the wagons. The bush grew thicker.

"Do you know where we are?" Abby asked, trying unsuccessfully to disguise her worry.

I'm in the sweetest place I could imagine. Sharing a warm afternoon with a pretty girl. And I'm in no hurry to return to the wagons and harsh reality. He'd surely encounter pointed looks from Mrs. Bingham but he didn't care. This moment was meant for enjoying.

"Are we lost?" Abby's trembling voice scalded his selfish thoughts.

"No, we aren't lost. Look at the sun." He pointed. The sun was midway down the western sky. "We just have to follow the lowering sun."

"Good to know. Except there are bushes in the way."

"Come on. I'll show you the way." He led her through the thick growth carrying the heavy bird in one hand.

They broke into the open. The wagon

train trundled along to their right and they hurried after it, though Ben felt nothing but reluctance at returning. If not for the responsibility of his sisters and his role as a committeeman he might consider asking Abby to stay right here with him. They could build a little cabin and live in bliss.

He knew such a dream was impossible, but he'd enjoyed ignoring reality for a few hours.

CHAPTER FIFTEEN

A few days later, Abby walked close enough to their wagon that Mother's words rang in her ears. Every time she tried to move away, Mother ordered her back to listen to her complaints. They'd intensified with every mile of the journey though Abby wouldn't have thought it possible.

"I wish we'd died in the river." Mother had perched in the wagon as they crossed the Big Blue a few days ago. She'd squealed in fright as the wagon swayed in the water but the crossing had been relatively easy compared to crossing the Kansas River.

Abby shuddered at the memory of those cold, dark waters but she quickly dismissed the thought in favor of the warmer, sweeter memories of Ben holding her to warm her. To that she added a litany of memories — walking with him each evening, talking of things near and dear to her though she guarded her most precious secrets, and picking berries. She chuckled softly as she thought of him struggling with that big turkey. It had tasted so good.

"Are you laughing at me?" Mother asked.

"Of course not."

Father half drowsed in the afternoon sun until the wagon jerked across another buffalo trail. They were in the Platte valley now. A wide desert of grass, patch-worked with wildflowers of yellow, blue and red. The Platte River ran wide and straight, through sandy soil. Buffalo country. The big animals walked single-file to the river for water, creating paths as deep as ten inches. Every wagon wheel had to cross those paths. It was rough, about snapped a person's neck out of joint.

"Mother, why don't you walk? It's much easier than riding on that hard bench." Mother tried to keep a pillow beneath her. Father often chose to walk beside the oxen to avoid the constant jolting.

"Look at you." Mother's voice rang with disapproval. "Your skirts are dusty. Your boots are worn thin. I wish you would ride in the wagon."

Abby had no intention of being shut up in the hot wagon. Her feet had hardened to the walking and she found she quite enjoyed it. She could talk to Emma or Rachel or

Sally or Delores without Mother hearing every word. It was freeing. She ran ahead to join the other ladies, ignoring Mother's call.

From where they walked, she saw Ben riding forward. My but he looked good sitting in his saddle. He turned checking on something slightly behind him.

Her heart leaped half way up her throat at how the light silhouetted his features. How strong and muscular he looked.

His attention slid down the line of wagons and he shifted to look at the group of ladies. His gaze burned into her mind, silently promising another evening of sweet, sweet communion.

She mistepped and had to catch herself. How could she enjoy his company so much when she knew how it would end? She'd never marry, not even to please her mother. Not even though her heart raced at the thought of another evening walk with Ben.

When she looked up again, he was riding away and she took several slow, steadying breaths.

She did her best to ignore Mother's complaints as they drew into a circle and as she helped prepare the evening meal. The turkey meat was long gone. Sam Weston had sent some men out to hunt for buffalo. She hoped they would come back soon.

Father returned from caring for the oxen. "We're in Pawnee country now. I hope they don't bother us."

Mother sat in her hard chair. Abby couldn't help but think her bottom must be getting calloused from so much sitting.

Mother kept her hands in her lap. Tried to appear she didn't care about the details of the camp but her white knuckles belied her concern. "I hope the sentries are armed to kill any savages that come near."

Father gave her a considering look. "Sam says we will pass through peaceably. After all, this is their land."

Mother pressed her lips together so tight a white line formed around them.

"I haven't forgotten it was an Indian who pulled Donny from the Kansas River." Abby spoke softly, musingly, but surely everyone — Mother included — should give credit where credit was due.

Mother didn't reply but gave her an accusing glare.

Rachel returned with a basket full of buffalo chips.

Mother rose and marched to the wagon and sat on the hard bench, pointedly ignoring the fuel they'd been forced to use since they'd entered the Platte valley, but she'd stopped saying what she thought after

Father had spoken to her.

Emma joined them. She crumpled to a heap in the grass and buried her head in her hands. Silent sobs shook her.

Rachel and Abby rushed to her side.

"What's wrong?" Rachel asked.

"The Turnbow baby died. I didn't realize he was so sick. I should have seen it." Her voice cracked with her agony.

The Turnbow baby had come down with measles two days ago. "Oh, how awful." Recognizing the weight of guilt in Emma's voice, Abby's guilt flared with fresh strength.

"I'm sorry about the baby," Rachel said.

"I should have checked on him earlier."

"Emma, you can't blame yourself for disease and accidents. They happen. A person can only do so much. After that, it's in God's hands." Rachel's words rang through Abby's heart but sometimes a person could blame themselves for an accident if they instigated a foolish action.

Emma dashed away her tears. "You're right. It just seems so unfair. Why do some people live long after their bodies have worn out and yet healthy babies with the future before them die? I don't understand."

Rachel hugged her sister. "Sometimes we simply have to trust."

"Trust what?" Ben's sudden appearance

278

sent a wave of awareness through Abby that made her face burn.

He squatted beside his sister and looked into Emma's tear-streaked eyes. "Emma, are you hurt?"

She explained about the baby. "I said I find it hard to understand."

He squeezed her shoulder. " 'I trust in your unfailing love.' Psalm thirteen, verse five." He met Abby's eyes over Emma's head and his gaze seemed to say, *remember when we learned this verse?*

How well she remembered. Pastor Macleod had suggested they break into pairs or teams to drill each other. She and Ben had slipped away to the corner of the churchyard. Right next to the cemetery. She remembered that detail so clearly because she could see Andy's headstone from where they sat. Ben said he could see his mother's. They'd reached for each other's hands at that moment, finding comfort in acknowledging their sorrow. All he knew of Andy's death was what everyone else knew — an unfortunate accident. Only she was aware of her responsibility.

If only she had told him about Andy then. But what good would it do except make it even harder to deal with her mother's demands.

He turned his attention back to Emma. "It's when we don't understand, or when we feel helpless or even when we could blame ourselves that we choose to trust."

"I know." Emma pushed to her feet. "And I do. I will." She brushed her skirts and smoothed her hair. "I promised to help prepare the baby for burial." She marched away.

Rachel stared after her but Abby watched Ben. Slowly he brought his gaze to her. They shared sorrow and something more — something deeper than her conscious thoughts. A connection with strands of steel.

Wasn't she getting fanciful?

The word of the death quickly spread and the travelers made their way to the Turnbow wagon.

"I'll get my mandolin." Abby retrieved it. "Are you coming, Mother?"

For a second, she thought her mother would refuse then she nodded. "I know what it's like to lose a son." Her eyes pierced Abby's soul, reminding her of who was to blame for that loss.

As if Abby could ever forget.

When we could blame ourselves, we choose to trust. She wished she understood what Ben meant. Or rather, how he thought it was possible.

280

Father helped Mother alight and Abby fell in at their side, following Ben and Rachel. The Littletons joined them, Martin's expression grim as he held Johnny. He knew what it was like to lose three children. Yet he remained kind, Sally remained cheerful. How had they found it possible to be so after so much sorrow?

They reached the spot. Most of the emigrants had gathered together, perhaps as much to rejoice that the hole hadn't been dug for their loved one as any other reason.

Rev. Pettygrove stood beside the open grave, the grieving parents at his side. He nodded to Abby who played and sang "Amazing Grace." Remembering Andy's death made it difficult to keep her voice from cracking but she wanted to do her best to bring a little comfort to the bereaved.

Rev. Pettygrove spoke a few words. " 'The Lord is my strength and my shield; my heart trusts in him, and I am helped.' May this Psalm comfort and strengthen those grieving and indeed all of us." He prayed. Once the amen was said, Father and Mother left, but Abby stayed with the others, standing at the Turnbows' side as the men filled in the grave. Rev. Pettygrove's wife hugged both the Turnbows and patted their backs even though the pair were still stiff with shock.

Abby and the others waited until the grave was covered over, then they slipped quietly away.

She joined the others at their camp. They ate their meal in relative silence except for Mother's complaints, but Abby barely heard them. Her mind was occupied with thoughts of Andy's death. Perhaps the others thought of their own losses.

Some deaths were accidental, disease or so-called natural causes. But Andy's death had been avoidable. If only she'd tried to dissuade him. If only she hadn't been more interested in showing her silly friend how wrong she was. She didn't blame God, only herself.

After supper that evening, Ben looked down at Abby, walking by his side as they circled the wagons. He regularly fought an inner battle, alternately thanking Miles for suggesting Ben ask Abby to walk with him each evening so he could keep an eye on the activities then wishing he could go back to that day and refuse the suggestion.

It was too late to go back and undo things. There was so much he knew he would regret later although he enjoyed it in the present. Like these evening walks. "You're awfully quiet tonight."

"I'm thinking about that baby and his poor parents."

He reached for her hand, knew a sense of rightness when she didn't resist. Seems she was learning a man could touch her without hurting her. "It's sad."

"Emma took it hard."

"She's so tenderhearted."

"Yes." She spoke somewhat distractedly he thought, and sensed she mulled over the recent events.

"What's really on your mind?"

She stopped, staring straight ahead.

He stood before her so she had to see him. "Abby?"

She focused her eyes on his. "I . . ." She shook her head. "Nothing."

He knew something weighed heavily on her mind. Something to do with the death of the Turnbow baby? Or had her mother been complaining again? Still. How that woman went on and on was enough to try anyone's patience. Over supper she had plenty to say about the hardships of this trip. Everything from burning buffalo chips to the mosquitoes to the talk of Indians all meant as a warning.

If God had meant us to go to Oregon, He would have made a proper road.

No one commented on the flaws in her

assertions.

Until Emma — quiet, sweet Emma — spoke up. *Instead, he sent us guides like Sam Weston, and brave men like my brother and your husband and Martin to lead the way.* Mrs. Bingham had been as surprised as any of them to hear Emma and for a few minutes kept her thoughts to herself.

Perhaps Abby worried her mother might be right.

"Do you think our trip is doomed to failure?" Ben asked.

She blinked and shook her head. "Absolutely not. I see it as the opportunity to start again. A new creature. Old things passed away, all things become new." She used the words of a Bible verse to explain her feelings. "We'll make it across the continent." She heaved out a deep sigh. "Or die trying."

He grabbed her by the elbows and drew her close. "You're talking like your mother."

"No, I'm not expecting to die. I'm simply saying that nothing short of death will stop me."

He looked into her green-gold eyes. Saw the depth of her determination and chuckled. "Let's make sure it doesn't come to that."

She continued to search his gaze.

He shoved aside the barriers, giving her access to his very soul. He thought of Queen Esther's brave words, *if I perish, I perish.* It would be the same for Ben. He'd allowed himself to grow close to her and he would pay the price when this trip ended.

Abby puffed out her cheeks and shifted her gaze to the middle of his chest. "If you must know, I was thinking of Andy, my twin brother."

"I'm sorry I never got a chance to meet him. Tell me what he was like."

They continued on their way. Ben took note of those coming and going, looked for anything out of the ordinary. Amos and Grant had been out checking the animals and gave a friendly wave as they returned to the circle. And there was Clarence Pressman glued to the wheel of the Morrison wagon. According to Emma, the wound on Clarence's back had healed well but still she spent time with him. Always apart from others. It bothered Ben no end but he'd stopped mentioning it. Every time he did, Rachel laid into him with protests and Emma ducked her head and ignored his concerns.

"Andy was brave and courageous. I suppose a bit of a daredevil." She shrugged. "Maybe even a show-off. But he could do everything he set his mind to do. Well, almost."

He turned at the tone in her voice. "Almost?"

She quirked a mirthless smile. "No one can do everything."

"Guess not."

"Mother and Father doted on him. He was everything to them. And he knew it."

"Everything? What about you?"

"I was his faithful shadow, but I didn't mind. I adored him. We were close. Like the Jensen twins. We could finish each other's sentences, know what the other was thinking. Maybe that was part of the problem."

She seemed to have slipped away into her memories.

"Part of what problem?"

A shudder crossed her shoulders. "Huh? Oh, just an expression."

He knew better. Something to do with Andy weighed heavily on her thoughts. "Did you ever tell me how he died?"

"Bucked off a high-strung horse." Every word came out clipped.

"Remind me. How old was he?"

"We were fourteen."

"Did you witness it?"

Even though they weren't touching, he felt her shudder clear through him and stopped walking. He took her hand but she pulled away.

"It was my fault." The words lacked emotion. Her face was blank.

As if she'd closed her heart and mind to the memory. How awful it must have been to hold her in such a vicious grip ten years later.

He reached for her again, wanting to hold and comfort her but she hurried past him and ran toward their campfire.

He followed more slowly. She'd shut him out even as she seemed to have shut out the pain of losing her twin. It bothered him and he couldn't say exactly why until he recalled something his ma had said. She knew she was dying, though the children had been spared the knowledge at the time Ben had in mind. But her words had comforted him and strengthened him after her death, after Grayson's wife and baby died and after Pa died. Ma said, "You can only overcome the power of grief if you lean into it and learn how to walk with it as your companion. It won't go away, but you get used to it at your side. But if you fight it, deny it, try to run from it, grief becomes like an angry dog, nipping at your every step."

So he'd leaned into his grief. Learned to walk with it.

That's what Abby needed to do. Tomorrow, Lord willing, he'd tell her this.

The next morning was Sunday. Rev. Pettygrove held his usual reading as he had since that first, long-ago Sunday when he'd been with the travelers still on the far side of the Kansas River. Only a handful of people gathered about. Most of them had decided to get on with the business of the day.

The Hewitts, Littletons and Binghams chose to have a Bible reading at their camp. It was Ben's turn to read again. Each man selected whatever passage he wanted. This morning, Ben selected Ecclesiastes chapter three and in part read, " 'There is a time to weep, and a time to laugh; a time to mourn, and a time to dance.' " He finished the chapter and took the Bible back to the wagon.

Somehow he managed to avoid looking directly at Abby though he meant the words specifically for her.

A sound of alarm raced across the camp and he jerked toward it. Men, women and children crowded toward the east side. Ben hurried that direction. He broke through the crowd into the open and ground to a halt.

A band of Indians on horseback stared at them.

"Pawnees," Sam said at his elbow. "From the look of hides they're carrying, I'd say they were returning from a successful hunt." Not only were the Pawnees strange to look at but the hides brought a pungent odor.

The camp dogs bristled and barked, and had to be restrained by their owners.

The lead Indian and a handful of others dismounted and strode toward them.

"What do we do?" Ben asked, wondering if he should have brought his rifle.

"Be calm." Sam turned to the crowd. "Stay calm. Be courteous."

The Indians poked their heads into the nearest wagon and pulled out a red shirt.

Sam approached him and by way of hand signals and words they communicated. Then Sam nodded.

"The chief will trade goods for meat. Bring things you think he'd like. Hurry now."

The crowd dispersed to their wagons and soon they began to return. The chief examined each item. He liked a mirror, a felt hat, a cooking pot and a set of forks which made him laugh.

He waved to the other Indians to come forward and soon mingled with the travelers freely examining items and offering trades.

A bit later, satisfied, they rode away, leaving the wagon train a goodly amount of buffalo meat. The women set meat to cook for the noon meal.

"We'll have to jerk the rest," Sam said, explaining how the Indians preserved the meat by cutting it into narrow strips and drying it over a low fire. So while dinner cooked, filling the air with a delicious aroma and making Ben's mouth water with anticipation, everyone helped slice the meat into strips. Sam showed them how to hang the strips of meat on ropes along the side of the wagons.

"We don't have time to dry it over a slow fire like the Indians would, but the sun will do the job for us."

It was past their usual nooning time when they finished and sat down to eat.

"It's gamey." Mrs. Bingham took a bit of the roast buffalo meat, but managed to eat her share.

As soon as they'd eaten their fill, Ben rose and began yoking the oxen in place. "Hurry and pack up. Sam is anxious to be on the way. Travel travel travel."

The bugle sounded and they moved out.

Ben rode beside the Hewitt wagon for a

bit as Emma drove the oxen then moved up to the Bingham wagon. Abby normally walked but this afternoon sat beside her father while her mother rode in the back. "Everything okay?"

She gave a smile that did not reach her eyes. "It is."

He waited a moment and when she offered no more, he rode on.

Everything was not okay. He knew it as clearly as he saw the line of wagons. Even more clearly because dust rose from every wheel clouding the sight of the wagons.

CHAPTER SIXTEEN

Abby watched Ben ride away. Everything was not okay but then she didn't expect it would ever be. A hole the size of the Platte valley sucked at her insides. Andy was gone. The hole would never heal.

She should never have started talking about him. It brought a fresh flood of memories and regrets.

Despite the uncomfortable bounce and jerk of riding in the wagon, she spent the rest of the afternoon beside her father.

The wind blew incessantly, but as they made camp, it increased in velocity. The only way they could build a fire was to dig a little trench in which to place the buffalo chips. The wind battered them as they assembled pots and food.

She tried to measure out flour for biscuits but the wind sucked it from the bowl.

Rachel laughed. "I don't think we'll be baking until the wind goes down. Even if you could get the flour to stay where you wanted, the oven would be blown clear back to Missouri."

They gathered up the meat they had hung to dry and stowed it safely in a cast iron pot.

The leftover buffalo meat from dinner would serve as supper.

Ben returned from helping people get settled. "Sam says we have to chain the wagons together so the wind won't blow them over." He showed Martin and Father what to do then turned to confront the women. "Finish up with the fire and put it out. It could easily get out of control." His gaze met Abby's for one intense moment. "Tie down everything that's loose." He strode away to spread the word as did each of the committeemen.

The wind tore at the canvas wagon covers. Father jumped inside and tied it tight. Emma and Rachel did the same in their wagon. Sally huddled inside their wagon holding Johnny while Martin tightened their canvas.

Abby turned her back to the wind and drew up her shoulders. Sparks from the fire flew past the wagons. She grabbed the shovel and quickly buried the smoldering buffalo chips before the fire could get away and cause further damage.

A shudder caught her whole body as she tried and failed to imagine how one would fight a fire in this wind.

"Abigail," her mother wailed. "Abigail."

Abby spun around in time to watch her mother's tent billow and bow then lift like a kite and sail over the wagon tongue. Mother lay wrapped in her blanket, her eyes wide, face pinched.

"My tent. Abigail, get my tent." Her mother sounded so fearful that Abby jumped over the same wagon tongue and raced after the sailing tent.

The wind pushed her along so her feet barely touched the ground. Bits of grass and dust swirled about her face, stinging her eyes so they watered. The tent sailed onward, with nothing to stop its flight. Laughter caught at the back of her throat at the sight she must make, her skirts billowing in front of her, the tent bouncing before her. Like some make-believe children's story about flying.

She caught her foot in one of those buffalo trails and landed facedown with enough force to knock the breath from her. She couldn't move. Black edged at her mind. She blinked in an attempt to clear her vision but it danced and shimmered.

"Abby, Abby. Are you okay? Say something." Ben's voice came from nearby. What was he doing out here? Surely she imagined it. Just as she had when he so often came to her thoughts over the years despite her intention to never think of him again.

Her lungs suddenly remembered to work and sucked in air hungrily. She lifted her head, turned. "Ben?"

He laughed and helped her sit up. "Were you expecting someone else?"

"I wasn't expecting anyone. I was — Mother's tent." She tried to rush to her feet but a wave of dizziness made her sit back down even before Ben's firm grasp pulled her back in place.

"Is this what you're after?" He held a bundled-up piece of canvas in one arm.

"Oh, thank goodness."

He sat beside her. "Abby, do you have any idea how scared I was when I saw you running across the prairie? I wondered if you'd sail clean out of sight. Don't you realize how easy it is to get lost out here? And then you fell so hard and lay so still —" He didn't finish but wrapped his free arm about her and pulled her to his chest.

He pressed his cheek to her head. She surely imagined he kissed her hair. But it was a nice thought and rather comforting.

He sat with his back to the wind, sheltering her from its batter.

A shudder shook him.

She tipped her head back. "Are you okay?" Perhaps he'd been hurt in pursuing her. Oh, how would she live with that added guilt on her conscience?

"I am now." He shoved the bundled up tent under his knees and held it in place. Then cupped his hand to her cheek. "Abby, don't ever scare me like that again."

Umm. It might be worth it to get him to touch her like that. "Why not?" some little imp prompted her to ask. She looked at him with wide eyes that likely revealed how much she wanted from him. A wayward thought that she would deal with later.

"Because, my sweet Abby, my heart would surely burst if you frightened me like that again." He lowered his head, and paused as if to give her a chance to duck away.

She had no such desire. She lifted her face to offer her lips.

He claimed them. Lingered. Not long enough to make her uneasy. Nor long enough to satisfy her desire to belong to him.

She pressed her hand to the back of his head. Claiming him. She realized he didn't wear a hat. Had the wind taken it? Not that it mattered at the moment. All that mattered was the two of them. Together. Belonging. Hearts melding.

He broke the kiss but only by an inch. His breath caressed her mouth. His scent filled her pores. Warm prairie grasses, leather, sage and the maleness of him.

"We need to get back before it rains."

Lightning flashed. Thunder shook the ground. How long had this been going on and she hadn't noticed?

He rose, grabbed Mother's tent and pulled her to his side. Together they fought the wind as they returned to the wagons only a couple hundred yards away. She thought she'd surely gone much farther.

Mother stood in the shelter of the wagon, watching their every step, her face pinched with disapproval.

It was too much to think she hadn't seen them kiss.

Ben lowered his arm from around her shoulders but caught her hand to help her face the wind.

They stopped before Mother, sheltered marginally by the wagon.

"I rescued your tent." Ben held it toward her mother.

"Abigail, take it and put it in the wagon. Benjamin, I'd like to talk to you." She gave

Abby a dismissive look and waited for her to climb over the tongue and step out of sight.

Abby's heart lay like a cold rock in the pit of her stomach. What did Mother intend to say to him?

She ducked through the narrow opening in the canvas and shoved the tent against the seat, straining to hear Mother. But she couldn't make out any words above the roar of wind, the continual claps of thunder and the creaking of the wagon.

Not that she needed to hear the words to know. *Abigail deserves better. She'll marry an important man in Oregon.*

Abby closed her eyes. Maybe this time Ben would stand up for her.

The wagon shifted, the canvas opened enough to allow Mother to crawl inside.

"What did you say to him?" Abby demanded.

"The whole camp could see you kissing him. What kind of conduct is that for a young woman who plans to marry another? If word of this follows us to Oregon, why, I don't know what a proper young man would think."

"Maybe I don't care." Only one man had ever mattered to her. "What did Ben say?"

"He said he'd honor your plans." Mother

caught Abby's arm and jerked her to within three inches of her. "Andrew would have made sure we were well taken care. It's your fault he's dead. I heard all about it from Isabelle's mother. How you forced him to ride that horse to prove he could."

Abby gasped. She hadn't forced him. But she hadn't tried to dissuade him, either. Her words of that day would live forever in her head. *Andy's the best rider around. He can ride any horse you have.*

She'd smiled confidently at her twin brother.

Andy had laughed. "You got that right, sister. I've never seen a horse that could get the better of me. Bring your animal. I'll show you."

It had taken two grooms to bring the horse out. When Abby saw the wild roll of the animal's eyes and felt the hatred from the horse, she'd gasped and reached out to stop Andy.

Mocking laughter at her side had made her drop her hand and keep her concerns to herself. Besides, Andy wasn't stupid. If he thought the horse was too much, he would say so.

Too late, she realized he was as driven by the jeers of the others as she.

"Mother, can you ever forgive me?"

"Oh, I forgive you." The words came far too easy. Abby knew they meant nothing.

"But I still expect you to make it up to me. Andrew would have never expected me to travel across this barren land."

Abby stared at her mother, struggling against the accusation and demand in her gaze. Now. Now was her chance to tell Mother she didn't want to marry a rich man. She didn't want to continue to carry this load of guilt.

"Mother, wouldn't you like me to marry for love?" Somehow the idea of marriage no longer frightened her. She'd seen enough in the weeks they'd traveled to know some men treated their wives well. Martin and Alvin, for example. And Ben? Would she be willing to risk her future happiness on it? Not that he'd asked. Even more importantly, not that Mother had released her from her foolish promise. Perhaps she would now. *Please, God, change her mind.*

Mother snorted. "It's just as easy to love a rich man as a poor one."

Abby rolled her head back and forth. Frank had proven that to be a lie.

Mother caught Abby's chin to still the movement. "Abigail, you listen to me and you listen good. You owe me for taking him from me and you will pay by marrying a man who can help this family."

"Mother." The word whispered from Abby's stiff lips. "Don't you care about my happiness?" *Don't you love me?*

"You lost the chance to pursue your own selfish desires when you let Andrew die. Now I'll hear no more about this." She shifted her back toward Abby and leaned against the pile of bedding.

At that moment, the skies opened and dumped rain on the miserable occupants of the wagon. The rain pounded at them. It blew through every crack, it dripped from the not-so-waterproof canvas.

Mother grabbed an oilcloth and huddled under it determined to keep as dry as possible while hating every minute of the journey.

And hating her own daughter?

Abby made no attempt to keep dry. She couldn't be more miserable if she tried. Her mother intended to continue to control her. Was there no escape?

She held on to one faint hope. If Ben were to say something to indicate his kiss had meant for him what it did for her, Abby would find the courage to break free of her mother's control. She'd fulfill her promise and responsibility some way other than marrying a man of her mother's choosing.

■ ■ ■ ■

Ben stared after Mrs. Bingham. Had she really said all those things?

You'll never be good enough for my daughter. Don't get the idea that she's spending time with you on this journey because she cares. You're just a convenience. When we get to Oregon, her plans are much bigger than a man without enough money to buy a decent hat.

His hand had gone to his head at those words. Where was his hat? It must have blown away at some point and he hadn't noticed. Never mind. A hat did not indicate a man's worth.

What concerned him was the thought that Abby was only using him. Rachel worried that might be the case.

How dare you kiss her? And in full view of the entire wagon train. Just goes to show what kind of man you are. No concern for propriety.

I'm sorry. I was simply grateful she was okay. Not that he regretted the kiss. Not for one second. He knew he wasn't mistaken in believing she welcomed it. Practically begged for more. His heart had danced against his ribs at the memory, but soon plopped back in dejection as Mrs. Bingham continued.

Leave Abigail alone. I don't want to see you with her again.

He'd stiffened at those words. *Isn't that for Abby to decide?*

Make no mistake. She'll do what's best for her.

She'd done what Mrs. Bingham thought best for her when she married Frank and the man had hurt her over and over. He couldn't believe that Abby's parents hadn't been at least a little aware of the situation. Was Mrs. Bingham really so uncaring it didn't matter if the situation was repeated?

Don't you want her to be happy? His words had been low but surely she'd heard the challenge in them.

Mrs. Bingham snorted. *You could never make her happy. You have nothing for her.* She'd climbed into the Bingham wagon, effectively dismissing Ben.

He drew in a shuddering breath. She was wrong. He did have something to offer — his heart, his care, his protection. But perhaps that would never be enough. He certainly couldn't provide her with a mansion in which to live, nor servants to do her biding.

Rain slanted against him and he trotted over to the wagon. Rachel and Emma huddled inside. He would not crowd them further and grabbed his slicker and shrugged into it. He hunkered down beside the wagon, which offered no shelter. There'd be no sleeping until the rain ended.

But he wouldn't have slept much anyway as he mulled over Mrs. Bingham's words.

Did Abby agree with her mother?

He wouldn't believe it unless he heard it from her own lips.

The rain battered all night. At some point, Ben pulled a waterproof sheet over him and dozed against the wheel.

Toward morning, the clouds blew away. The wind settled down to the constant breeze to which they'd grown accustomed. Ben rose, stiff in every joint.

He glanced toward the Bingham wagon. Mrs. Bingham peeked through the opening and her glare stung. He would not turn away though and finally she withdrew.

He waited a couple of minutes, but Abby did not come out and he must check on how the others had fared.

Sam, Miles, James and the other committeemen joined him and they made their way to a wrecked wagon.

"Looks like it was struck by lightning." James observed.

The smell of sulfur and burnt wood grew

stronger as they neared.

Ben poked his head into the wagon and met the wide eyes of a woman. "Are you okay?"

She didn't answer.

"Are you hurt?"

She blinked and shook her head. Her gaze darted past him and she shuddered.

"Ben," James called. "Come here."

He knew by the sound in James's voice that he wouldn't like what he saw and hurried around the wreckage of the wagon.

A man lay stretched out, partially hidden by the torn canvas. Sam bent over him and shook his head.

"Struck by lightning." Sam rose. "Best we check and see who else has been affected."

"What about this woman?"

People crowded about. "She can travel with us," someone said.

"We'll salvage what we can of the wagon," Clarence offered. For the first time Ben felt a thread of respect for the young man.

Rev. Pettygrove and his wife hurried over. "We'll take care of the details." He lowered his voice. "The burial and all. I'll ask Mrs. Black to play her mandolin and sing. It will provide a touch of comfort."

Sam moved on with the committeemen

accompanying him. They found two dead oxen.

"We got off better than I feared," Sam announced. "Let's get organized and move." He strode away. The men dug a hurried grave, waited for Rev. Pettygrove to say a few words then dispersed to their various directions for breakfast.

At seven, the bugle sounded and the wagons fought the mud to start rolling. The Bingham wagon struggled to pull out of the mire.

Ben jumped down to lend his assistance. But Mrs. Bingham saw him. "Leave us alone," she murmured.

Mr. Bingham, yelling at the oxen to move, didn't hear and Abby walking a few yards away never even bothered to look his direction.

He backed off and let Martin and a couple other men help. He stood rooted to the spot, watching Abby march on, her head down. Was she purposely ignoring him or avoiding puddles in the grass?

Slowly her head came up and she turned toward him. Her gaze hit him like a bolt of lightning. Full of power. And regret? Regret over her mother's words.

His heart slowed. Or regret over her choice to stop spending time with him?

Someone bumped into her. She turned her attention back to the trail.

He jumped to his horse and rode down the line of wagons. It wasn't as if he hadn't warned himself of the possibility since the first. But not until she said something would he accept it.

They pulled through mud for most of the morning giving Ben plenty to occupy him away from the Hewitt wagon which trundled after the Bingham wagon. Nevertheless, as he helped get wagons out of mud holes he had only to glance at the column of walkers to see Abby.

At the nooning, he hurriedly grabbed a bite of dinner then trotted away to check on those who had lost oxen and the woman who had lost her husband. Yes, he had responsibilities. But there was more to his hurry than that.

Mrs. Bingham had always before remained on her hard chair, never joining the others. Until today. She sat on a quilt close to the fire. Within reach of Abby. And she gave Ben a beady-eyed glare every time his gaze went that direction.

Ben couldn't abide her presence any longer than he must.

He had reached the end of the train when the bugle sounded to travel again and he remained there for some time. Bit by bit he rode forward. He tied his horse to the back of the wagon and climbed aboard.

Emma drove the oxen.

He took the reins from her. "Do you want to get down and walk?"

"Thanks." She joined the other women.

He sat alone with his thoughts, his gaze often slicing toward Abby. His insides were tight, awaiting a chance for her to speak her opinion of her mother's decision on her behalf.

Abby followed Sally and the Hewitt sisters without paying any attention to their surroundings. What had Mother said to Ben? Whatever it was, it couldn't have been more quelling than the words she'd spoken to Abby.

How was she to be free of her promise, her obligation, when Mother made it clear what her expectations were? Marry someone with prospects. The prospects being society and the appearance of riches. Did she have the courage to defy her mother? How could she when she'd given a promise and when God had commanded her to honor her parents?

Please, God. Give me a way out.

As they trudged along, she had lots of

time to consider how she could extricate herself from her promise. But none offered a solution.

She saw little of Ben throughout the day as he was kept busy with his duties.

The muddy trail caused an axle to break on one of the wagons and he stayed back to help the man repair it. Then there was a ruckus because someone was missing a valuable skinning knife and had accused his neighbor of stealing it, so Ben had to hurry through the noon meal and join the other committeemen in rendering a verdict of the case. She wondered if the man who robbed the safe on the day of their departure was on the train with them. But if he had $15,000 why would he want a knife?

That night Ben was one of the sentinels guarding the animals so he wouldn't be asking her to walk with him.

Mother watched her like a hawk and sat close, constantly demanding Abby's attention. Still, if circumstances were different and he'd asked her to walk with him, would she have said yes? She wished she knew the answer but she felt caught between duty and longing, between guilt and freedom. For a time freedom had meant the ability to choose to live a life on her own. Now she wanted the right to choose anything she wanted.

The next day proved hot and dusty. Not a hint of the mud of the previous day. The wind blew incessantly. Mother complained continually. The mosquitoes bit every inch of exposed skin. But all those vexations paled in comparison to the turmoil in Abby's heart.

They nooned on a level spot along the South Platte. To their left the banks rose to the high grounds.

Abby was heating the beans when she noticed Sally's milk can rattling on the side of the wagon. She stared. It wasn't possible. The wagon stood still.

"That's odd," Rachel said. "And I feel it in my feet. Is it an earthquake?"

"Buffalo stampede." Mr. Weston rode up in a lather.

The committeemen rushed over to Miles Cavanaugh's wagon, but Sam's words reached most of the travelers. "We have to act fast."

Grant Tucker trotted up to the group of men. Sam grabbed him. "Get your brother and head for the hill. Shoot the biggest bull and don't stop shooting until they turn. Do you understand? Don't stop until they turn."

Sam's voice filled Abby with fear and she clutched Rachel's hand.

"Mother, get in the wagon and stay there."

Mother looked ready to protest such a sharp order then looked at her vibrating feet and scurried inside. The wagon might not be enough protection in face of a stampede of animals up to two thousand pounds each, but there was nothing else to offer.

Emma hurried to join them and grabbed Rachel's other hand.

"You, you and you." Sam pointed to three men. "Go start a fire on the other side of the ridge." Another group ran for spades to tear up the grass behind the fire line to keep the flames from spreading down to the wagons.

Ben mounted his horse and, along with a couple other men, rode up the ridge.

"Where is he going?" Rachel's grip tightened. Or was it Abby who squeezed so hard?

"God, keep our brother safe," Emma whispered.

Abby silently echoed the prayer.

Then he rode out of sight straight into the face of the stampede.

She crumpled to the ground, pulled her knees close. She buried her head in her hands.

Was that the last time she'd see him?

CHAPTER SEVENTEEN

Ben crested the ridge. A black sea surged toward him as far as he could see, shooting up a huge cloud of dust. He had a handful of cotton rags. He couldn't even say where they came from. Only that someone had pressed them into his hand. He knew what he must do, though.

Turn those beasts before they crested the ridge. Otherwise they'd crush the wagons into kindling. And the people — ?

He couldn't think of what would happen. "Please, God, make 'em turn. Make 'em turn." He shouted the words but no one would hear him above the thundering stampede.

He rubbed a rag in powder and shot it out the musket. The flaming rag lit up the grass in front of the ridge where others created a fire line. Time and again he shot out a flaming flag.

"Please, God. Please, God." The word

came on each exhalation.

The animals surged forward, seemingly unaffected by the puny efforts of man. He glimpsed the pale, strained faces of those nearest him. Knew every one of them shared the same fear.

If the stampede reached the wagon train, there would be none of them getting to Oregon.

Then the black sea parted and the animals flowed past them on the right and left. He rode to the ridge to watch the animals thunder past the wagons. The two columns rejoined, plunged through the river and flowed across the plain.

Ben slouched forward in his saddle. Would his heartbeat ever return to normal?

Sam rode along the line of men. "It's over. Go eat your dinner so we can move on. Travel is what we need to do."

Ben laughed. Travel had never sounded so inviting. He rode toward his sisters and Abby and the others with a heart so light he laughed for the sheer pleasure of being alive, of seeing all those he cared for alive.

Abby and his sisters hurried toward him, expressions full of gratitude.

Martin rushed past and enfolded Sally and Johnny in a grateful hug.

Mr. Bingham went to the wagon. "Mother,

we are safe. Thanks be to God. I have never prayed so hard in my life."

Ben didn't hear Mrs. Bingham's reply. His entire attention was on those waiting to greet him.

He swung to the ground as his sisters rushed to him. Emma broke into tears and he pulled her to his side to comfort her.

"I'm glad to see you're safe." Rachel gave him a playful punch. "Don't ever scare us like that again."

He laughed and pulled her to his other side. "I'd like to make such a promise, but I can't."

He met Abby's gaze as she stood two feet away. Her eyes were wide and dark. Of course she'd been frightened. They all had been.

But was she frightened for him?

"Abby." Her name was but a whisper on his lips.

She shuddered.

His sisters reached for her and drew her close.

Ben was almost nose to nose with her. Close enough to see the strain about her mouth, the tension in her eyes. He could smell the campfire smoke, and the fear clinging to her. "We're all okay," he murmured, wanting nothing more than to pull her into his embrace.

He dropped his arms from his sisters' shoulders. They edged back a few inches. "Abby." He lifted his hands, pressed them to her shoulders. Felt her lean into him. "Oh, Abby." Her name came from deep inside, from a place of needing, wanting, a secret sacred place reserved for her and her alone.

"Abigail Bingham Black, what are you doing? I need your help." At her mother's voice, Abby sprang back. The color drained from her face. She lifted her eyes to Ben.

"I can't. I can't." And ran to the wagon.

Ben stared after her, as wave after wave of shock, disappointment and confusion shuddered through him. He could fight an unseen prospect in Oregon, even a suitor on the wagon train.

But how did he fight the hold her mother had over Abby?

He hugged his sisters again. The Binghams and Littletons joined them for a hurried meal.

Ben couldn't help but notice the little furrow in Abby's forehead as she bent over her plate. Why did she let her mother control her so firmly? There had to be more to it than fidelity but what?

He wished he could get her alone to talk

315

to her but life suddenly became very busy. They had reached the point in the trail where they had to cross the South Platte River. Sam suggested a way to do it. Remove as much stuff as possible from the wagons, cover them with skins and float them over. The job took a long time.

Ben grew tired of listening to the men and women bicker about what they would take and what they would leave behind. Thankfully Emma and Rachel had already chosen wisely so only had to leave behind a chest of drawers.

They moved from the river crossing to Windlass Hill. The path down looked perpendicular. How would they get the wagons safely down without them ending up splintered at the bottom?

"Cast off anything that will make your wagons heavier," Sam called. "Unless you've got a wish to see everything you own broken and scattered at the bottom."

It surprised Ben to see that people still carried extra stuff. Soon belongings were scattered across the landscape. Some enterprising fella could make a nice living collecting all the things and selling them.

The oxen were taken down, then the wagon wheels chained to stop them from rolling. Small trees were tied to each wagon to hold it back then men attached ropes and by means of pulleys lowered the wagons to the bottom.

Ben's palms bled from the ropes. But he couldn't stop.

One wagon hit a stump on the way down and snapped one of the ropes holding it. The wagon flipped over and over and shattered on the ground. Thankfully no one was hurt and the occupants who had watched helplessly from the top of the hill were taken in by another family.

With no time to nurse sorrow, the men prepared another wagon to lower it. To one side, Clarence Pressman fell back and let his rope slacken.

"Hold tight," Ben called. "Or we'll have another wreck."

Clarence sat on the ground, spent.

Ben shook his head. What was a weakling doing on this trip? His own muscles strained to the breaking point under the added weight of trying to hold the wagon back.

Suddenly, a mountain of a man grabbed Pressman's slack ropes. He nodded at Ben as if to say everything was under control.

"Thanks," Ben called, and turned his attention back to his task.

As soon as the wagon was down, he strode over to thank the man again.

"Nathan Reed, at your service."

Ben immediately liked the man despite his unkempt look. Black hair to his shoulders. Ebony eyes. And a way of looking directly into one's gaze as if he saw the whole world there.

"Where are you headed? We could use a man like you on the train."

Nathan shrugged. "Going to Fort Laramie to stock up."

Ben took that for agreement to join the wagon. After a few questions, he ascertained the man was a hunter and trapper who spent much of his time exploring the great plains. "I'll introduce you to Mr. Bingham. He needs someone to help him."

"Don't mind being that someone."

Nathan grabbed a rope as they prepared to lower the next wagon.

They finished up by dark and Ben introduced Nathan to the others at the camp. "Nathan is going to accompany us. Mr. Bingham, he's willing to partner with you."

Mrs. Bingham's mouth pursed like she'd bitten down on a lemon but Mr. Bingham held out his hand to Nathan. "Glad to have some help. I fear I struggle with the oxen, among other things."

Ben sat back, weary clear through. Emma dressed his palms and wrapped strips of cotton around his hands.

"You'll have to keep them clean until they heal."

He leaned his head back against the wagon wheel and half closed his eyes. But he couldn't resist letting his gaze slip to Abby.

Her mother clung to her side, hands clawing at Abby's sleeve as if afraid Abby would run off.

Abby looked directly at Ben, her expression guarded perhaps so her mother wouldn't take note of it. But he saw the longing that filled her eyes.

At least he told himself he did. He was too tired at the moment to contemplate any other reason for the way she looked at him.

After supper, James moseyed by and signaled to Ben.

Ben joined him outside the wagons.

"Look what I found." James showed him a piece of scrap wood with *H.P.* burned into it. "I believe it means Henry Plante. This is from his wagon. Remember, the robbers back in Independence stole his wagon. I'm even more certain that the man who robbed the safe is among us."

"Where did you find it?"

"Up the hill. It was part of a broken chest. I'm guessing whoever threw it out had no idea the initials were on it. We need to keep a sharp lookout for this man."

They walked the perimeter of the circle as they talked but could detect nothing amiss.

"I have to say this for the man," James said a couple of hours later. "He's cunning."

A little later, Ben bid him good-night and returned to his family. Everyone had already retired except Nathan who wrapped himself in a fur and lay under the wagon.

"Trouble?" he asked.

"I hope not." He wouldn't be sharing any secrets with Nathan, for despite his help this afternoon, Ben had no reason to trust him. Just as he had no reason to trust Abby.

He wished he could convince his heart it didn't matter.

Abby listened for Ben to return. Heard him wishing James a good night. So he preferred James's company over hers.

Or had Mother's words quenched his interest in her? She brushed her lips. How could he kiss her with such warmth if he didn't care? But he'd managed to avoid her since that night. Oh, she understood he was busy but was it more than that?

Then he'd assigned Nathan to help Father. That meant Ben wouldn't need to in the future.

Was it just another means of staying away from her? She shuddered.

Was this to be the punishment for her guilt over Andy's death?

Her insides coiled and tightened so that she had to lie on her side and draw her legs up.

She pulled the covers over her mouth lest anyone hear her sigh.

Oh, God, how I long for Your peace.

Did she deserve it?

The next morning when she arose, Ben was already gone. He returned a little later to eat breakfast. But he and Nathan talked together.

"It's July Fourth," Emma said.

Ben chuckled. "And we are free to travel."

"You mean we aren't going to celebrate?" Rachel sounded disappointed.

Ben and Nathan were on their feet ready to leave. Ben paused to answer his sister. "Maybe Sam will let us stop early this evening." His gaze slid to Abby. Stopped there long enough to make her heart rattle against the roof of her mouth. Then Mother jerked on her sleeve and Ben turned away.

They moved on. Travel travel travel. Was that all there was to life?

But by late morning, a ripple of excitement hurried down the line of wagons. "Ash

Hollow. Sam says we'll camp here."

Abby and Rachel rushed ahead to see what was so special about Ash Hollow.

They stopped and stared. "It's the most beautiful campsite I've seen," Abby said. Thick, shady ash trees and a spring of water.

Rachel laughed and caught Abby's hands, swinging them round and round in a crazy, happy dance.

"This is where we're celebrating the Fourth." Ben's voice sounded amused.

Abby stumbled. She hadn't seen him stride up and he was gone again before she could gather her thoughts together.

"A celebration!" Rachel cheered. They hurried back to camp, and under Rachel's watchful eye, Abby made a spice cake while Rachel and Emma made currant pies. Everywhere, the women worked hard preparing a special meal.

The children played in the water. The men filled the water barrels.

Rather than each group eat separately, the women spread the food down the center of the camp on barrels and upturned tubs. Everyone was in high spirits at having made it this far.

"We must be halfway," young Jed Henshaw said.

"We've come five hundred miles," Sam said.

"Only a quarter of the way." Jed sounded dejected.

"And the worst is yet to come."

Sam's words robbed the celebration of its joy. Then they dismissed his warning. How could it be worse?

Emma looked about. "Have you seen Delores Jensen?"

Abby searched the crowd. "I don't see any of them." She'd been so caught up in her own concerns, she'd forgotten everyone else. Except for Ben and he was enjoying himself down the row with Miles and James.

She hurried back to the wagons, Emma at her side. They ran past several until she located the Jensens.

The two older girls sat holding the babies.

"Ma's inside," Annie said.

"The twins are poorly," Betty added.

"Delores?" Emma climbed up to peer in. "What's wrong?"

"They're fevered."

She scrambled inside. "How long have they been this way?"

"Since morning, I guess. I confess I didn't notice at first."

Abby watched from the back as Emma examined the twins.

"Could it be the measles?" Delores asked.

Emma stared at her. "I thought all your children had them."

"The girls did." Delores looked troubled. "When the twins didn't get them when the babies did, I assumed they were going to be spared."

Emma nodded. "It could be measles, but there's no way of knowing until the rash comes out."

Delores glanced about, her expression tight. "I don't know how I'll manage what with the babies . . ." She shook her head.

"I'll stay and help," Abby offered. It's not like anyone would miss her at the celebration. Mr. Henshaw had a fiddle. He could play for them.

"I'm grateful. The baby needs nursing, but the twins won't let me leave."

Abby swung into the back. "Will you let me take care of you?" she asked the twins.

Cathy nodded, but Donny barely looked at her.

"Do what you can to lower the fever," Emma said. "I'll check back in a little while." She sighed. "I'd really hoped this was done."

Abby sponged the twins. She sang to them. And she remembered when she and Andy were sick. Always at the same time.

Always competing for attention from the nurse. Mother would visit once or twice a day. She'd hover over Andy, brushing his hair off his forehead. She'd pause at Abby's beside and nod.

"You're doing fine."

Abby had longed for a warm touch from Mother. She still did. But those, for the most part, had been reserved for Andy.

Cathy's fever lowered with sponging, but Donny grew warmer, tossing and turning and muttering nonsense.

Delores returned from nursing the youngest baby. She shook her head after touching Donny's forehead. "I don't like this."

Nor did Abby. But she wouldn't let the boy die. *No, God. Not again.* She dashed from the wagon and scooped icy water from the spring. She hurried back, unmindful of the water sloshing from the bucket and wetting her skirts. Back at the wagon, she found the oilcloth Alvin used and spread it on the ground. She briefly wondered where the man was. Perhaps it was his turn to be on guard duty.

"Give me the boy. It will be easier to fight his fever out here."

Delores did so and saw what Abby meant to do. She quickly stripped Donny's clothes off until he lay in his underwear.

Then she and Abby sponged him with the cold water. After what seemed like an hour, they sat back, relieved that he was no longer dangerously hot.

Emma returned. "So far these two are the only ones with these symptoms. How are they doing?"

Delores explained what they'd done.

Emma squeezed Abby's shoulder. "Good job, but I expect his fever will return." She turned to Delores. "Watch him carefully. Sponge him again when necessary."

Twice more Donny's fever grew and twice more he responded to the cold water sponge.

At the moment, he rested comfortably. Cathy had insisted she be with him, so they slept within reach of each other.

She and Delores sat a little way from the children so they could talk freely. Delores nursed the baby again. Annie and Betty had taken the other little one and gone to bed.

"I had a twin brother."

"Had? What happened?"

"He died." Realizing this was not the time to talk of a twin dying, she added. "But that's in the past."

Delores squeezed Abby's hand. "Not so far back it doesn't still hurt. Why don't you tell me about it?"

Abby hesitated. "I don't want to burden you with my concerns."

"Nonsense. I promise I won't let it upset me."

"Very well. Andy was thrown from a horse. I confess I encouraged him to ride the animal even though everyone knew it was a man-killer." She'd found that out afterward.

Delores squeezed Abby's hand again. "My dear, you have to forgive yourself."

Somehow, Abby wasn't surprised that Delores saw right to the heart of the matter. "I will never forget."

"I didn't say forget. I said forgive."

Abby didn't respond. How did one forgive when it was their fault?

"I lost a baby, between Betty and the twins. I blamed myself. I heard the baby fussing in the night, but I was so tired I didn't get up. In the morning, she was blue and cold. She'd vomited. If I'd checked on her she would be alive today."

Abby found Delores's hand and squeezed it. "I'm sorry."

"For a long time, I didn't want to live. Poor Alvin didn't know what to do with me. He got my mother to come and care for the girls while I lay on my bed and stared at the wall."

Abby had no words of comfort to offer the woman. She knew the feeling of such despair.

"But I recovered. I found the strength to continue and to forgive myself. You can, too."

Abby didn't say anything. She could never forgive herself.

"It was the Easter season and my mother made me get up and dress to attend church. My, but I resented her at that point but she knew what I needed. I saw the picture at the front of the church of three crosses. The preacher read the story. The only words I heard were those spoken by the one thief, 'We receive the due reward of our deeds.' I knew the due reward I deserved for neglecting my baby. I thought if I never enjoyed life again, I might pay a big enough price. But Jesus forgave that man. He wanted to forgive me, too, but I had to let Him. I found peace from my guilt at that service and God blessed me doubly with my twins and two more little ones." She turned to Abby. "You see, my friend, if a righteous God can forgive us, we need to forgive ourselves."

Abby nodded. The words made sense, but could they apply to her? Could she forgive herself?

CHAPTER EIGHTEEN

Ben looked about for Abby. Where was she? Didn't she want to join in the celebration? He made his way through the crowd. The women were busy cleaning up from the meal. Perhaps Abby had gone back to the campsite but only Rachel was there putting away dishes.

She glanced up as he neared. "How are your hands?"

"Oh, fine." He'd almost forgotten his sore palms. "Where's Emma?"

"The Jensen twins are sick. She's checking to see if any others are ill. I think she fears sickness more than a buffalo stampede. Abby is helping with the twins."

He hadn't asked after Abby and wondered that Rachel would offer the information.

Mrs. Bingham sat on her wooden chair. "She shouldn't be nursing the sick. That's what servants are for. I will hold your entire family responsible if Abby gets sick."

Rachel rolled her eyes, but wisely kept her opinion to herself.

On the far side of the circle, Mr. Henshaw picked at the strings of his fiddle as he tuned them. Music soon filled the air. Many grabbed a partner and danced.

Ben didn't care to be among the merrymakers. There was only one person he wanted to share the celebration with and she was busy elsewhere. He stepped over the nearest wagon tongue and began his evening walk around the circle.

His footsteps slowed as he neared the Jensen wagon. There she was, sitting near the fire with Delores. He took his time passing, long enough to watch Abby hurry to the twins and start sponging young Donny.

He moved on, satisfied she was safe.

He finished his tour and returned to the camp, intending to wait by the fire until Abby returned. Mr. and Mrs. Bingham had retired to their tent. The others were enjoying the evening festivities.

A little later Alvin Jensen hurried toward him.

His heart hammering, Ben jumped to his feet. "Is something wrong?"

"The twins are sick, but Delores assures me they'll be okay. I don't know if she's saying it for my sake or hers. Abby wants me to inform her parents that she plans to stay and help my wife as long as she's needed."

"Mr. Bingham," Ben called.

"Thank you. I heard."

Muttering came from the tent. Mrs. Bingham protesting, no doubt.

Ben resumed his position. He'd sleep on the ground beneath the wagon with Nathan, but for now, he waited for his sisters. They didn't return until the music ended. As soon as they were safely in their tent, he rolled up in his bedding, as did Nathan. Soon the other man snored softly.

Ben slept lightly wondering if Abby would return.

When he wakened the next morning, she had not. They set out on the day's journey and still she did not go to her parents' wagon. She spent the next day with the Jensens, as well, and returned in time for supper looking weary but triumphant.

"Both of them have measles, but apart from the rash are feeling more like themselves."

"You've worn yourself out," Mrs. Bingham said sharply. "And for what?"

"To help others." Abby's reply, although soft, sounded abrupt.

Ben smiled. Abby had exerted more independence in the past two days than he'd ever seen before.

They departed for the day. Ben rode down the line of wagons then returned to the Hewitt one. He tied his horse to the back and swung to the bench.

Rachel drove the oxen. He would have preferred his quieter sister sat beside him. She would have respected his wish to sit and contemplate.

"Do you want to get down and walk?" he asked, hoping she'd take his hint.

"Maybe later." She turned to give him her full attention.

"You're staring at me," he said after they'd traveled a few yards.

"Guess I am. I'm trying to figure you out."

"What's to figure?" He would not be drawn into one of her I see a problem and you're it mind games.

"Well, let's see. You and Abby have gone from 'can't keep your eyes off each other' to 'can't look at each other.' You act like you got a burr under your saddle and Abby . . ." She sighed sorrowfully.

He jerked about to watch Rachel. "What's wrong with Abby?"

"I'd like to know. What did you do to her? What did you say to make her so unhappy?"

"Me? Why would you blame me?"

"Because it's obvious, dear brother, that

something is amiss between you."

"Maybe it's like you said. She's only taking advantage of my assistance until we get to Oregon."

"Ben, forget what I said earlier. What did you do or say to offend her?" Rachel tapped his knee for emphasis.

"Rachel Hewitt, what kind of man do you think I am that you can blame me for Abby's problems?" He snapped the reins even though the oxen were trudging along at their normal pace. One of them swung his head in protest. *Sorry, old chap. It's not your fault.*

"I may be but nineteen, but I know a lover's quarrel when I see it."

His mouth fell open and he stared at her.

"Shut your mouth before your brains fall out."

He shut it. Opened it again. Then gave up and shook his head. "Lover's quarrel? That's rich." He meant to sound amused but feared he sounded bitter instead.

"That's how I see it."

"Well, you are wrong. Abby's mother doesn't want me to spend time with her. Abby does what her mother says."

Rachel didn't reply. They rode in silence for the space of two minutes.

He was the one to break the quiet. "You

didn't expect that, did you?" Any more than he did. Oh, he should have seen it. The signs had been all there. But he chose to ignore them, to believe things had changed.

"Her mother is very controlling and Abby does her best to keep the woman happy. I admire her for that." Rachel shifted to confront him. "But what I didn't expect, Benjamin Hewitt, was that you'd let her go so easily."

His mouth fell open again. Would his little sister ever stop surprising him?

She touched his chin. "Brains. Don't want to lose what little you have."

He clamped his mouth closed. "I don't give up easy." But did he? Or did he act out of caution, wisdom and experience? Besides, he had no desire to add misery to Abby's life by antagonizing her mother.

"So what are you going to do?"

He didn't answer. What could he do?

"Bear in mind, you've only got four or five months before we reach Oregon. And at the rate you work, it doesn't seem as long as it does when I think of all the steps I have to walk."

"Are you the same sister who warned me about Abby, saying she was only using me?"

"Maybe. But she isn't how I remember her."

"Hmm." She was exactly as he remembered her.

Rachel leaned her head to Ben's shoulders. "There's many a mile between here and Oregon. Plenty of time to heal wounds and learn new ways of being."

Did she mean wounds between him and Abby? But what else could she be talking about? "When will you stop surprising me?"

She grinned. "When you no longer look at me as a kid sister." She jumped down and joined Emma and Abby.

Abby glanced his way. Her gaze riveted his for one heartbeat and then skittered away. As if to warn him that she wasn't interested in spending time with him. He understood he couldn't compete with the hold her mother had over her. No reason he should be disappointed. It was exactly what he'd expected from the time he realized she was on this journey.

For two evenings, they watched the sun set behind Chimney Rock.

The first evening, despite her mother's protests, Abby hurried off to join the Jensens and help with the children,

The second evening about twenty Indians camped near them.

Some of the women came close to the

camp. They wore deerskin dresses with tiny beads sewn into the sleeves. Their hair was braided and one of them carried her baby in a basket on her back.

His sisters and Abby — again against her mother's protests — went out to greet the shy women. Abby brought corn cakes to offer them.

One of the women offered a small square of deerskin in which were several chunks of cooked meat.

The Indian ladies touched both Abby and Emma's blond hair and giggled.

Ben leaned back against a wagon and smiled. He, too, found Abby's hair fascinating and so often longed to reach out and touch it

The Indian entourage slipped away and his sisters and Abby returned to the camp. He continued on his way around the circled wagons, often glancing at Chimney Rock and slowly a plan grew.

When they reached the place he'd ask Abby if she'd like a closer look at the rock formation. He'd ask her to answer his concerns clearly. Did she intend to follow her mother's wishes? Was he only a convenient diversion on this trip? And if she said yes to the latter, what would he do?

He hardened his heart against a desire to

try and woo her. If she wasn't truly interested, he could find hundreds of ways of keeping away from her.

Abby stood with Emma and Rachel staring at the huge pile of rocks that rose from the plains like a chimney.

"It's amazing," Emma said.

"Let's go closer." Rachel grabbed their hands and tried to drag them toward the formation.

Emma pulled back as did Abby.

"We have to let Ben know our plans," Emma said.

Abby knew Mother would disapprove. Mother had grown more critical of Abby with every passing day and Abby had no wish to aggravate her. But she longed to see the rock close up.

"Then let's tell him. And Abby can tell her father." Rachel turned them about and dragged them back to the wagons.

Abby nodded. Her father wouldn't object. And if she spoke to Father privately she could avoid having to deal with Mother's objections.

She slipped away from Rachel's grasp and went to the Bingham wagon. Nathan drove it. Father walked by the oxen. Mother must be resting inside. Good. This was better than she'd expected. She hurried to her father's side.

"The Hewitt girls and I are going over to the Chimney for a closer look."

He smiled. "You go right ahead. Enjoy yourself."

With a free heart, she joined Emma and Rachel who were still talking to Ben. They appeared to be arguing but stopped as soon as they saw her.

"You go on and have fun," Ben said, waving them away. He raised his eyebrows at Abby as if asking her something.

She hesitated. If he wanted company she'd gladly stay behind. She could see Chimney Rock well enough from here. It would have been nice if they could have gone together — just the two of them. But in the past few days he'd made no attempt to talk to her alone. She could only assume that whatever Mother had said to him had the effect Mother desired.

She turned away. It certainly did not have the effect Abby wished for. Though she wasn't even sure what that was. Had she hoped Ben would refuse to bow to Mother's orders? But then why would he? Her words six years ago had disguised her feelings in dislike. Yes, she'd hoped these past weeks had shown him how false they were. But even if he cared she was bound by her guilt over Andy's death. An ache as familiar as her name sucked her breath from her.

Her thoughts quickly turned to Delores's words. She had to forgive herself. If only she knew how.

Rachel caught her hand. "Stop worrying about things. Don't be discouraged. Everything will work out. I know it." She laughed and pulled Abby along.

Abby had no idea what things Rachel thought would work out, but her laughter was infectious and Abby put away her problems for the moment and enjoyed the afternoon with the Hewitt sisters.

They joined the many others going to have a closer look and went right up to the Chimney, tipping their heads so far back they almost fell over which sent them into gales of laughter. Some of the boys scratched their names in the base.

Rachel begged a knife off Jed Henshaw and scratched her name there. She handed it to Emma who scratched hers.

Emma held the knife out to Abby. She shook her head.

She didn't want to remember Abigail Bingham Black. She wanted to be new. Free. According to Delores she could be if she but forgave herself.

But how?

The question hounded her the rest of the day, had her tossing and turning on the hard ground throughout the night. Her lack of sleep was evident on her face the next morning.

"Abigail, you've overdone it," Mother scolded. "That's what you get for hiking off to some wild place like some sort of —"

"Mother, don't say it." She didn't know what word Mother had in mind, but knew it would be insulting to those who shared their campfire, and who had been so helpful and patient with the entire Bingham family.

Mother's eyes snapped her disapproval. She did not care for Abby challenging her.

Not that Abby ever did.

Later the next day, they passed Scotts Bluff, which looked all the world like Abby imagined a castle would.

The bluff walls hugged the river so they had to pull around it and climb a rocky ridge.

Abby couldn't stop staring at the wild formation.

"Do you know how it got its name?" Ben's voice came from behind, startling her and at the same time sending a wave of hopeful anticipation coursing through her veins.

"No, I don't."

He stepped to her side. "It was named after Hiram Scott. He worked for the American Fur Company about fifteen years ago. He was deserted by his companions after he was injured, some say by an arrow. Others say he broke a leg. His bones and boots were found here sixty miles from where they'd left him. He crawled the whole way."

She jerked around to stare at him. "Crawled? Sixty miles? That's incredible."

"Yup, it is. Just goes to show what a man can do if he sets his mind to it. Or a woman for that matter."

She couldn't turn away from his look; didn't want to — finding a secret source of strength and encouragement in his presence and the offering of his words.

"Like crossing the continent to get to Oregon?" she said.

"Yup. And even more, confronting opposition and criticism to do so."

"Like turning aside a stampede of buffalo?"

He nodded, his smile soft upon his lips. "Like choosing to follow our own plans."

"Like jumping into a river to save a child." *And like you jumping in to rescue me.*

"I hope you don't do that again."

"I hope there isn't a need."

"But you did it because you saw the need.

You're one brave lady."

"Am I?" She tore her gaze from his though it pained her to do so. "I don't know."

He touched her shoulder. So gently that it was a mere brush that triggered within her a yearning as big as Scotts Bluff.

She brought her gaze back to his, felt herself drawn into his look. "Some things are very hard to overcome."

"This journey is bound to give us all the chance to deal with our inner challenges. A chance to get past them. Start over. Start new." His hand on her shoulder, riveted her in place, filling her with hope and strength.

Did he refer to something Mother had said? Horror clouded her vision. Had Mother told him she was responsible for Andy's death? Horror darkened her thoughts.

She spun away and hurried to catch up to the Hewitt wagon.

She couldn't bear if he knew the truth.

You have to forgive yourself. It sounded so inviting. *Forgive. Be free. Start over. Start new.*

But how? *How do I forgive an endless pain?*

CHAPTER NINETEEN

Ben stared after Abby. He'd hoped his words would make her see that she could be free of her mother's control. Could start anew.

He swallowed back a bitter taste. Just hinting at it had sent her running.

He rehashed what he'd said. He wanted to help her. He wanted her to be free. He wanted to know the truth about her feelings and why her mother had such a firm hold on her even after she'd been married.

How could he get past her defenses?

A verse they'd memorized came to him. *If the Son therefore shall make you free, ye shall be free indeed.* Something had her chained to the past, to her mother's control. Perhaps if he could learn what it was he could help her see the grip it had on her.

Lord, I'm powerless to help her. Only You can free her of whatever this is. Guide my steps in trying to get through to her.

They would reach Fort Laramie in four days. The trip would be one third over. That left them many miles yet to go, but in some ways it seemed far too short.

He wanted to rush after Abby and demand an explanation but an inner voice warned him she had a battle to fight that she must fight on her own if she was to ever be free. So for the next four days, he stayed his distance, watching her, seeing the way she kept to herself, the way her forehead furrowed. Often she sought out Mrs. Jensen and the two appeared to be in earnest conversation.

Ben waited and prayed. Although he chafed under the strain of holding back his questions, he knew it was what he must do.

The wagon train reached Fort Laramie. A time to restock and rest. A time to resupply and repair wagons and harnesses and shoes. Built from logs, the fort was owned by the American Fur Company and mostly traded with the Indians, many of whom camped outside it. Trappers and mountain men dressed in leather congregated, as well. Nathan Reed seemed to know many of them and was greeted with much shouting and shoving.

"Like overgrown children," Emma observed as they set up camp then made their way into the fort.

She gasped at the prices. "Coffee, a dollar fifty a pint, but we're almost out."

Rachel examined some calico. "A dollar a yard and it's inferior."

Ben was likewise shocked at being charged a buck fifty for gunpowder. But what could they do? He left the women trading for goods and went in search of a blacksmith. Their wheel rims needed to be tightened.

He stepped aside to make way as Mrs. Bingham marched into the dry goods store with Abby at her side. Abby spared him a quick glance, then turned back to her mother. Was he mistaken in thinking she appeared to offer a silent apology? And if so, was it over her mother's dismissive behavior or —

He tried to quell the thought. Did she regret that they'd spent no time together for four days?

He touched the brim of his hat in greeting. Maybe he'd purchase a new one while he was here. His was battered out of shape after being on the prairie in the rainstorm. James had found it caught on some sagebrush and laughed. "It's seen better days."

"Sure enough has." And he hoped it would see better days ahead, as well. But a new one might help brighten his future.

The day was busy with purchasing and repairing. The camp at evening was noisy with excited children running about, men checking equipment and the women comparing purchases.

If he'd hoped for a chance to speak privately to Abby, he wouldn't be getting it. The commotion of camp didn't subside until long after dark.

The next morning, he rose early. Others staggered from their tents, paying the price for their late-night revelry.

The ladies immediately set to work over the campfire. Soon the table they used was crowded with all sort of bowls and pots

"Looks like a lot of breakfast," he commented.

"We plan to use the time to bake up biscuits and beans and sweets and —" Rachel gave an expansive wave. "Everything. We'll eat like royalty for the first little while at least."

Abby chuckled. "Not everything, surely?"

Rachel shrugged. "Just some extra baking. We never had time on the trail for anything but necessities."

Ben's duties relaxed as they camped at the fort so he sat back and watched them cooking up a storm. He would relax a lot more when they discovered who was responsible for the robberies both on the wagon train and back in Independence.

Johnny toddled over and held out his arms. Ben scooped him up and tossed him in the air. Johnny giggled with delight.

Ben caught Abby's gaze upon him and stopped tossing the baby, who protested loudly.

Her gaze seemed to beg him to do something. What? And then it hit him. He pushed to his feet. Handed Johnny to his mother and murmured to Abby as he passed her. "Walk with me this afternoon? Right after dinner?"

She nodded, her eyes guarded.

"I'll meet you at the gates."

He sauntered off, waited until he was out of sight to jump for joy. She'd agreed. She wanted to spend time with him. Even against her mother's wishes.

He jumped again and hollered, "yeehaw." The Indians gave him a puzzled look and shook their heads at each other. He could almost hear them saying *Crazy white man.* But he didn't care.

Abby hid her smile. Mother had retreated to the wagon but should she look out and see Abby smiling, she would demand a reason. Of course, if she knew the true cause, she would forbid Abby to go. Abby could not bring herself to outright defy her mother. But if her mother didn't know, she couldn't forbid.

Abby had made up her mind, although it had been a long torturous journey before she came to her conclusion. Verse after verse had circled a path through her head until she thought there must be a trench inside her brain as deep as the buffalo trails.

Verses she'd memorized filled her every waking hour. There was a moment she wished she'd never committed them to memory, but she didn't believe it for even a minute. Those words had been her sole comfort for years.

If we confess our sins.

"Confess therefore your sins one to another . . . that ye may be healed."

She knew there was more to it than that, but those particular words were beacon lights in her brain.

She'd talked to Delores, seeking her wisdom.

"God forgives if we but ask," Delores said.

Abby had asked but her heart ached for more. That's when she knew what she must do.

She meant to tell Ben the whole truth. Every ugly bit of it. And if he still wanted to walk with her . . .

Not that he'd asked her for several days. She'd prayed most earnestly for a chance and here it was.

She could hardly keep her thoughts on the tasks at hand as she helped the others cook up as much food as they thought would keep for few days. Every couple of minutes she glanced up hoping to see Ben, but he didn't return until noon.

He sported a new hat, a wide-brimmed felt hat that gave him a rakish look. He took it off, spun it around on his finger and hung it from a hook on the wagon.

His sisters watched and laughed.

He grinned at them, including Abby in his look.

At the welcome in his eyes, her heart forgot to work.

The Littletons had camped close to them perhaps out of habit and little Johnny wandered over and begged to be picked up.

At the tender way he lifted the child and rubbed noses with him, she thought her heart might explode from her chest and pressed her hand to her throat in an attempt to calm her reaction.

Somehow she managed to eat her meal without attracting unwanted notice from the others. The last thing she needed was for Mother to think she picked at her food. No doubt she would order Abby to have a rest. As if Abby was still a child.

The meal ended. The men left to tend to their business of getting the equipment ready for the next stage of their journey and finally Abby could breathe easy.

Only she couldn't. Ben waited for her to join him.

Her arms felt too long, her hands uncooperative, as she washed the dishes. Surely Mother would notice. She sucked in air and held it until she felt calmer.

Suddenly they were finished. There was nothing to stop her from heading to the fort. Nothing but a bout of nerves that made her tongue stick to the roof of her mouth.

She gave herself a little shake and went to the wagon to retrieve the coins Father had left for her.

"Where are you going?" Mother's sharp words knifed along Abby's spine.

"I need to buy some thread." She worked on quilt squares almost daily and had run out of both thread and fabric. One square she made had a dark brown hat on green prairie. The hat caught on a gray-green bit of brush. Blue patches signified the puddles of water. She'd watched James find Ben's old hat and bring it back to Ben. To others it represented the windstorm. But for her, it reminded her of Ben running after her in the wind, worried and concerned. And then kissing her.

That memory gave her courage and strength to continue with her plans. "Father gave me money to buy the supplies I need."

She dropped the coins in her pocket and strode toward the fort without a backward look.

She stepped through the open gates and looked around.

Ben uncoiled from the log wall of the nearest building and smiled, sending her pulses into drum beat.

"I need to make a few purchases." Her words sounded thin and airy. Like she was excited or nervous. She was both.

"May I accompany you?"

She nodded graciously. "It would be my pleasure." She meant it more sincerely than he could guess.

They crossed to the store and stepped inside. She hurried to the section where the yard goods were displayed and ordered two yards of white muslin and a bit of green-and-blue percale.

Ben stood close by, watching her examine the fabrics. It made her less certain of herself, so she turned to him.

"Do you think this is a good color for grass?"

"Grass is green. This is green. Seems simple enough."

She laughed. "Put that way, yes." Was this a habit she'd been unaware of — making things complicated when they were simple? If she could convince herself it was true then perhaps this afternoon and the things she meant to say were the same. This is what happened. This is my part in it. Simple enough.

She would have liked to purchase more colors but the selection was limited. She added a spool of thread and paid for it. The man waiting on her wrapped her purchases in brown paper and tied it closed.

Ben took the package and tucked it under his arm. "Let's go for a walk."

"Yes, let's."

A heavily bearded man strode past, bumping into Abby.

Ben pulled her close and tucked her arm around his, her fingers on his forearm. "I'll keep you safe."

She liked the sound of that and the feel of his powerful arm beneath her palm. He was strong. But he possessed the kind of strength that displayed itself in gentle kindness. Not in brutality. Of that, she was certain.

They stepped out of the fort and turned to the right, walking in the shadow of the log walls. They reached a spot where they could no longer see the covered wagons and she tugged on his arm.

"Let's stop here."

They leaned against the rough wood. The plains rolled away as far as they could see. The cloudless sky matched the cornflower blue of her thread. She planned how to make this scene into a quilt block.

"Ben, do you mind if I ask you a question?"

"I'd consider it a privilege."

He might not after she said all she meant to say. "What did my mother say to you the other day?"

She felt his surprise in the way he stiffened.

He took his time answering and every second of waiting measured out a drop of dread. Was it that bad?

Finally he sighed. "Mostly the same stuff she said six years ago. That I wasn't good enough for you. That you had plans for your betterment in Oregon. That you would do what's best for you."

Abby groaned. "Mother wants me to do what is best for *her.* She thinks I owe it to her."

Ben turned to study her. "Do you agree with her?" His tone revealed nothing, and she dare not look at him for fear she would lose her determination.

She'd thought how to explain to him and prayed for the opportunity. She didn't intend to let it pass.

"I never told you the whole story about Andy's death and my part in it." She recounted to him that fateful day, not glossing over her neglect in thinking about Andy's safety rather than impressing some friend she wished she could erase from her memory.

At some point he had taken her hands and held them to his chest.

She still couldn't meet his eyes and kept her gaze on his shirtfront. "I wish I could take that day back. I always believed Mother didn't know just how guilty I was but the other day when she talked to you, she told me she knew everything and blamed me."

"Abby —"

"Let me finish before you say anything." And if, when she was done, he wanted nothing more to do with her, she would understand. She'd die inside. But she'd been half dead the better part of a decade anyway.

"I was consumed with grief and guilt. If only I'd asked him not to do it. If only I

hadn't cared so much what that girl said."
She could never bring herself to say her
name. "I knew Mother would never forgive
me. Her whole world centered on Andy. If
we were sick, she fretted something would
happen to Andrew. When Father took us
places, she made certain Andrew had the
best place and gave Father a dozen warnings about keeping him warm, making sure
he got a treat, letting him play in the park."
She'd never minded too much. After all,
she'd adored her brother.

"Knowing how upset Mother would be,
and how she'd never get over it, I did the
only thing I could think of. I vowed to her
that I would do my best to take Andrew's
place. I'd take care of her and Father just as
she expected Andy would." Abby stumbled
on the words and took a moment to push
her emotions into the dark hole where they
constantly lived. "Mother got a Bible and
made me swear on it that I would take care
of her. She's never let me forget my promise.
I married Frank —" Her voice broke and
she couldn't go on.

Ben pulled her toward him but she shook
her head. She had to say it all. Only then
could he make a decision based on who she
really was.

"I never loved him, but Mother thought

him a man with prospects." Every word shivered up her throat at the memory of those awful days with Frank.

Ben had his hands on her upper arms, providing strength even as he waited for her to continue.

"I thought when he died, I'd be free of my vow. But Mother has other plans. She will find a rich man for me to marry. It won't matter if I care for him in the least."

She brought her gaze to Ben's then. "I will never be free."

Why did she even think it possible? A vow given on the Bible was unbreakable.

CHAPTER TWENTY

Ben stared past Abby as she talked. The prairie shifted and wavered as if stroked by unkind fingers. The same cruel fingers that raked through his heart leaving it in shreds.

Abby blamed herself for Andy's death. She labored under a load of guilt that would have made two yoke of oxen stagger. *Lord, heal her. Comfort her.* If only he could offer something.

"I will never be free." Every word carried so much hurt his knees buckled.

Her eyes met his, the pupils wide and unfocused.

He saw clear to the depths of her soul, felt every pulsing beat of pain.

His hands gripped her shoulders.

She leaned toward him. He had only to bend his arms to bring her to his chest, but his own emotions raged. He feared he would crush her.

Barring anything he could hit, he wanted

to shake his fists into the air. How could anyone treat her this way? Her own mother, no less.

"Ben?" His name was a sob and released him from the grip of his rage.

"Oh, Abby." He pulled her to his chest and crossed his arms over her back, enfolding her as if he could protect her from the pain of her life. But the pain lurked inside, where he couldn't attack it. He bent his head and pressed his cheek to her hair, breathed in the sweetness of her. A sweetness that had been sullied by undeserved guilt. At least she allowed him to hold her. Surely a sign of trust. But could he help her find the healing she needed and deserved?

Lord, help me.

"Abby, I am so sorry about Andy. I wish I'd known him. I imagine him as an adoring brother who would sooner spend time with you than anyone else."

She nodded against his chest. "He was."

He continued, letting his thoughts flow into words. "What a hole his death must have left in your heart. I don't expect it can ever be filled."

Her shoulder shook as she sobbed almost inaudibly. Hot tears wet the front of his shirt.

"Punishing yourself won't fill that hole."

She grew quiet. Perhaps waiting. Perhaps disagreeing. He didn't know but continued.

"If he'd lived he would be your biggest defender, I expect."

She nodded.

"I believe he'd look at you and tell you he didn't blame you. He'd want you to enjoy your life to the fullest. He'd want you to be happy, wouldn't he?"

Again a little nod.

"Can you be happy if you continue to live in guilt?"

She tipped her head back. Her eyes were dark. Her pupils wide. "But I am guilty."

"Of what?"

She blinked. Opened her mouth. Closed it again. Cleared her throat. "Of his death." He caught the note of uncertainty in her voice.

"Really? It seems to me you only acted like a fourteen-year-old. As did he. We all make foolish mistakes. We all do things we regret. Is that reason to punish ourselves?"

"Delores says I have to forgive myself." Her words shivered from her.

"I agree."

"I've tried. I don't know how."

The despair in her voice closed off his throat and for a moment he was unable to speak. Then it hit him. He didn't understand the bond between twins but it seemed she'd had an especially strong one with Andy. She needed Andy to forgive her.

That was impossible. Andy was dead. But perhaps —

He dropped his arms and put her from him. Only an inch away but his arms felt empty. He must try this for her sake.

"Abby, close your eyes." She did so. "Now pretend I'm Andy and tell me you're sorry."

Her eyes popped open. "Why?"

He explained.

Her eyes pooled with tears. "I wish I could tell him how very very sorry I am. If I could go back, I would do things so differently."

"I know you would."

She held his gaze with such hungry longing that he felt hollowed out inside. He ached to press her next to his heart and hold her until all her pain went away. But he didn't want to be sidetracked before they did this.

"Andy can't be here, but you can use me as a substitute. Close your eyes and say to me what you need to say to him."

She swallowed loudly, nodded and closed her eyes. A shudder shook her from head to toe.

He longed to hold her but not while she was imagining him to be Andy.

"Andy, I miss you." Her voice quavered. "I will always miss you. Every day I see things I know you'd enjoy and want to tell you about them. But I can't. And it's my fault. I should have stopped you from riding that horse." She shivered. "Please forgive me for letting you down. For putting my pride ahead of your safety. It robbed you of life. I am forever sorry."

He dared not make a sound, not even the sound of his breathing for fear of ruining the moment.

"I know you're in a better place. I know I will see you someday and we can talk about all these things." She nodded as if she heard a voice. Her expression went from pain to regret to peace. "Thank you for forgiving me. And yes, I'll live my life the way you would want me to." She laughed a little, the sweetest sound Ben had ever heard. "You'd want me to enjoy it to the fullest and be willing to take risks. Reasonable ones, of course."

Her eyes opened and she smiled like the heavens had poured into her a secret store of sunshine.

He opened his arms and she went into them. She wrapped her arms around his waist and pressed her face to the hollow of his shoulder. "Thank you," she whispered.

He didn't need thanks. "I only want you to be free."

She groaned. "How can I be free of my vow? I swore on the Bible. I can't pretend I didn't."

He held her close a moment then tipped her back to look into her face. "Abby, what do you want in life?"

The way she looked at him practically invited him to kiss her but he must know she was prepared to accept him over her mother's wishes.

She quirked an eyebrow as if reading his thoughts. "I want to be free to follow my heart."

He dared to think the way she looked at him, she meant him. But first she had to be free.

She lowered her head so all he saw was the golden halo of her hair. "I gave my word."

He held her but said nothing. This was something she had to figure out on her own. Otherwise she would never be truly free.

She slumped against him. "What am I to do?"

"Only you can answer that question."

She straightened, putting distance between them. "I will go to Mother and say I have paid my price and want to be free from my vow."

"And if she refuses?" As she most certainly would for the woman appeared to have no natural affection for her daughter.

She contemplated his question. "I pray she will release me."

He caught her hands and brought them to his chest. They bowed their heads together and he prayed for Abby to be free of the vow she'd given in haste.

"I want to do it now, while I feel like I'm strong enough to face her."

They retraced their steps to the circle of wagons and he reluctantly let her go alone to her mother.

Abby looked for Mother. She normally didn't go further than her chair parked by the campfire. The campfire was dead. The chair empty. "Mother?" She called again. Perhaps Mother was in the wagon. But silence answered her. Perhaps she'd gone to buy something, though she'd been in the store with Abby yesterday and declared all the merchandise of inferior quality and refused to purchase a thing. Knowing this was her last chance for many miles, she might have reconsidered. Abby sighed. Likely she'd gone looking for Abby to make sure she didn't wander off with someone unsuitable, like Ben.

Abby trotted back to the fort and asked at the store.

"I remember your mother. Yes, she was in. About an hour ago. Asking about you. Haven't seen her since."

Abby went around the fort asking after Mother but no one had seen her for some time. How strange. Mother never wandered far. She paused by the woodpile and heard the rattle of a rattlesnake. Her heart raced and she backed away and hurried on by.

Perhaps she and Mother had missed each other and Mother was back at the wagon fretting over Abby's absence.

She made her way back there, stopping several times to speak to others. Finally she reached the campsite. No sign of Mother. She called her. No answer. On the off chance Mother might be so sound asleep she didn't hear her call, Abby poked her head in the wagon. There she was, curled up like she'd been sleeping.

"Mother, didn't you hear me call?"

"It's cold out. Put your coat on." Mother's words were slurred and made no sense. Had someone given her a strong drink?

The sour smell of vomit hit Abby's nostrils. She scrambled inside. "Mother, you're sick. And your arm." It was swollen to the size of a melon and when Abby touched it, her mother moaned.

At the way her mother struggled to breathe, Abby knew there was something seriously wrong. She leaned out of the wagon. "Emma? Where's Emma?"

Ben appeared so suddenly she knew he waited nearby. Waited to hear her mother's answer to Abby's request. Abby had forgotten it as soon as she saw her mother's state.

"What's wrong?" Ben asked.

"Mother is sick. Very sick. I need Emma."

"I'll find her." He trotted off.

Abby didn't know what to do apart from offering Mother water and pressing a damp cloth to her forehead.

It seemed like forever before Emma and Ben returned. Emma climbed into the wagon and looked at Mother's arm, turned it gently. Shook her head. "Snakebite." She pointed to the marks. "If I'd known sooner, I could have helped. If only she'd sought assistance."

Abby stared at Emma, trying to make sense of her words. "Are you saying you can't do anything for her?"

"Abby, I'm sorry. The poison has gone clear through her body."

Ben reached in and squeezed Abby's arm.

"I'll find your father." And he was gone.

Father arrived, but Mother was already unconscious. She convulsed shortly afterward.

"She's gone," Emma said.

Someone helped Abby from the wagon. Someone put a cup of tea in her hands. People came by and said they were sorry. Rev. Pettygrove arrived and he sat beside Father while his wife sat beside Abby.

She barely noticed them. Barely heard the hum of conversation around her.

Mother was dead. Was this the answer to Abby wanting to be free of her vow?

Somehow she made it through the rest of the day. Because of the heat and the plans to travel in the morning, the funeral was held that evening. Abby couldn't say if it was before supper or afterward.

"I made a simple coffin out of bits of wood people donated," Ben said, speaking at her elbow.

"Thank you." The words were spoken out of habit. She felt nothing.

Father thanked him, too.

Abby clung to her father as they followed the coffin, born on the shoulders of Ben and Martin, Nathan and James, to an open grave.

Rachel held Abby's mandolin. "Abby

taught me how to play. This is for you, Abby, my friend." She played and sang "Amazing Grace."

Rev. Pettygrove spoke a few words, none of which registered with Abby, and then the coffin was lowered into the ground. Dirt shoveled in to fill the hole.

One by one, the people filed by and spoke to her and Father. She hoped she responded appropriately for she could not think.

She and Father were alone.

"Come, Abigail. It's time to say goodbye."

"Please leave me. I need time."

Father hesitated, then walked away, his steps heavy.

She turned back to the fresh grave. The hopelessness of her situation consumed her. She fell to the ground.

How long she sat huddled by the freshly turned sod, she couldn't say.

Gentle arms lifted her. Ben. "Come back."

"Why? What's the use? I am forever chained to my vow."

He wrapped his arms about her shoulders and led her toward the wagon. "Abby, you're free now."

"No. Don't you see? I should have been here when Mother needed me. Instead, I was looking for a way to get out of my obligation. It was wrong. I swore on the

Bible. I can never be free."

Abby had mentioned hearing a snake at the woodpile and Ben and Martin had hunted it down and destroyed it. It might not be the snake that bite Mrs. Bingham but it was a danger, nonetheless.

Ben didn't say anything more to Abby. She was in shock. When she'd had time to think the situation through, she'd see that her mother's death released her from her vow. Not that he rejoiced in the fact. It would have been better by far if Mrs. Bingham had freed Abby from her promise. But would she have done so? They'd never know.

Abby would forever wonder what her mother would have said. He would have pulled her to his chest and held her close even in this public place but he sensed how fragile she was at the moment.

He released her to his sisters' care. They made sure she ate and drank, then pulled her into their tent for the night so she wouldn't be alone.

Nathan watched it all from a distance until the girls left then scooted over to sit by Ben. "Do you suppose they will go back?"

Ben's whole body jerked at the question. He'd never considered the Binghams might turn around. If they did, he'd never see

Abby again. "I can't say." His voice croaked like he'd burned his throat raw.

"I can." Mr. Bingham stepped over the wagon tongue and joined them. He had left a short time ago. Ben assumed he had gone to visit his wife's grave. "There is nothing for me back East. I will go on." He looked toward the east and shuddered.

Ben's breath eased out. He understood it would be hard for Abby and her father to go on without Mrs. Bingham but he was glad he could continue to enjoy Abby's presence.

From the girls' tent came the sound of quiet humming. Emma comforting Abby. He wished he could do something to help her but for now he must stand aside and let others do it.

He rolled up in his bedroll only because he knew he must sleep as they were hitting the trail again tomorrow, but sleep did not come easily. His mind lingered on one thought.

Abby did not see her mother's death as an escape from her vow. Surely that was only shock talking. When the shock wore off, she'd see it differently.

How long before she realized the truth?

The sound of the morning wake-up call pulled him from a restless sleep. He hurriedly rose and waited for the girls to leave their tent.

Emma came first, her eyes swollen from crying and lack of sleep.

Ben waited. Murmurs came from the tent but neither Abby nor Rachel exited.

"Abby's upset."

At Emma's words, Ben took two steps toward the tent then forced himself to stop. He couldn't burst in and take Abby in his arms as he wished.

"Rachel's comforting her." Emma began preparing breakfast.

Sally joined them. "It's got to be difficult."

Emma nodded. "She blames herself. Says if she'd been there, her mother might still be alive. She keeps saying things like 'I shouldn't have tried to excuse myself. I knew it was wrong.' "

Ben stared at the tent as Sally and Emma talked about how Abby would cope.

Please, God. Let her see that she is no longer controlled by her vow.

Finally Rachel and Abby emerged and Rachel led Abby to Emma's side. Abby sank to the ground and sat like she was carved of wood. Her red-rimmed, unfocused eyes stared into the distance.

Ben edged closer. "Abby?"

Her shudder was the only sign that she'd

heard him.

He squatted at her side. "Abby, everything is going to be okay. I know it."

She barely moved. And gave no sign of having heard him.

He closed his eyes. It would take time.

How much time?

As long as it would take. Days. Miles. He'd stand by and wait as long as necessary.

Sam, Miles and James, along with the other committeemen, approached them. They were accompanied by the little Frenchman who ran the fort.

"Ben, we need to talk." Sam tipped his head to indicate they would adjourn to a spot outside the wagons.

Ben reluctantly rose. He patted Abby's shoulder, felt the tension in her muscles and hesitated. But duty called and he joined the others a distance away.

The Frenchman jammed his fists to his hips. "I 'ave been robbed. My safe, he is empty."

"Are you accusing us?"

"I saying it not happen until the wagon train, she come. My friend, the chief, he not rob me. I follow some tracks. They come dis away."

"Ben, all the evidence points to someone

on the wagon train. Like I said, once a thief, always a thief."

"You find dis *homme.* You find my moneys and gives it back." The Frenchman stalked away.

Sam stared at the wagons. "It's certain someone among those fine people is a thief."

James stood at his side, arms crossed. "But who and how do we find him?"

"Let's spread out and see if we can discover anything suspicious," Sam said.

James shrugged. "Seems unlikely we'll find anything but it doesn't hurt to try." He turned to Ben. "Come along. Let's have a look."

In pairs, the men trooped off to inspect the wagon train.

"We could ask to look in each wagon." Ben only wanted to find the thief, return the goods and be on their way.

"I've taken the liberty of looking in a few, but this thief is too cautious to leave money out in plain sight. If you wanted to hide money, where would you put it?"

Ben thought of his hiding spot. Before they'd left Independence, he'd cut away the center of a few pages of a book, folded the paper money into it and glued the pages together so it wasn't visible to any casual examination. He wasn't about to tell James of his secret but one thing was certain. "We'd waste hours, maybe days, looking for it."

"I don't think we're going to be welcome to stay much longer." James indicated the fort. The gates had been closed. An armed guard stood his post.

They completed their tour of the wagons and rejoined the others.

"We found nothing." Everyone reported the same thing.

"Let's get this wagon train moving." Sam studied the closed-up fort. "One hour." Sam left to attend to his own tasks.

They had a hurried breakfast and left right on schedule. Ben was glad to leave the fort and his dashed hopes behind.

Day after day, they continued on their weary way dealing with dust that clogged a man's nostrils until he could barely breathe. They suffered rain that soaked their bedding. A sort of numbness came over the camp at the sameness of every day.

But worst was the dead look on Abby's face. She seldom walked anymore, choosing to sit on the hard bench of the wagon, whether Nathan or her father drove.

"She never speaks a word," Nathan reported. "Just stares at the switching tails of the oxen."

Abby had quit playing her mandolin, had stopped reading aloud from her book. Many people said how much they missed it.

None more than Ben. He drove the Hewitt wagon and attended to his responsibilities as a committeeman. And he waited and prayed.

His lungs worked a little better the day Abby got down from the wagon and walked alongside his sisters. They chatted away to her. She contributed nothing. But it was a start.

When they stopped that night, Abby slipped away and went to see Delores Jensen.

Ben prayed the woman would help Abby understand she was free — free of her vow, free to love, free to enjoy life.

CHAPTER TWENTY-ONE

Delores saw Abby coming toward her and held out her arms. Abby went into her warm embrace, letting the woman rock her and murmur comfort.

"Come sit down a spell. Annie and Betty, take the little ones to play."

The older girls shepherded the twins away and took the two-year-old. Eddy. Though they never called him that. Only Baby Two.

Abby's gaze followed the twins. She'd once been that free and secure.

Delores squeezed Abby's hand. "Now tell me how things are going with you."

"I'm fine." What else could she say?

Delores made a sound of disapproval. "You aren't fine. You mother has recently died, and that is a sorrow you must bear. That is understandable. But I see in your demeanor it is more than that." A beat of waiting silence. Abby knew her friend had more to say. If she had the strength she would have changed the subject. But she couldn't pull a single protesting word from her mind.

Because she wanted help to understand how she could move forward with this burden of guilt.

Delores continued. "I had such high hopes for you. I saw you with Ben and thanked God you were moving past your guilt and accepting the good things God has offered you."

Abby shook her head. "I can't. You don't understand. I made a vow and meant to break it." She explained.

"Oh, Abby-girl, I would not want my children controlled by guilt and obligation. I would not want them caring for me with those emotions. What's more, I could not be the mother they need and deserve if I was blinded by guilt and obligation."

Blinded. That was exactly how Abby felt.

"I want my children to love me. I want to be free to love them without the burden of guilt. The good book says 'love covereth all sins.' My dear, isn't it time you let God's love wash away all your guilt?"

"It's not a matter of letting God cleanse me."

"Then believe that if God removes our guilty stain He remembers it no more."

"But I vowed on the Bible."

Delores gave her a steady look. "Abby, did you vow to God or to your mother?"

"I swore on the Bible to take care of Mother and Father."

"Perhaps you should ask your father if he wants you to look after him. Or don't you want to be free of this burden you have carried for so many years?"

"Of course I do."

"Are you sure you aren't bearing a cross of your own making with the mistaken belief that by so doing you can compensate for the harsh things that come into your life?"

Abby stared at the fire. Was she doing that? Thinking she could pay for her mistakes by carrying a cross of her own making? Wouldn't that be foolish, indeed, when Jesus Christ had carried a cross so she might be free of guilt and judgment?

She rose and thanked her friend. "I have some thinking to do."

Delores chuckled. "Try thinking less and trusting more."

"I'll try."

For the first time since Mother's death, she slept in her own tent that night, despite objections from Emma and Rachel. She felt Ben watching her, saw in his eyes the depth of his caring.

"I'm fine," she said to all of them, but kept her gaze on Ben as she spoke.

He nodded and smiled. Trusting her.

Where had that thought come from? Yet she felt it so strongly that she smiled as she prepared for bed. She mulled over Delores's advice.

She considered her mother's death. She might have been able to prevent it if she'd been there. Or she might have been on the other side of the canvas and if Mother didn't ask for help, nothing would have changed.

Ben had helped her see an enjoyable future free of so many negative things she'd learned to associate with Andy's death. She hugged her arms around her. Andy would never have blamed her and would have been angry at her for blaming herself.

It was time to put the painful past behind her.

Only one thing was necessary in order for her to be able to do that.

The next morning she suggested to Nathan that he should drive the wagon, then asked her father to walk with her.

They moved far enough away from the others that she could talk to him without being overheard. "I want to tell you about Andy's death." From there to her vow to her mother, she spared no details. "I swore on the Bible and I cannot forget my vow. I'm asking you to release me from it."

"Your mother was so afraid of being poor. It had been drummed into her from childhood that poverty was a fate worse than death." His voice choked. "I regret she placed such a burden on your shoulders. I would never want such sacrifice from you." He hugged her. "I haven't told you this, but I love you and I want only for you to be happy."

She'd never been certain of her mother's love, but felt blessed clear through by her father's.

They walked on with Abby tucked into the shelter of his arm.

"Abby, I see how you and Ben are together. He's waiting for you. Has been for some time, I expect. Go to him."

"Why, aren't you the romantic?" She laughed, her heart so light it seemed to float within her chest.

She looked about her for the first time since they'd left Fort Laramie. They traveled along the Sweetwater River. Ahead of them lay a sloped rock like a bear sleeping.

"That's Independence Rock," Father said. "We'll be there by early afternoon."

Independence Rock. How appropriate.

Ben watched Abby and her father walking some distance away. Was he mistaken in thinking she laughed?

Oh, wouldn't it be wonderful to hear the music of her laughter again?

The pair walked arm in arm the whole morning.

"Only an hour to Independence Rock," Sam called as he rode along the line of wagons. "We'll noon there."

They reached the massive rock and stopped for dinner.

Abby and her father joined them. There was something about the way Abby acted that made him want to cheer. She moved with energy, like she'd found a reason to enjoy life.

Oh, Lord, please let me be part of that reason. Though he'd be almost content just to see her ready to put her past behind even if he didn't play a part in it.

After the meal he hung about. Was it too soon to ask her to walk?

She solved his quandary by turning to him. "Ben, why don't you show me the rock?"

He was on his feet so fast he had a moment of light-headedness.

They were among many who had the same idea.

She laughed at the young men scrambling to the top of the rock. She picked a wild daisy and tucked it behind her ear.

Ben could not find his tongue. Was afraid to speak for fear of sending her back into her shell.

The others were intent on reaching the rock. He cared only to ask Abby about this new, joyful person she'd become.

The one he thought had vanished after her mother's death.

They reached the base of the rock and had to stop unless she suggested they climb it.

She didn't. Instead, she turned to face him. "Ben, I wanted to be here, at Independence Rock, when I told you I am free. I have my independence."

She correctly read his confusion.

"Father said I am under no obligation to keep my vow. He doesn't even want me to. Says he'll take care of himself if I don't mind."

"What about your mother?"

She sighed. "I might have been able to help my mother if I'd been right there. Or not. In the end, her pride was responsible for her not asking for help."

He nodded.

"Don't you see? I'm free. Free to live and love and enjoy life the way I choose."

"Does your choice include me?" He barely managed to get the words out as his throat threatened to close off.

She smiled up at him. "I kissed you back on the prairie. What do you think that meant?"

He tried to sort out his scrambled thoughts. "I don't know what it meant to you, but I know what it meant to me." He opened his arms and she came eagerly, wrapping her arms about him and sighing as if she had also wanted this for a long time.

"My sweet Abigail, I love you and have since we first met. I've never stopped loving you, even though I tried after you married Frank."

"I have never stopped loving you, either."

"Will you marry me?"

"I will."

He bent his head and claimed her lips. It was like coming home after a hard day. Like seeing sunshine after a long storm. Like everything good rolled up in this one sweet gesture.

They eased back, but couldn't bear to part and kissed again.

He lifted his head. "I have an idea. Let's

find Grayson's name." They searched until they did. He pulled his knife from his pocket and carved his name. Ben Hewitt. Beside it he added Abby. He began to carve a *B* when she stopped him.

"No more Bingham or Black. I want to forget the past and look to the future."

He kissed her again before they returned to the wagon.

Emma saw them approach. "I think you have an announcement to make."

"Abby and I are to be married. Not right away, because it's too soon after her mother's death."

He went immediately to Mr. Bingham. "Sir, I would like your permission to marry your daughter."

The man grabbed his hand. "I heartily approve. She deserves every bit of happiness you can give her."

Friends and family gathered round them and offered congratulations.

"This is reason to celebrate," Emma said. "Let's have a party." She looked at her soiled apron and pulled it off. Rubbed her hand over her hair. "I'm going to fix my hair." She went to the wagon and let out a squeak.

"What's wrong?" Ben called.

"Someone's been rifling through our

belongings. My silver and tortoiseshell hair combs are missing." She barely contained a wail. "Mother gave them to me. They were hers. Who would take them?"

James and Sam were present.

Sam looked around the assembly. "Did anyone see anything suspicious? Speak up if you did. It's time to expose the thief."

Rev. Pettygrove stepped forward. "I saw someone with dark hair and kind of tall looking in the wagon."

Only a half a dozen men fit the description Rev. Pettygrove gave and they all had alibis.

Except Nathan Reed.

He stared at the crowd with fierce eyes, but spoke not a word of defense.

"He's guilty," Ernie Jones called. "Let's deal with it here and now."

Ben groaned. So much for a celebration.

Miles Cavanaugh heard him and took pity on him. "First we celebrate the engagement of Ben and Abby. We'll deal with this matter afterward."

"I'll watch Nathan," James said and indicated the big man should precede him to the Cavanaugh wagon.

Miles clapped to get everyone's attention back on him. "Now let's enjoy the evening and Ben and Abby's love."

That evening there was much rejoicing amid music and dancing but none enjoyed the evening nor had more reason for joy than Ben.

He pulled Abby into his arms. "Are you sure you want to give up your newfound independence to marry a man like me?" He half teased, but waited for her answer with a measure of trepidation.

She tipped her head back and smiled sweet. "Freedom to follow my heart is the greatest freedom I could ask for." She pressed her hands to the back of his head and pulled him close. Just before their lips met she whispered. "I am free to love you the rest of my life."

Dear Reader,

This story is based on a very real event. The first wagon train on the Oregon Trail indeed crossed the country in 1843. Historical experts might find some discrepancies in my tale. My aim was to tell a satisfying story within the limits of the acceptable word count.

I am so often amazed when I read of the early pioneers. They faced incredible challenges with resolve and extraordinary courage. This is no more evident than in the first wagon train on the Oregon Trail. I wonder if I could have embarked on such a journey. And yet it isn't the physical challenges but dealing with the emotional baggage that so often proves the bigger hurdle. In that, I don't think the travelers were much different than we are. My prayer for this story is that it will help the readers find healing and wholeness from any personal burden they have.

I love to hear from my readers. You can contact me at www.lindaford.org where you'll find my email address and where you can find out more about me and my books.

Blessings,
Linda Ford

ABOUT THE AUTHOR

Linda Ford lives on a ranch in Alberta, Canada, near enough to the Rocky Mountains that she can enjoy them on a daily basis. She and her husband raised fourteen children — four homemade, ten adopted. She currently shares her home and life with her husband, a grown son, a live-in paraplegic client and a continual (and welcome) stream of kids, kids-in-law, grandkids, and assorted friends and relatives.